ACKNOWLEDGEMENTS

Once again, special thanks to David Kopp. I would be remiss to omit thanks to Earl and Vi Haake, Bonnie Murphy, Val Telman, Diane Carson, and Gene Culver for the various ways they have helped in getting me this far. And a special mention to my nephews, John and Scott Bradshaw, my wonderful brother-in-law and sister-in-law, Jack and Jean Sydnor, and pals who have given me a leg up; Brian Kowert, and Tom Campbell.

DEDICATION

This book is dedicated to my grandson, Mark Bettencourt, Jr., and all of our men and women in uniform, whom I look forward to him joining when he comes of age.

1.

Jim Scott froze as he glanced at the television and saw the flames pouring out of the tall building on the screen. He turned up the sound and then went ahead and took off his boot just as a plane slammed into the other building. Without really taking time to think—as his stomach knotted up in anger—he said aloud, "Boy, oh, boy, bin Laden, you jackass. You stepped in it this time."

He had just come in from the barn after riding with his wife, Holly. She and their two dogs, Lady and Bowser, were still in the barn. Jim had turned on the television and sat down to take off his riding boots.

Now he quickly put on his sneakers and was standing up as Holly and the dogs came romping into the house. Jim raised his hand in a motion to silence her; Holly saw the expression on his face and instantly quieted down as she, too, looked at the television.

After a few minutes of watching and listening, with tears welling in her eyes, Holly asked, "Oh, my God. Jim, what kind of insanity is this?"

Jim put his arm around his wife and hugged her. "If I don't miss my guess, Usama bin Laden just started a chain of events that may, in time, lead to us cleaning up the Mideast mess once and for all."

"Should we pack for Washington?"

"Yes. But we'll wait for General Bradley to call. May be a day or two. I'll get everyone else on the team ready to go."

"Why don't we just go? I for one am ready for some blood."

"Honey, you know I feel the same way. But I'm sure the government will shut down the skies in short order. Probably already have the process underway."

The "team" Jim referred to had been formed at the request of the President. The previous administration had a four-man secret committee that took care of "off-the-books" situations as they arose. Stanley James Scott, a former Marine and former CIA field operative, had been recruited to handle those jobs. The last one had been the elimination of Saddam Hussein—though few in the world knew Saddam was dead. Two of his generals, Haitham Al-Shahristani and Hussain Al-Majeed, had put forward one of Saddam's doubles in his stead moments after Jim had blown the top off of the real Saddam's head.

Jim had the foresight to have a long-range listening device pointed in the direction of where that had taken place and managed to get a recording of the plot to replace Saddam. The President was well aware that Iraq was now being run by the double and two generals, but chose to keep that information close to his vest. He felt that what was needed in Iraq was a regime change. Therefore, the ruse of the fake Saddam was allowed to go on without exposure.

While the previous administration—via a super-secret four-man committee set up by the President—had authorized the elimination of Saddam, the event itself had actually happened after the new President was sworn in. While he was still President-elect, the current occupant of the Oval Office had signed off on the deed. However, when it was completed, he ordered that the secret committee be disbanded. The President recognized the many talents of Jim Scott and those nearest him whom the President had come in contact with. That led to his request that Jim form his team of advisors—with the understanding that any "off-the-books" items needing attention would be the handled by Jim and/or his team. No government funding would be used on the team's existence.

The team picked up the nickname "Jim's Janitors" because they more often than not would be cleaning up someone else's mistakes. In fact, the only "mission" to date for the new administration had been to extract a general's wife from a ticklish situation in a supposedly

Dear Reader

Jim Scott and friends (now called Janitors—as in they clean up other peoples messes) are back for another kick at the can. All the folks who helped Jim and Holly in *Baghdad Butcher* (available at www.new-we.com) are back with a few new additions. The basic team set up at the end of *Butcher* is augmented by a new character. We also have a briefly mentioned character in this book who will become prominent in later books.

This time around, Jim and team are headed for Iraq within 72 hours of 9/11. For all of you who enjoyed *Butcher* and have been making requests (in some case *repeated* requests) for the next book, here it is…enjoy.

1/13/06

To Steve,

Thanks for

your service.

Best Wishes,

Mike John

Forward

For years it was rumored that a secret protocol to the SALT treaties between the United States and Soviet Union called for the banning and destruction of any and all small nuclear devices that were easily carried, thus suitable for terrorist acts.

This is the story of four such devices, which were never destroyed and made their way from the Soviet Union (or Russia after the fall of the Soviet Union) to an al-Qaida facility within the borders of Iraq.

friendly Mideast Muslim nation. The woman had gone off base in attire ruled not proper by the locals. She had been subsequently beaten, then, to show the mercy of the host nation, taken to a local hospital, where all access to her was denied.

Jim managed to enter the country on "other business" and rather forcefully removed the lady from both hospital and country before anyone really realized what was happening.

•

Holly went up from the expansive living room to their bedroom and commenced packing, her movements nearly robotic until the tears streaming down her face made seeing difficult. Then her anger returned and she heaved the bag she had been packing against the nearest wall.

Meanwhile, Jim got busy on the phone. First he placed a call to Drew Hollins, his father-in-law and former CIA legend, who had trained Jim Scott in clandestine work (long before Holly Hollins became Holly Hollins Scott). Jim said, "Drew, are you aware?"

"Yes, have the television on as we speak. These sons-of-bitches are gonna pay big-time for this! I've already called Boris. He's walking up the street to my place right now. See him out the front window. Thought we'd drive to Washington, since the skies will soon be cleared of traffic. By the time General Bradley gets to you, we'll more than likely be there. Boris and I aren't as slick on your computer set-up at the Joint as you are, but we should be able to do something worthwhile."

"Good idea, Drew. You might start by getting up to date on that place we've been monitoring in Iraq. Since the guards we've spotted there aren't wearing army uniforms, and we've all agreed they're probably terrorists of some stripe, that might be a good place to start extracting some revenge."

"More interested in that than in Afghanistan?"

"Yes. I have an idea the military will be all over Afghanistan if the President gives the okay, and I'd bet big bucks that he will. I'm thinking a raid on that obviously secret facility might be in order, and soon. I'd like to send a fast message to these bastards, and I'm sure the President will agree…even if it isn't al-Qaida. "

"Right you are. Boris or I'll give you a call when we get there."

"Thanks. See ya."

"Bye."

Drew's reference to the "Joint" was a facility built on Andrews Air Force Base outside Washington, D.C. for the Janitors. The construction costs of the Joint had been totally funded by Jim, at a cost of well over two million dollars, with another twenty million spent on the computers at the facility. The President had authorized building it on the Air Force base, and had also authorized the lease of a one-acre plot for it and the surrounding security perimeter. The building itself had a massive work area with all the latest in computer systems, which could access the CIA and FBI systems, with certain limitations. There was also a large combined lounging and kitchen area, and eight grand bedrooms, each equipped with a king-sized bed and full, well-appointed baths.

The name "Joint" came about in joking fashion when the building was finished. Jim had invited the six other members of the team to see it. As they walked around the spacious building, team member Boris Telman had tried his best at American slang when he said, "Nice joint." The name stuck.

Boris Telman was a retired Russian spy. He and Drew Hollins had been Cold War adversaries, though Drew never knew the true identity of Boris until the Soviet Union dissolved and Boris opted out. Once he saw the mess in Russia, as the nation tried to come to grips with the switch from communism to capitalism, he decided he was simply too old to put up with the hooliganism and left for the United States.

During his years as a master spy, he had opened literally hundreds of bank accounts around the world for his and his spy network's use. When the Soviet Union suddenly was no longer a nation, Boris, who had carefully and wisely always converted the accounts into U.S. currency, decided his paltry retirement funds just wouldn't do and, with no Soviet Union to turn the banked money over to, he kept it.

He had visited his old "friend" Drew Hollins and the two former spies hit it off quite nicely. He joined up with Jim Scott and his group during the aftermath of the episode that saw Jim eliminate Saddam Hussein. Jim had a practice of splitting any "found money" that happened to turn up during his capers with those who were part of the mission. On that particular occasion, the retirement fund of Boris Telman had grown greatly. Therefore, he had eagerly agreed to join the Janitors when offered the opportunity. He bought a home across the street and two doors up the block from Drew Hollins in the town of Belleville, Illinois.

That was where he was walking from while Drew had been on the phone with Jim. Now as they drove toward Washington, he said, "I suspect we are going to be quite busy for some period of time. This time the pay will probably be even less than the pittance the Soviets paid me…not that I'm complaining, Jim has taken quite good care of me."

Drew laughed. "Knowing Jim, I'd bet we stumble onto some money somewhere along the line. Money comes to that boy like rain to the ocean."

●

While Drew and Boris had been getting ready to leave, Jim had also been busy. His next call had been a brief one to Billy Longbow, his longtime friend and former comrade-in-arms when both were in the Marine Corps.

Billy had been a Marine master sergeant when he joined Jim's Fox Team for insertion into Iraq during Desert Storm.

When Billy answered the phone, Jim said, "If you've heard, you know we'll be heading east soon."

"I have, and Sally—between her tears—is packing for me right now. How long do you think it'll be before the general calls? I'm ready to rock-an-roll. I'm so damn mad I could spit."

"Yeah, me too. My stomach's a big fat knot of anger. To answer your question, I'd say a day or two. Guess we'll have to ask him to get us an escort, so we don't get blown out of the sky. How about checking the Gulfstream out and making sure it's ready to go. If you don't mind, you could stop by and get our stuff and get it and yours loaded."

"Sure. Talk to you later."

"Bye."

Jim's next call was to Hector Garcia. Hector had also been a Marine master sergeant and member of Jim's Fox Team. That team had been a ten-member group that had been dropped behind enemy lines to call in air strikes and cause as much trouble for the Iraqis as possible. The team had actually been split into two five-man groups: Fox Team One, headed by Jim, and Fox Team Two, headed by Ted Kuntz, who was now part of the White House staff as an assistant to General Bradley, who in turn held the White House post of Military/Intelligence Advisor to the President. That was a newly created post of some importance that carried with it the ability to contact the President at any time, and without prior appointment.

The call to Hector took a while to get through, since Hector wasn't at his home, office, or reachable on his cell phone. Finally, one of the messages Jim had left got through and the phone rang, just as Holly was coming back downstairs. Jim answered it. "This is Jim."

"Hector here, Jim. Got your message, and know why you're calling. I'm on my way home. I'm afraid Rosa's brother was in one of those buildings. She's beside herself, so am I. A guy couldn't ask for a better brother-in-law…just a hell of a nice guy."

"Oh, God, Hec. Sorry, pal. Do you want to stay with Rosa for now, join us later?"

"Naw, Rosa and I talked it over on the phone. She was taking the kids to school and then doing some shopping. She's more than ready for me to go into action…said she wished she could come along and shoot one of these Arab jerks herself. I can be ready in about two hours, though I don't know how I'm gonna get from Los Angeles to Washington. How do you plan to make it from your Montana retreat?"

"Fly. However, not until I talk to the general. Probably have to get military escort or some such. Same thing for you and Tom. Speaking of whom, will you call him?"

"Sure, amigo. Not real happy that I'm the one to ruin his fun. He just got back from his honeymoon two days ago. Wonder if he's told Jessie what he does in his spare time."

Jim chuckled, in spite of his anger. "I'd bet against it. I'd forgotten he was just now going on his honeymoon. Hell, with that fox he married, I bet all the time since the wedding has been like a honeymoon. Speaking of his wedding, I still have a headache from his bachelor party…even though it was over a month ago. I'll call you after I hear from the general, or Ted. Now that I think of it, the general is going to be real busy, so I'll probably be hearing from Ted first."

"Nah…ten bucks says it's the general."

"You're on. Talk to you."

"So long, amigo."

When Jim hung up the phone, Holly grinned and raised an eyebrow. "Nice way to be talking about another man's wife in front of your wife of less than a year."

"The girl is a fox...but not nearly as foxy as my gal."

"Nice try, buster. Ah, from what I heard of your end of the conversation, I take it Rosa is pretty upset, too."

Jim nodded and explained about Hector's brother-in-law.

Holly shook her head. "God, how awful."

•

Tom Wilson was the seventh member of the Janitors. He was a former Marine pilot who became involved with Jim under less-than-ideal circumstances. In a desperate effort to keep from losing his plane when had he fallen behind in his payments, he had turned to flying drugs. Due to the efforts of Jim, Tom was arrested but never charged. Not only did Jim get him out of a severe mess, he took Tom on as his pilot during the Saddam Hussein elimination process. During that overall operation, quite a bit of money had fallen into the hands of Jim...a good portion of that money was passed on to Tom. With that money—and a sizable loan from Jim—Tom had opened a flying school in Los Angeles.

By mid-February of the current year, Tom was doing well enough with the business that he decided to hire an office manager. The ad he ran for the position offered free flying lessons as a perk. The first—and last—day the ad ran, Tom had over a hundred applicants. One of those was Jessica Howard. Jessica was employed in the hi-tech field and was bored out of her mind. She didn't simply want this job; she decided she would have it. Sharp young lady that she was, she didn't just call. She found out who the phone number belonged to, took a deep breath, thought for a few seconds, and quit her job. Then she drove out to the small plane airport where Wilson Flight Training was located.

Jessica Howard was a tall, thin young lady who was very well-proportioned and was either beautiful or very pretty, depending on who was doing the looking. That fact was not lost on her. As she told Tom once after they had become involved, "I came out to apply for your job in person because I have a mirror and know I'm not the ugliest person around."

Tom was impressed by Jessica's initiative, her hastily drawn résumé, and personality. That she was quite attractive was not lost on Tom, but he felt certain she could do the job and do it right. He hired her on the spot and told her to commence answering the phone at once to inform any further job seekers that the job had been filled.

Over the next few months their relationship developed from employer/employee, to good friends, to romance. At their wedding, Jessica met those closest to Tom. She almost laughed outright when she met Billy Longbow and Jim Scott. Seeing those two with Tom was like "looking at three peas in a pod." All almost exactly 6 feet tall and none more than a pound either side of 185. The shorter, stockier Hector, she had long known since he handled security for the flying school. The two older men, Drew and Boris, she found quite entertaining.

She took to the three wives, Holly, Sally Longbow, and Rosa Garcia, at once, and them to her. While not threatened by the comparison, Jessica did admit to herself that Holly was well above the norm, in all respects. However, her wonderful body and knockout good looks almost seemed to dim in comparison to the person. She also found Sally and Rosa to be attractive, charming, and warm-hearted.

In short, every one of Tom's friends had impressed her. There was one thing, however, she did not know, and that, she was about to find out. Like a vast majority of Americans, Tom and Jessica were watching television, with tears rolling down Jessica's face, Tom clenching and unclenching his fists and swearing quite often. After news came in about the plane going down in Pennsylvania, Tom reached over and turned off the small office TV set. "Jessie, there's something we must discuss."

Jessica pointed at the TV and said, "But, Tom..."

"Sorry, honey, that will have to wait. Sometime soon, I'm going to be getting a phone call. Not much after that—my guess would be a day or two—I'll be going to Washington and probably will be gone for an extended period of time."

Jessica Wilson was not a naive little girl. From the time she had known Tom, about every six to eight weeks he would announce he was going away on business and always left her in charge of the business for the ten or so days he was gone. Now she said, "Those ten-day trips you've been taking every two months didn't have a damn thing to do with 'business.' I knew something was up with that, but didn't know what. I like all your friends, but they all seem to have a certain edge to them. Now that I think about it, so do you. Are you CIA or something?"

"Or something. Jim Scott heads up a group of 'advisors' to the President. I'm part of that group. The 'business' trips were for training. Jim wants all of us to be able to mesh as a unit, if and when we go into the field."

"Wait a minute! Advisors to the President…the President of the United States? The guy in the Oval Office?"

"The same."

"Just what do you *advise* him on, and what does that have to do with going into the *field*? Field as in going out and getting shot at? Like some Army guys or something?"

"Or something."

"You say that again and I'm going to punch you."

"Jessie, simmer down. Let me explain the whole thing," which he did.

When Tom was finished, Jessie took his face in her hands and kissed him. "Wow! I'm scared for you, but proud of you, too. And if you go after the guys responsible for this…this abomination, kill a couple of them for me! When you go to Washington, I know I'll have to stay here and keep the business running, but will you be able to stay in touch and let me know what's up?"

"To a degree. Our phone obviously isn't a secure line, so I'll have to be guarded in what I say. I doubt I'll be able to tell you much if we head off on some mission or the other. I'll ask Jim what I can and can't say. If we're going to be in the Joint for an extended period, I'm sure Jim will let you come out on weekends if you want."

"Wouldn't miss out on that for anything in the world. You said Holly was part of the team…Janitors. What a dumb name. What about Rosa and Sally?"

"No, just Holly. She was in the FBI when she joined up with Jim on the mission that got me involved. When they became engaged, she quit. Of course, by then she had already been to Baghdad with Jim, when he killed Saddam."

"He's really dead? I just saw him on television last week."

"He's dead. There's a double in his place. Two generals are really running Iraq…just have the fake Saddam as a front."

"Wow, this is neat. I know…not one word of this to *anyone*."

That conversation had taken place while Hector had been talking to Jim. Now Hector looked at his phone, smiled, and thought, *"Well, pal, hope this doesn't cause you too much trouble."*

He then made the call. Tom answered on the first ring. "Wilson Flight Training, Tom speaking."

"Hi, Tom. It's Hec."

"I've been expecting your call. When?"

"Jim guesses a day or two. I agree. Uh, have you told Jessie about us…the Janitors?"

"Just finished."

"Everything?"

"Yes."

"How'd she take it?"

"Fine. Jess is a pretty level-headed gal."

"Agreed. Okay, get packed. Jim or I'll call you when it's time. See you, amigo."

"So long."

2.

While Jim had been organizing things, Holly had been thinking. She was four months pregnant with their first child. She was concerned that Jim would be over-protective and not want her to remain part of the Janitors if things led to field action, as she was sure they would.

That night in bed, she finally decided to talk to Jim about her concerns. "Darling, I want to be with you through what's to come, as long as I'm able. I know when I get big as a house, I can't be bouncing around in Humvees or whatever, but in the meantime, I don't want to be left behind, just because I'm pregnant."

"Wouldn't dream of it. In the first place, there would be no living with you. In the second place, you're too valuable to leave behind. *You* tell *me* when the time has come to lighten up. After the baby is born, we'll have to play things by ear. I'm sure you realize that we're in for a long battle with these guys, now that they've opened the dance."

"Do you have any plans thought up so far?"

"Possibly. But we'll just have to wait for Washington to summon us…see if they have anything in mind."

"I wish it would be sooner rather than later."

"As I told you, it'll probably be a day or two."

The call came sooner than Jim had anticipated. Eighteen hours after Jim had taken off his first boot, the phone rang. Jim was sound asleep, but instantly awoke and answered on the first ring. He said, "Hello," in a surprisingly clear voice.

"Hi, Jim. Bradley here."

Army Major General Ellis G. Bradley was the Military/Intelligence advisor to the President and the Janitors' direct link to the President.

"Damn, General, you cost me ten bucks."

"How's that?"

"I bet Hector you'd have Ted call."

"Tough luck, pal. You can afford it. I think that underground facility you've been monitoring in Iraq needs some further attention. The boss agrees…even if we can't publicize it. He wants to send a message, and soon. Needless to say he's pissed, as we all are. We're already sure it was asshole bin Laden and his al-Qaida scum. It'd be wonderful if that facility in Iraq was theirs. I presume you're ready to go."

"Yes, sir. We'll probably need some sort of escort. So will Hector and Tom from Los Angeles."

"Already arranged. Your plane and theirs make it without fueling stops?"

"No. Probably need a stop. Maybe Scott or thereabouts."

General Bradley did some fast mental calculations and decided Scott Air Force Base in Illinois would work well with the change in escorts he'd planned. "Okay, I'll arrange it for Scott. I've got a number for you to call when you're ready to roll. Pass it on to the boys in LA…separate escorts for both of you. What about Drew Hollins and the Russian?"

"They're driving. Probably at the Joint by now, or soon will be."

"Good. Talk to you when you arrive," General Bradley replied before giving Jim the phone number to use for his military escort.

General Bradley always referred to Boris as "the Russian" because he was not all that comfortable having an ex-KGB agent working so close to White House matters. This in spite of both he and the President having agreed to the inclusion of Boris in the Janitors.

•

At about the same time that call was concluded, Generals Al-Shahristani and Al-Majeed were busy in Iraq. After lining out a few things they expected "Saddam" to do during the day, Al-Shahristani said to his counterpart, "We better make sure the al-Qaida operation at Hit stays underground as much as possible. You know the Americans will increase surveillance of us now. They will know it was bin Laden, but to be on the safe side will monitor us closely."

In that, he was correct. However, the surveillance on the activities just north of the Iraqi town of Hit had been increased for months, after Drew Hollins had noticed some unusual goings on in that area while scanning photos from spy satellites over-flying Iraq. Soon, increased observation of the area was requested. A joint services special ops team, lead by Army Sergeant Major Bruce Edmonds and including two Navy SEALS and a Marine gunnery sergeant, was sent in for a fast "look-see." They reported back that the facility was *not* an Iraqi army outpost.

When Drew and Boris arrived at the Joint, they both did palm and retina scans at the guard shack that was the only break in the electrified security fence surrounding the facility. They did the same thing at the entrance to the building itself. Only the seven Janitors and Ted Kuntz, their liaison to General Bradley and the White House, could get into the grounds and building. All had their palm prints and retina characteristics on file. For anyone else to enter, it required one of those authorized entry to punch in the correct security codes, and go through the normal procedure for their own entry.

Once inside the Joint, Drew and Boris immediately went to work compiling all the information they had on the Hit facility, and updating their database from the last time the Janitors had been in the compound.

As Drew and Boris worked, Jim, Holly, and Billy Longbow were airborne, with a two-plane military escort. Hector and Tom had left Los Angeles with their own escort an hour earlier. During the flights, other military aircraft replaced all four escort planes. Hector and Tom reached Washington twenty minutes before Jim and his two companions did, and were already hard at work when the others arrived.

After greetings all around, Jim said, "Either I, or General Bradley, is becoming too predictable. He mentioned the Hit location as a place for us to zero in on. I presume all eyes have been checking that area, so does anyone have anything of interest?"

Drew and Boris, having been there the longest, looked at each other, and Boris answered, "Activity aboveground seems to be ceasing. My guess is the Iraqis don't want to draw any attention to the area and expect us—I just said 'us'—you folks have made an American out of me. Anyhow, they expect *us* to give them a closer look now that bin Laden has struck in this manner."

Jim nodded. "Drew, do you agree?"

"Totally."

"Okay, here's the drill. All of you—except Billy—continue to monitor things there, while I contact the general. Billy, you lay out an attack plan. I'm thinking airdrop, do our thing, head south, and use helo extraction. If you come up with something better, great."

Billy just nodded, then he and the others got busy.

Jim placed a call to the White House line of General Bradley, and got Ted Kuntz instead. When on the line, Ted said, "Hi, Jim. The general is in the war room. He told me to get him out if you had anything."

"Nothing new. We're cobbling together a plan for insertion. If you can get away, we should have something on paper in a half hour or so. If you like it, you can take it back to General Bradley and see what he thinks."

"No problem getting away. I'll come over shortly. See you then."

"Right. Bye."

"So long."

Off the phone, Jim went to look over what Billy was doing. He made a few suggestions, and then checked in on the progress the others were making. The latest satellite photos, taken less than an hour previously, showed almost nothing. The only thing of note was a few extra guards at what had been previously determined to be the two entrances to the Iraqi facility.

With nothing new to see, Jim went back to help Billy. When they had finished the rough outline of an attack plan, Jim made seven copies and placed them and the original at different locations around a large conference table. Next, Jim told his team to take a break.

Everyone found something to drink—coffee, in most cases; water for Tom and vodka for Boris. A few also found something to munch on as they waited for Ted's arrival. Just about the time Jim was starting to wonder where Ted was, they all heard the soft bell that told them someone was at the fence line entrance. Every room in the facility had at least one bank of monitors showing the extremity of the building. At the sound of the bell, all except Boris glanced at the nearest monitor and saw Ted walking through the gate.

A short time later, he came in. "Sorry I took longer than planned. General Bradley came up for air just as I was leaving. Told him I was headed here, Jim, and what we had discussed on the phone. From what he said, it may be a week or three before we hit Afghanistan. However, he also said if your plan is okay, no reason to wait on implementing it. Assuming, of course, that it is of a clandestine nature."

Jim smiled. "What else would it be?"

After a few chuckles, Jim said, "Grab yourself something to drink, and something to eat if you're hungry, then let's get down to business."

Ted made a sandwich, got a cup of coffee, and joined the others at the conference table. The next half hour was spent going over the plan. A few suggestions were offered, changes made, and general comments followed.

The plan basically called for the Janitors and their equipment to be airlifted by Hercules C-130J transport to Saudi Arabia with other cargo. Once there, the other cargo would be deplaned, while the Janitors remained onboard and out of sight. Then the transport would head for Turkey, but follow an irregular route, west of the normal flight path from Saudi Arabia to Turkey.

About 20 miles west of the target, the Janitors and their equipment would be dropped. The airdrop would take place at night, with all equipment, rigging, and parachutes being either black or camouflage colored.

After raiding the facility, they would drive the two Humvees airdropped with them south toward the Saudi border. Theater circumstances would determine their extraction. The plan offered the possibility of driving into Saudi Arabia or being picked up by helicopter.

Satisfied they had a sound enough plan to approach General Bradley and the President with, Jim said, "Okay, Ted, that's it. Off you go to the White House. We'll need no more than an hour to get ready."

"Looks good to me. Wish I could go along. I'll contact you…or the General will."

•

The Janitors were not the only ones making plans. Saddam Alwash, an al-Qaida-trained Iraqi, was in charge of the targeted facility. With him were a mixed nationality group of 72 al-Qaida members. The underground man-made cavern was huge. The main corridor was thirty feet wide and over two hundred feet long. It was used for vehicle parking and had two sandbagged two-man machine gun defensive positions in the unlikely (they thought) event that they were ever attacked. Four different areas off the main corridor had from 3,000 to 5,000 square feet of space. One of them was for berthing, one was for eating and recreation, one housed weapons, and the largest contained a vast array of computer equipment.

The entire encampment had poured concrete floors. They had running water, a sewer system, and a self-contained power system. The two entrances were manned twenty-four hours a day, normally by two guards each at both ends of the edifice. One of these led out into the surrounding desert; the other led to an underground boat dock off the Euphrates River, about ten miles north of the Iraqi town of Hit.

Immediately after the glorious attack on the infidels, Saddam Alwash ordered that the entrance guard be increased to four men during night-time hours and three during daylight. He also ordered that the two machine gun pods be manned at all times.

While Alwash really didn't expect any trouble, it didn't hurt to be prepared. What he did not realize was that a man he hated (without knowing who he was) would be the very man to bring trouble to his doorstep. Aras Alwash, his cousin, was in Federal Prison in the United States, where he would remain for the rest of his life. Jim Scott had been the person responsible for that, though neither Alwash cousin was aware of that fact. Jim had busted up an Iraqi drug ring led by Aras, and had been responsible for his arrest and subsequent conviction. Now Saddam Alwash was about to come face-to-face with the very same man, though neither Jim nor Alwash would ever be aware of the unusual facts of fate involved.

Even if he would have known that he would soon be in contact with Jim, Alwash would have proceeded just as he did. He had, to him, more important things on his mind. One of his men was about to leave the facility with a small nuclear device. He was to take it to America, deliver it to al-Qaida members there, and help them deal the United States another blow. The bomb, in a suitcase-sized container, was one of four that would be used on America within the next eight weeks…one every two weeks.

•

When Ted returned to the White House, he went into conference with General Bradley. The general liked the plan and took it into the President when the President's time permitted. He said, "Jim Scott has drawn up a plan to take out that underground facility in Iraq near the town of Hit that we have discussed a few times already."

"Will it work?"

"I think so, sir. You know Scott…he seldom misses… Make that never misses, as far as I know."

"Can he bring it off without it becoming public knowledge?"

"I'm sure he can. Who would broadcast the fact? Certainly not the Iraqis. Whatever that place is, you can bet that it is something that shouldn't be. On our end, only you, I, Ted, and the Janitors will know. Oh, some of the support people they have asked for—airlift types et cetera will know—but what will they really know? Only that the Janitors went in and came out.

"Sir, if we're lucky, this is an al-Qaida facility and we can hit bin Laden where he least expects it…and soon. I can lay on the things Scott needs in about two hours. He said he needs about an hour's notice. It sure would be nice to smack bin Laden back within 36 or so hours. Just a damn pity we'd have to keep it to ourselves. The public could sure use that kind of a boost. However, it would make the job of coalition building very difficult if it leaked out."

"That was my real concern when I asked if we could keep it under our hats. Do you see any reason not to give him the go ahead?"

"None, sir."

"Do it."

"Yes, sir," a very happy General Bradley said as he turned and left the Oval Office.

Four hours later, the Janitors were on their way to Iraq.

3.

When the long flight to Saudi Arabia was over, Jim ordered his team to find the most comfortable place they could on the plane and try to sleep. It was early afternoon, and Jim wanted the drop to happen after full darkness.

While the Janitors slept—or at least tried to—the Hercules flight crew ate, showered, and slept. Meanwhile, the cargo that was to be off-loaded in Saudi Arabia was removed from the plane, and a few lightweight articles were placed on board…presumably to be taken to Turkey.

At 8 pm, the plane took off for the journey to Turkey, via Hit. By the time they reached the drop zone all of the Janitors were more than ready to deplane. The two Humvees, loaded with their equipment, went out first, then all of the Janitors jumped, Jim being the last to leave the plane.

Being less-experienced parachutists, Tom and Boris were the only team members to land more than twenty feet from one or the other of the Humvees. By the time they buried their chutes, as had the others, and made their way back to the Humvees, Tom and Boris found the others ready to go. A few joking comments were made about their tardiness, but the entire team was soon off. Jim, Holly, and Tom were in one Humvee, with Billy driving, while Hector drove the other with Boris and Drew aboard.

General Bradley had arranged to have air cover for the operation. That consisted of a constant patrol of two attack aircraft assigned to the Janitors. There was also an Airborne Warning And Control System (commonly called AWACS) plane hovering over the general area. However, it was not there for the sole purpose of assisting Jim's team. It was flying a normal flight plan and would also do its normal job of assisting any aircraft patrolling the no-fly zone over Iraq.

The Janitors had been outfitted with communication capabilities that allowed direct communication with their air cover and the AWACS plane. The latter had a call sign of "Big Brother" for all planes in the area. The two attack planes assigned to cover the Janitors had call signs of "Cop One" and "Cop Two." Jim and his team were to use the call sign "Robber."

Jim had made an unfriendly comment when told of the call signs, but was now using them as he used the communication gear to say, "Cop One, this is Robber. Over."

"Hello, Robber, this is Cop One. Over."

Assuming they might be overheard, it had been pre-arranged that communication would attempt to give the indication that "Robber" was airborne also, therefore Jim asked, "Do the skies look clear tonight?"

The pilot understood that Jim was asking if there was anything ahead of him to worry about and answered, "Clear as a bell, except for Cops and Robbers and Big Brother, too. Your heading is fine, by the way."

"Thank you, that was going to be my next question…over and out."

"Roger that. I'll call if I get lonely. Out."

By pre-arrangement, "lonely" meant that trouble was approaching the Janitors.

•

A number of ears had listened in as Jim and the pilot conversed. In the underground facility near Hit, the technician manning their radio gear sent someone for Saddam Alwash. When he arrived, the radioman said, "I think you should hear this. I don't understand it."

Alwash listened intently, then said, "I do not understand it either. However, it doesn't sound like their normal chatter. I think I will send out three teams of four men, one team each to the south, west, and north. On the river we should be able to detect anything unusual with the men we already have at the east entrance. Thank you for being so observant."

Shortly after this conversation, the three teams were sent out. All were on foot so as to avoid detection by any noise a vehicle would make.

•

Cops One and Two spotted the foot patrols almost at once and Cop One engaged his communication link to Jim by saying, "Say, Robber, I'm getting lonely. Almost said 'hi' to a bird dead in front of me. How go things there?"

Billy instantly stopped his Humvee and turned off the engine. Hector, able to listen in to the conversations of Jim and the aircraft, had his Humvee turned off within a second of Billy.

Jim replied, "Not lonely here. Having a blast doing loop-de-loops with clouds. Call back if you run into any birds. Out."

"Roger, out."

Hector was already walking toward Jim's Humvee as the pilot signed off. Billy and Jim got out, soon followed by the others in both Humvees. Hector said, "Sounds like we have company coming."

Jim nodded. "Okay, who volunteers?"

Hector looked at Billy. Billy looked at Hector and said, "Indian scout take first shift."

That drew a few chuckles as Billy went to get out a silenced rifle, checked it out, and put on a communication set that was locked in on a channel that matched the sets of everyone else on the team. Next he checked his sidearm, a silenced Walther pistol identical to the ones used by all members of the Janitors, looked at his compass, and headed off across the sand and up a dune that was only a few feet from where they had stopped.

After his first few steps, Jim said, "Uh, Billy, no prisoners. That team General Bradley sent out reported these guys are terrorists of some strips. We sure as hell aren't leaving any live terrorists behind to come blow up more of America…and we aren't taking them home."

Billy nodded as he headed off. As he did, the others all put on their communicaton sets. Those sets were quite small, similar to those worn on the sidelines by NFL coaches, but smaller and much lighter. They were transistorized, but had a range sufficient for the job at hand, as Jim had no intention of anyone getting anywhere close to out of range, as he didn't want anyone to risk getting separated from the team.

All members of the team were already wearing night vision goggles, an item that gave them vast superiority during the night to anyone not wearing similar gear.

About five minutes later, Drew said, "I'll follow Billy. When I think we're far enough out that you can start up again, I'll holler."

Hector said, "I can do that, Drew."

"No. I'm not so damn old that I can't pull my weight."

"That's a lot of weight to pull, old man," joked Boris.

Drew just gave Boris a dirty look and headed off in the tracks Billy had left.

The remainder of the Janitors just stood around the Humvees or sat in them for what seemed a lifetime before Drew said, "Okay, start up. If I can hear you, I'll let you know."

Jim got into the lead Humvee and replaced Billy as the driver. He started up and waited to hear from Drew. When he heard nothing, he started driving ahead. Hector soon had the second vehicle started and followed.

After about fifteen minutes, Drew said, "Can hear you. Shut them down."

Jim and Hector both immediately stopped their vehicles and turned them off. Then Jim said, "Billy, we aren't more that ten miles from the target. You should be about half that close."

Billy didn't reply, but Drew did, "He's onto something. I can tell by his body language."

The "body language" Drew spoke of saw Billy dive to the ground and sight in on the nearest of the four men who had just come over the crest of a sand dune. He waited until all four men were halfway down the dune before he re-sighted, this time on the man who was the longest distance from him, in the back of the fanned out procession.

His shot took the man in the throat, just above where neck joined torso. The man was dead before he hit the ground. The second shot took out the man next nearest Billy. By now, the other two realized they were under attack. Both dove to the ground. One died on the way down, the other seconds later.

After expelling a deep breath, Billy said, "Four found and down. Drew, is that you behind me?"

"Yes."

"Move on up to my position, then I'll go check them out."

"Right," replied Drew and did as requested. When he got there, Billy left and went to check on the four dead men.

Once he verified that all four were indeed dead, he went to the top of the dune, saw nothing, and said, "Okay, Jim, looking good. I don't see any others. I have a pretty good range of vision from here…why don't you go ahead and move on up?"

"Roger."

As the vehicles started up and headed for Billy's location, Drew joined him.

About the same time, Cop One keyed his mike and sang, "I'm not lonely anymore, but I would be just about as lonely as I was if I flew north or south." After humming a bit he simply closed his mike without further comment.

Jim got the message, as did the others in the Humvees. Into his headset he said, "Billy, our friendly escort tells me there are four more south and another four north. Something to watch out for when we go in. I don't want any surprises coming up behind us."

"Agreed," Billy replied.

Then Jim asked, "Speaking of things, which we weren't, do any of those birds have any kind of communication gear?"

"Yeah, radio. No requests for a report or anything yet. Wonder if they had check-in times?"

"Be my guess," Hector said.

"Mine, too," added Jim.

When the Humvees reached Drew and Billy, the rest of the team got out and Jim said, "Their call-in time worries me, but not much we can do about it. Okay, here's the drill. I checked our on-board navigational equipment and we're closer than I thought. Billy, you moved pretty fast, and Drew, you did fine keeping up."

"Especially for an old guy," joked Boris.

Jim smiled. "That as it may be, he did a good job and we're only about two miles from the west entrance of the facility. Which means a few things. One, according to our friends in the sky, we have four men two miles north of us, and another four two miles south. The other thing is we are through driving…at least for now. So, Billy and Boris, I want you two to go about half a mile straight ahead, then angle north. When you cross the tracks of that group, park and wait for them. Hector and Drew, you do the same, only head south. I don't know how many men they have, but our estimates are between 50 and 100, as you know, so 12 off whichever number is a good thing.

"Tom, you and Holly stay here. When I tell you, bring the Humvees in closer. I'll head straight for the entrance. When I can see it, we'll probably be as close as we dare bring the Humvees. This desert on a calm night, sound will travel pretty far, so we have to be careful. Any questions?"

There were none, and soon Hector, Drew, Billy, and Boris headed out on their respective missions. Jim got his silenced sniper rifle, picked up the radio that had been carried by one of the dead al-Qaida operatives, and headed toward the entrance of the target.

When they were gone, Holly got into one of the Humvees to monitor the communication gear that connected them to their air cover and Tom found the highest ground he could to keep a lookout for any approaching trouble.

Billy took the route outlined by Jim, with Boris walking about 100 feet behind him. He spotted their targets before he was seen and dropped to the ground. When he did, Boris dropped down and crawled up near him. By the time Boris reached Billy, the al-Qaida men were less than 50 feet away, evidently retracing their steps toward the facility. Billy motioned that he would take the two on the left; Boris acknowledged that and sighted in on one of the men to the right.

They fired within a second of one another and instantly sighted in on another target. Within three seconds, all four foes were down. Billy told Boris to hold fast as he went forward to check the four men. Two were dead, the two others soon were also, as Billy dispatched them with his silenced Walther.

After reporting that they had accomplished their task, the two men then set out to intersect with the path Jim had set out on.

Hector and Drew used the same procedure. However, things went a little less smoothly for them. Hector crested a sand dune at precisely the same time as the last four al-Qaida operatives. He reacted faster and was able to shoot two of the four before they could get off a shot. But, the other two both fired and hit Hector in the chest. All the Janitors were wearing bulletproof vests. Hector's saved his life, but the force of the two shots knocked him back down the dune. The severity of the shots also rendered him unconscious.

Meanwhile, Drew hurried a shot that hit one of the two remaining enemies in the leg. The other pulled his companion down and behind the top of the dune. Holly and Tom heard the shots fired by the al-Qaida operatives, started up the Humvees, and headed in the direction of Hector and Drew.

Drew decided against going to check on Hector and set off after the two remaining targets. Rather than charging straight at them, he started to circle around. The unwounded al-Qaida terrorist looked up over the top of the dune he was on, saw Drew, and fired. His shot just ticked the camouflage jacket Drew wore, without hitting flesh. Drew hurriedly sought cover.

As Holly crested a sand dune in the lead Humvee, she instantly saw her father pinned down, and soon saw Hector lying at the bottom of a dune. Without a second's hesitation, she headed for Hector.

Tom, right behind Holly, saw what she had, noticed where she was headed, and headed for Drew. When Holly reached Hector, she stopped and got out. After feeling his pulse and finding him still alive, she took out her Walther, ducked down as a shot whined off the Humvee, and fired back. She too missed, but headed up the dune. Both the wounded man and the other sighted in on her as first Tom, and then Drew, fired at the men.

Unfortunately, both aimed at the same man. Both shots hit the man and took him out of things. The other, already wounded man, sighted in on Holly even as Tom and Drew were turning their attention to him. She saw the man also and fired. Tom was just slightly faster than Drew in swinging toward the other man and he fired about the same time Holly did. Again, both shots hit home. Seeing all four men down, Tom headed in their direction, while Holly and Drew went toward Hector.

Jim heard the faint sounds of gunfire. He thought he had heard some firing earlier, when the first shots had been fired at Hector and Drew. Now he was certain of what he heard. Knowing all his people had silenced weapons; he knew someone was firing back at the Janitors. Using his headset, he said, "Report, please."

Drew replied, "Hector's down. The four bad guys are, also."

"How's Hector?"

"Just getting to him," replied Drew

"Alive," Holly added, as she neared Hector for the second time.

Drew quickly determined that the vest had saved Hector from serious injury and said to Holly, "Get the smelling salts out of the Humvee."

Holly did as told and handed the small vial to Drew, who quickly broke it open and held it under Hector's nose. Hector coughed, groaned, and opened his eyes. Groggily, he said, "God, I feel awful."

That utterance caused a number of smiles to break out and six people to exhale a larger breath than they had been.

Jim, who had stopped to listen in as Hector was being tended to, saw Billy and Boris approaching, so just stood and waited as they walked up. Then he asked, "How's the patient?"

Hector, whose headset had fallen off, was putting it back on after Tom, who had retrieved it, handed it to him. He answered, "Not worth a damn, amigo. Having trouble breathing. I'd bet on a couple of broken ribs. But, before you ask, Jim, I'm good to go."

"All right," replied Jim, "Billy and Boris are with me and we'll move forward until we can see the entrance. Somebody try to tape Hector's ribs…and you might give him a shot. When you have him patched up as well as you can, move out in our direction."

Without much conversation, Drew helped Hector off with his vest and took the emergency first-aid kit from Holly. Then he began to tape around Hector's torso in the area of pain. Once that was done, he gave Hector a shot of morphine.

In all the excitement over Hector, Holly had forgotten that she had just shot her first man. Now that they were moving forward in the Humvees, she started to think about it. She was in one Humvee with Tom driving; Hector was in the other with Drew driving.

After a few minutes of thought, she asked, "Tom, that last guy….did we both hit him?"

"Yes," answered Tom, who, when checking the man to make sure he was dead, had noticed that his shot with the much higher-caliber weapon had hit the man in the left lung, a shot that almost surely would have been fatal, in time. Holly's shot, on the other hand, had hit him square between the eyes.

He told Holly, "I'm pretty sure my shot was the one that killed him."

"Nice try, Tom…and thanks. But I know my shot was a head shot, just wasn't sure if I hit him or not."

They drove on in silence, until Jim suddenly said, "Stop."

Both vehicles stopped at once and were turned off.

As Jim, Billy, and Boris had gotten closer to the entrance, the ground had started to flatten out and become firmer. They found a small rise to hide behind and waited for the sound of the Humvees. After telling them to stop, Jim waited a short interval as the sound stopped, and then said, "We're about three quarters of a mile from the entrance, behind some sort of a knoll. We have four guards in sight. If you come due north from where we heard you, you'll more than likely find us."

"Roger," replied Hector, as he headed off in search of Jim, with the others following him.

4.

At about that time, the radio Jim had picked up crackled and Saddam Alwash asked for his three teams to report in. They were ten minutes past the time they should have called. When Alwash got no return call from any of the three units, he was perturbed, but not unduly alarmed. He felt that his men, in their eagerness to please, had just gone further than they were supposed to, and had gotten out of radio range.

Alwash was not as familiar with his equipment as he should have been. The radios had a far greater range than he imagined they did. One of those with Alwash felt certain that the men should still be well within range. However, he kept it to himself, because Alwash was known to have a violent temper and he did not feel inclined to have it lavished on him.

•

Jim looked at Billy and shrugged. "Well, it appears the cat is out of the bag. Let's keep a close eye on those four guards and see if their body language will give away their knowledge that we're coming."

By the time the others had joined those behind the knoll, the slovenly demeanor of four guards not really expecting trouble had continued. Leaving Billy at the top of the hill to keep watch on the guards, Jim slid down to the others, with Boris right behind him.

Jim kissed Holly. "Your first kill, honey. Nice shooting."

Holly didn't know if she should hit him, puke, or smile. She smiled, lamely.

Then Jim asked, "How are you holding up, Hector?"

"Awful. Let's get this over with so I can find a nice warm bed…halfway around the world."

Everyone smiled or chuckled and Jim said, "Well, if you're sure you can go, here's the plan. Hector, since you're not moving too well, you take Holly and Tom and try to work your way around to the river entrance. My guess is any guards there will be as bad as these out front…or worse. If you can take them out without causing a disturbance, by all means do so. Wait until the rest of us cause the shit to hit the fan, then work your way inside from their backside."

Hector nodded and asked, "You gonna take out the front guards from here?"

"Yes, in part. Billy and I'll stay here and let Drew and Boris get in as close as possible. If they get detected, we'll just blast away and hope for clean kills before any alarm goes off."

Hector nodded. "Okay, amigo, we're off."

After Hector, Holly, and Tom left, Jim told Drew and Boris to move in, but very carefully.

Drew grunted and Boris said, "Like snakes in the grass, we shall slither hither and yon."

Billy and Jim took up positions atop the knoll and agreed that Billy would take the two men on the right, Jim the two on the left. Then they waited. As they watched, Drew and Boris inched nearer and nearer the entrance.

Hector, Holly, and Tom meanwhile circled wide around the front entrance, until they came to the river. Then they headed upstream. When they saw the first of the guards, Hector halted them, watched, and waited. The man was smoking a cigarette. When he finished, he tossed the butt into the water and headed down a path. That path led to the boat docks, which were underground and out of view of Hector and his team.

After the man disappeared, Hector eased forward, with Holly and Tom close behind. When he reached the path taken by the guard, he went partway down it and had a good view of all three guards, three boats, and the rear entrance to the cave-like structure.

He motioned Holly and Tom forward, took out his Walther, and signaled them to do the same. All three then gently laid down their rifles and crept forward. The guards were doing a very poor job of guarding. For that laxness, they paid with their lives.

Hector and his cohorts got within twenty feet of the nearest guard without detection. At that point Hector stood up and shot the man. Well before the other two could react, they died under a hail of bullets from three guns.

Hector gently felt his ribs, motioned the other two to check on their victims, and said, "Jim, backdoor secure. Three down and out."

Jim replied, "Roger. Drew, Boris, you're close enough. You're both in easy pistol range. Drew, you take the one on the extreme left; Boris, you have at the one nearest him. Billy, you take the guy on the far right; I'll take the other one. On three. One, two, three."

All four men fired within a second of one another. All four hit what they were aiming at. Jim and Billy rushed forward, as Drew headed to check bodies while Boris stood his ground looking all around to make sure there were no surprises.

By the time Jim and Billy reached Boris, Drew had reported all four targets dead, though he had to help one on his way.

Hector heard Drew report the success of the front entrance operation, took his rifle from Tom (who had retrieved all three of them), and headed toward the rear entrance. There were two large metal sliding doors that came together in the middle. Those doors were closed about halfway, a fact that pleased Hector to no end.

When they reached the doors, Hector went to the end of the one they stood behind and peered around the edge to see the vast cavern before him. He also saw the nearest machine gun nest, which was manned. He quickly pulled his head back and whispered, "Jim, we have a machine gun, manned by two men, not twenty feet from us.

My guess is you'll run into the same thing. We'll wait here, until you start the dance."

"Roger. Thanks for the warning."

Drew was standing behind a door similar to the one Hector stood behind some two hundred feet distant. As Jim, Billy, and Boris approached, Drew peered around the edge and saw basically what Hector had at the other end. He whispered to Jim, "Same thing. Two-man machine gun encampment."

"Well," replied Jim, "this isn't good," just before replacing Drew and peeking around the door's edge himself. The two men at the machine gun were talking and not paying the least attention to the things they should have been.

Jim saw no one else nearby so he boldly walked around the door and shot both men. As their dead bodies slid down next to the gun behind the sandbagged enclosure, Jim raced forward, with the others following suit.

They all knelt down behind the sandbags and Jim whispered, "Two more down. Hector, take out the two guys you saw, then report."

"Roger," Hector said before peeking around the door again. He saw both men looking at each other as they talked, stepped out, and shot each man in the head, then rushed forward with Holly and Tom close behind.

He checked the pulse of both men, needed another shot to finish the job on one of them, then reported. "Both down and out, Jim. We'll hold here at the gun pit until you tell me otherwise."

"Roger."

Due to the lateness of the hour, most of Saddam Alwash's remaining force was asleep in the berthing pod. Of the eight (besides Alwash) who were up and still alive, three were in the radio room with Alwash, who by now was starting to worry just a bit more than he had been earlier. The other five were eating: two soon to take over one of the machine guns, the other three to take the watch in the communications center.

At night, the number of lights left on in the main corridor was reduced to a scant few, just enough to see one's way around. They were enough, however, to negate and render useless the night vision goggles the Janitors had worn. With all seven members of the team now sans goggles, vision was on an equal footing.

Not being one to sit around and think when all the thought in the world would bring little in the way of results, Jim shrugged and started down the corridor. The first opening they came to was the dining/recreation area.

Jim looked around the corner of the opening, saw the five men inside, pulled back, and held up an open palm. When he wiggled his fingers and thumb, the others understood there to be five targets inside. Without further hesitation, the four men walked into the dining area. When the first of those eating saw them, they opened fire. It was over in seconds, with next to no noise.

They quickly dragged the five dead men behind a counter, where they were unlikely to be seen by a casual observer walking by. Then, as Jim walked back to the opening, the other three carefully searched the remainder of the pod to make sure it was empty.

Back in the corridor, they went on to the next opening. This one contained the sleeping quarters, which were in total darkness except for the small amount of light from the dimly lit corridor. After peeking around the corner and finding darkness, Jim put his night vision goggles back on and peered in. He saw several bunks, some filled, more empty. He pulled back, slid the goggles up on his head slightly, and motioned sleeping men inside by putting his hands together and resting his head on them at a slight angle. The others understood at once and put on the goggles.

All four men went in and commenced a slaughter. Jim had no intention of trying to take prisoners. For one thing, it wasn't practical. For another, he still had visions of watching a plane intentionally fly into a tall building. They found forty men sleeping. None would ever wake up. After searching the entire area to make sure there was no one left, they went back to the opening and removed their goggles.

After checking the still-empty main corridor, Jim whispered, "Hec, we've found their sleeping quarters. About forty or so guys here, now dead, but about a hundred bunks. Don't know how many are actually in use. Several had no bedding, or next to none. We're in the second pod off the main corridor that we found. If you want to move up, do so. Just be careful. When you come to any pods, check them out. My guess is there will be at least one more. The way this thing is laid out, probably two or three more."

"Roger," Hector replied as he motioned for Holly and Tom to follow him.

When he stood up from inside the machine gun pit and looked down the main corridor, he could see Jim and his group approaching from the other direction. He just gave a little wave, which was returned by Jim. Hector reached the armament pod before Jim got to the communications pod. He peered around the corner, found it dark, put on his goggles, and saw what appeared to be an area with no one in it. He quickly stepped inside, followed by Holly and Tom, who had put on their goggles as well.

He whispered, "Jim, I've found their arms cache. Other than weapons, it seems empty...I mean, no one about."

Jim didn't answer because he was peeking around the opening of the communications pod. Jim saw four men and quickly pulled back. This time he paused to think. He was sure now that this was the last pod—hence, the last of the enemy was inside.

He whispered, "Four inside. Looks like their com center…let's try to take one or two alive…but not at the risk of getting our asses shot off."

The other three men smiled and all four walked in. When seen, Jim shouted, "Freeze," in perfect Arabic.

Saddam Alwash went for his sidearm, as did his men. All four died in seconds.

Jim said, "Damn. Well, no one to question, so let's see what we can find out on our own. Tom, Holly, guard the back entrance. Billy, how about taking the front."

Billy nodded and asked, "What about the Humvees?"

Jim thought just a second and said, "Good point. Drew, Boris, you guys feel like getting them?"

"No," joked Drew, then added, "Come on, *old* man."

While Jim started investigating the computer equipment in his pod, Hector found the light switch in the armament pod and started searching there. It didn't take him long to find something he wished he hadn't. He walked down the corridor to where Jim was, walked in, and said, "You ain't gonna like what I think I found."

"What?"

"Nukes."

"You're shitting me."

"Wish I was. Looks like those satchel ones the Ruskies had."

Boris, who could hear the conversation quite well in spite of bounding along in a Humvee, said, "That'll be 'Russians' had, Mexican rodent."

Everyone laughed, but the mood only lasted a few brief seconds. Then Jim said, "Boris, when you get back, check this out with Drew. Hector, stay here and help me with these computers. I'm finding some interesting stuff. I think we may have just stumbled onto bin Laden's financial center…or a good portion of it anyhow."

Drew laughed outright. "See, Boris, as I told you 'Like rain to the ocean'."

Boris laughed at the joke between him and his friend, but said nothing. He was too busy hoping against all hope that what he would find in the pod uncovered by Hector was not what he feared it was.

As Hector and Jim searched on through various floppy discs and paper records they could find, trying to uncover any access codes, they heard the loud noise of the Humvees pulling into the facility.

When they were turned off, Jim said, "Drew, if you remember, there was that one walled-off sleeping area with nicer accommodations. My guess is that was the main guy's sleeping quarters. Since he wasn't there, he's probably one of the guys here or one of the guys we dusted in the dining room. Before you help Boris, how about tossing that room and then checking the bodies of those guys in the dining room. I've found some nice accounts belonging to asshole bin Laden, but can't find access codes."

"Will do."

"Tom, please go relieve Billy so he can come down here and help me. Besides me, he's our best computer geek."

"On my way."

"That's Indian 'geek,' sir," joked Billy.

When Billy arrived, Jim told him to check the bodies in their pod before helping on the computers. The third body Billy checked was that of Saddam Alwash. In a pocket of the tunic he wore, Billy found what had eluded Jim to that point. He handed the list of codes to Jim and asked, "This what you're looking for?"

Jim scanned it and replied, "Bingo! Drew, call off your search. I've got what I need."

Boris said, "Drew, you better get down here. We have a catastrophe."

Even as Jim started accessing various accounts of the al-Qaida network, he asked, "How so?"

"I found what Hector referred to. He was correct. There is a rack here that contained four small, portable nuclear weapons of Russian design. There are three bombs remaining. All have dust on them. The empty space has no dust."

Jim sighed. "Get them loaded."

Just as Jim said that, Hector, who had been working on another of the computers, trying to see what he could find of interest, said, "Sweet Jesus!"

Jim glanced over at him and asked, "What?"

"Jim, you can't believe all the intelligence data we've got here. We're gonna have to load up all these computers and discs. God knows how much data we can pull off the hard drives."

"Okay, get to it. Pull one of the Hummers down here and start loading."

Jim got back to work on his task, which was using the access codes Billy had found to transfer as much of bin Laden's money as he could.

Just as he had cleaned out one account, Holly said, "Uh, Jim...a boat's coming down the river."

"Guys, I'm trying to liberate two hundred and seventy odd million from bin Laden and I could do so much better without all the interruptions," Jim said, sighed, and then added, "sorry, honey. Drew, go help your daughter. Holly, stay out of sight."

"She's your wife."

"Not for long, if he's going to be a jerk."

Jim shook his head in dismay and kept at his task without responding to father-in-law or wife. Transferring money from someone else's account into his without leaving a trace took time. Jim had a prickly feeling on the back of his neck that time was going to be a precious commodity.

The next interruption proved him correct. The radio sounded as General Al-Shahristani said, "Hit Station, this is headquarters. Over."

Jim instantly recognized the voice of Al-Shahristani from two previous encounters. He looked at Billy. "You take it. He'd probably recognize my voice."

Billy looked at Jim in a funny way, until the light dawned that *Jim* recognized the other voice. He quickly nodded, picked up the radio hand mike, and—in the fluent Arabic he spoke—said, "Hit Station here. Over."

"Do you have any signs of trouble?"

"None. We have posted extra guards, but nothing of note has happened."

"I just received word that not too long ago there was some strange radio traffic from the infidels that no one here has been able to decipher."

"Yes, we heard that, also. We have sent out foot patrols who have been reporting in regularly, without any sightings of trouble."

"Very well. Headquarters out."

"Roger. Out."

•

Two things bothered General Al-Shahristani. He had never heard the voice on the other end of the radio—normally only three men used that radio and he knew all three voices. In addition, that voice never said "sir" during the entire conversation.

After consultation with General Al-Majeed, they agreed that the matter should be investigated. The nearest force of any size was an Army Battalion at Ramadi, some 40 miles southwest of Hit. They decided to send a force of a hundred men to the Hit facility as quickly as possible.

•

Jim meanwhile was making progress. However, he had twelve separate accounts to "liberate." The largest of those, containing over $100,000,000.00, was safely tucked away in an account of Jim's. He had been working his way down the list in the order of the size of the account. The account he was working on when the radio message came in had been for about $14,000,000.00. With still over $42,000,000.00 to go, spread over five more accounts, Jim knew he was pushing his luck. He had no illusions that General Al-Shahristani would be fooled by Billy's best efforts.

As Jim worked, Hector determined that the first Humvee was as full as it was going to get and still be able to haul two or three people. Without bothering Jim, he got in and drove it to the front entrance and drove the other one back.

Jim, of course, heard the racket, but kept on working. With another account transferred, he had that prickly feeling on the back of his neck again and said, "Tom, get in that Humvee and call our air cover. I have a feeling we are gonna get company before long."

"Roger," Tom replied as he came in from outside and climbed into the Humvee.

To be sure of a clear signal, he pulled it out of the entrance opening and then keyed the radio as he said, "Cop One, this is Robber. Over."

"Go ahead, Robber. Over."

"I had the feeling you might be getting lonely. Over."

"No, not right now, but thanks for the thought. Over."

"Roger. Out."

Knowing Jim heard the entire conversation since he had left his headset on, Tom said nothing further. He wondered why Jim was worried, but decided not to bother him now with any idle questions.

5.

The force out of Ramadi turned out to be closer to a hundred and fifty men than 100, but they moved fast. Within ten minutes of getting the call from headquarters, they were underway. Less than five minutes later, the cover aircraft saw them.

Cop One keyed his mike and said, "Ah, Robber, I got lonely after all, *very damn lonely*. I guess you're still southwest of me. Over."

Before answering, Tom said, "Jim, you heard. What should I do?"

"Find out how much time we have?"

"How much do you need?"

"At least fifteen minutes, maybe more."

"Okay," Tom replied before returning the call from Cop One.

"Cop One, this is Robber. If you're real lonely, you can dance with my wife when you get back to base. I've slowed down some in my old age. Wouldn't ask you to dance with the old hag longer than about fifteen minutes. Over."

Cop One instantly picked up on a request for time of arrival of the Iraqi force and replied, "Oh, I'm not as old as you, so I can probably handle her for *about* half an hour. Over."

"Roger, you got her. Out."

"Jim, you get all that?"

"Yes. Listen up, everybody. Pack up and get ready to roll. When I'm done, I'll bring this computer with me. Without the hard drive, they'll never figure out where their money went. Plus which, God knows what else might be on it. Billy, Hector, see if you can rig this place to blow when we split. I'd just as soon they didn't know what we took."

"No problem," replied Hector, and he and Billy headed to the armament pod.

With the amount of explosives in the armament pod, it was easy to rig for an explosion. With the help of everyone except Tom and Jim, they quickly moved large quantities of explosive material to each of the pods. Billy took a keg of gunpowder and laid a line of the material to each of the piles of explosives, then one long connecting line of the powder to the front entrance.

As Jim continued to work, the others finished loading up. Hector and Billy carefully checked over the inventory of weapons, found some hand-held rocket launchers, and loaded twelve of them—six in each Humvee. Since Boris wanted to stay with the nuclear weapons, he, Billy, and Tom got into the Humvee nearest the entrance and waited.

The next call from Cop One added urgency to the situation, as he keyed in and said, "Robber, Cop One here. In about ten minutes, I'm gonna head for home so I can dance with your wife. Over."

"This is Robber. As I think about it, I may have forgotten to tell you something. She's a bit fat. Out," Tom replied.

Jim said, "I heard. I'm on the last one. Be done in a few minutes."

Holly, sitting in the Humvee outside the opening into the communication pod with Hector and her father, wondered just how close Jim was going to play it. "A few minutes" off of ten didn't leave much room for error.

Finally, Jim was done and he grabbed the computer tower from the unit he had been using and ran for the Humvee. As he got in, he handed the tower to Drew, started the engine, and drove to the end of the corridor, where Hector told him to stop. Hector leaned out the door, fired a shot at the gunpowder (which ignited it), closed the door, and said, "No damn detonators. Let's make tracks."

Jim swung around the Humvee in front of him and headed northwest, away from the complex. Billy, driving the other Humvee, followed close behind. As they drove away with as much speed as possible, Jim keyed the radio and said, "Robber here, Cop One. How are things looking? Over."

Cop One could see the Humvees speeding away and could also see the approaching Iraqi force. The closeness of their departure to being caught had him almost holding his breath. He replied, "In about another minute, I have to go get a drink for this bird. Your heading looks fine to me. Over."

"Roger. Thanks. Out."

"You cut that a little close, husband."

Jim smiled and replied, "A minute is better than thirty seconds. By the way, what about your boat?"

Holly grinned. "Thought you'd never ask. Went on by."

The Iraqi force *was* close enough to see the Humvees depart, but they didn't have enough speed to catch up. The force commander was trying to figure out his next move when the earth erupted just in front of him. Debris from the mammoth explosion rained down on his column. By the time things settled down, the Humvees were out of sight.

In the Humvees, the Janitors felt the shock wave of the explosion but were unimpeded by it and drove on. The Humvees had been equipped, in addition to the radio link to their cover, with a secure communication link with Big Brother, the AWACS plane also flying overhead.

Jim now used that link. "Big Brother, this is Robber. I need to be patched through to the White House, General Bradley, ASAP. Tell him Fox One is calling. Over."

The communication commander aboard the AWACS had been observing all the goings on below and had a feeling that whoever in the hell that was down there probably had the heat to be calling the White House or he wouldn't have asked for the link in so firm a manner. He replied, "Right away. Over."

It took a few minutes to get General Bradley on the phone. Ted Kuntz had taken the call and had to pull the general out of a priority meeting. When told who was calling, General Bradley hurried to the phone in his office and said, "Bradley here."

"Hold on while I connect you, General," the communications commander replied.

"Robber, your party is on the line. Over."

Jim said, "General, Jim here."

"What is it, Jim?"

Knowing the call could be heard aboard the AWACS, Jim answered, "The worst. I've got stuff with me that *MUST* get back to Washington. An Iraqi force is pursuing me. We have lost them for now, as best as I can tell, but I'm sure more will try to box us in. I'll never make the Saudi border. I'm heading northwest now, but plan to swing around and head for that highway that leads from Baghdad to Jordan in a short while. I need you to get our Hercules, or another one, to land on that highway and pick us up.

"I don't have a secure link to my air cover, but I can get directions out of harm's way from them. We've established a pretty good rapport with them and have had no trouble getting messages across without giving away the game. Well, not totally. I don't know if the AWACS and the fighters have a secure link…"

"We don't," interjected the communications commander aboard the AWACS.

"…okay, that idea just went to hell. Thanks, Big Brother. So, General, we'll have to use plain language. However, I think everyone involved can bring this off. I do need you to get that Hercules airborne soon. And, sir, I'd like you to get the President to authorize an attack on the Iraqis if all else fails. What I've got is that serious."

General Bradley knew Jim well, and knew if he was willing to risk a potential war over the information he had, it was probably worth risking. That in mind, he said, "Okay, Jim, hold the line. The President is in a serious meeting, as you can imagine. I'll get the Hercules up first, then get the President."

"Yes, sir."

General Bradley put the call to Jim on hold, and placed another secure call to find out if the Hercules Jim had used to get to Iraq was still in Turkey. It was and he said, "Alright, I want it airborne and headed for the location of their earlier drop site at once. Within ten minutes. This is a national security matter with capital N and S."

After a prompt "Yes, sir," General Bradley hung up and went after the President.

The President was in the White House "Situation Room"—or War Room as it was commonly called. General Bradley entered as the meeting Ted had pulled him out of was still going on. He said, "Sorry for the interruption, Mr. President, but I must speak to you privately, now, on an absolutely urgent matter."

The President looked around the table, which included the most senior members of his administration, the intelligence community, and military, and knew feelings would be hurt if he kept them in the dark about whatever General Bradley had on his mind. He also remembered that Ted Kuntz had used Jim Scott's name when pulling the general out of the meeting. He stood up and said, "Excuse me, I'll be right back. Time for a short break anyhow."

As they walked out of the War Room, General Bradley said, "Thank you for the trust, sir. My office, if you don't mind."

"Lead the way."

As they walked toward General Bradley's office, the general said, "Sir, Jim Scott has found something in his raid that is so hot he's going to meet a Hercules on the highway leading from Baghdad to Jordan. He's under pursuit. He wants you to authorize an attack on the Iraqi force, if it comes to that."

"Attack on ground forces?"

"Yes, sir."

"Do you know what he has?"

"No, sir, but he used the term 'the worst.' My sickening guess would be nuclear."

"Knowing Jim, you're probably right. He isn't the type to go off half-cocked and ask us to risk a war we're really not ready for…and God knows what kind of diplomatic fallout…unless it's real serious—and nuclear weapons would fall into that category. Either that or bio."

"That possibility is also viable, sir. But I have a feeling it's nukes."

Just as they reached General Bradley's office, the President said, "All right, whatever he needs."

General Bradley picked up the receiver, punched the hold button down, and said, "Jim, the President is here. I'll let you talk to him."

"Yes, sir."

Taking the phone, the President said, "Another nice mess you bring me. Why is it every time you go off on one of your missions, you bring a pile of cow dung back with you?"

"Just lucky, sir."

The President smiled. "Just what is your situation and just what do you want done?"

"My situation is we have completed the mission, but have hot pursuit after us. For now we have lost them, but I don't know for how much longer. They, the Iraqis, will almost certainly try to seal the borders as well as they possibly can. General Bradley has a Hercules on its way to us and it will land on a highway, pick us up, and away we go.

"The catch is, if they, the Iraqis, find us, we may not have enough fire power to get out with our skin. Right now, our skin is the least of my worries. We have a gold mine of intelligence, and have three out of four devices you are going to be very unhappy about. The fourth one, I fear, may be headed your direction."

"Jim, are you telling me what I think you're telling me?"

"Sir, yes, but hold on just a second. Big Brother, are you still with us? And if so, are you the only one listening?"

"Yes on both counts."

"Mr. President, can you give this fellow a direct order, as Commander-in-Chief, to take what he's about to hear to his grave?"

"I can, and hereby do. Do you have it Big Brother? Do you want these verification codes that General Bradley has around here somewhere to verify who I am?"

"That won't be necessary, Mr. President. I recognize your voice and I placed the call to the White House. You can rest assured I will *never* repeat anything I hear of this conversation."

"Thank you. Now, Jim, are we talking nuclear?"

"Yes, sir. We found a rack that held four satchel-sized devices—three had dust on them. The fourth slot was empty, and no dust on the rack."

"God Almighty."

"My thoughts also, sir."

"Very well, Big Brother, if it comes to it, do *not* let these people be captured. That includes direct attack on anyone needing to be attacked to stop that potential capture."

"Yes, sir."

"Uh, Mr. President."

"Yes, Jim."

"If all else fails, and we are about to be captured, please authorize Big Brother to take us out. I mean, blow us all to hell. Now that we have these three away from them, I don't want them to get them back. Also, while the intelligence boys will be denied the other information we have, al-Qaida will be dealt a severe blow in not having it either."

"Big Brother, you heard him. I don't like this one bit, but agree with you, Jim, that they don't need to get their hands back on those weapons. However, please do me a favor and don't let it come to that. In fact, get on that airplane without incident…that's an order."

Jim chuckled and replied, "Yes, sir."

The President handed the phone to General Bradley and said, "See you back downstairs," and left the general's office.

General Bradley said, "Okay, Jim, I heard most of that…(the President's end of the conversation, at least)…and could figure out about what you said. I'll get more planes scrambled from Saudi. Good luck."

"Thank you, sir. Goodbye."

"So long…hope to see you soon."

•

By the time that conversation ended, General Al-Shahristani had received the report of the total destruction of the Hit facility. When he received that report, a chill went down his spine and a thought flashed through his mind…Jim Scott.

Dismissing that thought as groundless, he conferred with General Al-Majeed and ordered all available forces out to cut off escape. There was a small garrison at the town of Rutba, which was the nearest force to the Jordanian border. It was ordered out to seal that border.

Garrisons at Al Qaim, Ana, and Sinjar were ordered to seal the Syrian border. A much larger force from the more distant Mosul was ordered to assist those groups as quickly as they could reach the border area.

Small garrisons at Ash Shabicha, As Salman, and As Busalya in the south were ordered to seal off the Saudi border. The remaining force at Ramadi was also ordered south, to the Saudi border.

Finally, all available patrol craft on the Euphrates River were ordered into action. Since the invaders were in the southwest, Al-Shahristani wanted them kept there.

The generals considered sending a larger force toward the Jordanian border, but decided instead to have their fake "Saddam" call the Jordanians and ask for assistance.

They felt that was really an unnecessary risk, because any invading force would be least likely to head for Jordan, due to the relationship between Iraq and Jordan. The Syrian border also seemed less likely than the Saudi border. So all extra available forces were dispatched in the direction of the Saudi border.

It was also ordered that any helicopters sighted should be shot down at all costs.

6.

As Jim drove, he had a thought and called the AWACS. He keyed the secure line and said, "Big Brother, this is Robber. Over."

"Big Brother here. Over."

"I just had a thought. You said you don't have secure communications with Cops One and Two. How about a transponder?"

"One-way communications only. Us to them."

"That'll work. How about telling them what's up, with limitations, and tell them to warn me if I make a turn toward trouble. My plan is to double back on myself, drive in circles, and just generally make it difficult for those guys we left at the target site to gain on us."

"I can handle that without bothering the Cops. We have a visual on you. Not a great one, but enough to keep you out of trouble."

"How'd you find us?"

"Honed in on your signal while we were talking to the big boss."

"Well done. Thanks. I still think the Cops should be given a little info so they don't get surprised by the Hercules or orders to shoot at whatever."

"I agree. By the way, if I ever meet you, I'd like to buy you one hell of a big drink. I don't know if I would have balls enough to ask for my own destruction in a worst case scenario."

"Sure you would. But it helps to be a little crazy, which we obviously are by being in our current predicament in the first place."

"If you say so…but you still have my respect. Out."

"Roger. Out."

The AWACS communications officer realized that guy down there's final request made on the President to order his own death was the bravest thing he had ever heard, and he would never be able to tell anyone the kind of man America could produce.

From time to time, the AWACS would tell Jim to alter course one way or the other, but for the most part the Iraqis never came close to the Humvees. As the Hercules neared, Jim was directed to the highway and was sitting alongside it when the big bird landed.

The Hercules was designed to land on any surface smoother than a cornfield—and with a good pilot…and Major Timothy Scalley was a *very* good pilot—maybe even a cornfield. A well-surfaced highway was no problem for it, and it pulled to a stop about three hundred feet past where Jim had been waiting. Even as the plane landed, the Humvees were moving and as the cargo hold dropped down, they arrived and drove right up the ramp.

They were airborne in a matter of minutes. Jim got out of the Humvee and went forward to the cockpit and said, "Thanks," glanced at the insignia on the pilot's jacket, and added, "Major."

The plane's captain replied, "You're welcome. The name's Tim, Tim Scalley. How'd you manage no traffic on that road?""

"Just lucky," Jim said jokingly, then added, "Home, James. Oh, I'm Jim Scott. My team and I are forever indebted to you and the Air Force."

"Nice to meet you, Jim. 'Home, James,' I know about. Andrews or bust. General Bradley from the White House talked to me personally and said that if I crash this baby, I better die in the crash or he would kill me himself. I take it your mission went well."

"You might say…especially now that you've plucked us from a potentially ticklish situation. I need to make a phone call, if possible."

"Sure. Give our comm officer the number and he'll get it for you."

"To Israel."

"No problem."

Jim went back to the communications officer, told him what he wanted, and gave him the number. Soon the phone was ringing, and the phone was handed to Jim.

Awakened from a sound sleep, Benjamin Schiller, the number two man in the Israeli Mossad, said, "Schiller."

"Hi, Ben. Jim Scott here."

"Who else? I know few people that care little for my sleep patterns, except those I work for."

"Ben, I need you to come to Washington ASAP. Big-time serious."

"Do I get a hint?"

"You remember those items Sid got a line on in our former main foe's backyard? The ones you put a little surprise in?"

"Read you loud and clear."

"I need you to look at something similar and tell me if it was one of the items you had fun with."

"I'll be on a flight within the hour."

"Thanks. See you there."

"Right."

Earlier in the year, Jim found out that several nuclear weapons of the former USSR were sold to Iraq and other similar countries, and that Israel knew of the sale and had not informed the United States of the transaction. The President had asked Jim to find out what he could about the matter. What he found out was that his old friend Ben Schiller had sabotaged the weapons and made them useless. Their only danger was to anyone using them.

Now Jim was hoping that the devices he had—and the one he did not have—were part of the group sabotaged by Ben. He had a sick feeling that would not turn out to be the case, but it was a base that had to be covered.

•

When the C-130 landed at Andrews, General Bradley was there to meet them. After backing the Humvees down the ramp, they pulled to a stop and the general walked up to Jim as he got out of the vehicle. "What now, Jim?"

An airman standing nearby was signaled over by Jim, who tilted his head in Hector's direction. "I've got an injured man. Can you take him to the base infirmary for me?"

Seeing General Bradley in full uniform nearby, the airman at once answered, "Yes, sir."

Jim called out, "Hector, go get checked out."

Hector, who was in a great deal of pain, readily agreed. As they drove off, Jim said, "Sorry, sir. Had to take care of that first. Now, I suggest you come over to the Joint with us. I see you have an escort, so I propose that we give you the nukes, the hard drives from their computers, and you can send them off to wherever. Tell whoever looks at the nukes to be careful. They may have been booby-trapped…by Ben Schiller."

"Oh, do you think these are part of the bunch the Israelis fixed?"

"No, but best to be sure. I called Ben from the Hercules and he's on his way here."

"Without clearing it with the President first? Do you think that wise?"

"Maybe not wise, but fair. If these things are operational, the missing one could be headed for Israel."

"I'd bet against it."

"Me, too. However, only fair to warn them of the possibility. If Ben says he didn't fix these, then we can give him the warning verbally while he's here and that will be out of the way."

"Okay. Not sure the boss will be thrilled with you on this one, but I see your point…and I guess he will, also. Let's go."

With that, General Bradley went back to his car and told his driver to follow the Humvees. Jim got in and headed for the Joint, with Billy following in the other

Humvee, the general next in line, followed by two half-ton trucks he had brought with him.

When they reached the Joint, Jim and the other Janitors got out and, as General Bradley walked up, Jim said, "Okay, here's the drill. The weapons we appropriated, including the nukes, to the general. The computer towers with the hard drives in them also go with him. The floppy discs and hard copy printouts—and all the other paper stuff, we keep."

To the general, he added, "Sir, please have one of your guys guard our front gate. Nobody but you and my people should be allowed to pass. After we go over all the paper, we'll copy what we want and send it all over to you at the White House. You can deal with what agency gets what…same for the discs."

"If I read the President properly—and I'm pretty sure I do—we'll make copies of all of it and give it to each of the intelligence organizations. By the way, what type of weapons, besides the nukes?"

"Some stuff—hand-held rockets and so forth— that we took in case we had to make a fight of it with the Iraqis. Since we didn't, maybe your guys can track down where it came from. Some of it looks like our stuff, so the serial numbers might offer a clue."

"Good idea. Maybe we'll get to bust some balls. What about the information on the discs?"

"If you want, we can forward what's on them as we put each in our computers for review. Just give me a list of who you want to get it, and we'll work up a program so that each time we put a disc in it will automatically get forwarded to all on the list. Along with the list, have directions for each computer that will receive it all."

"All right…let's get going."

By the time the two men had finished talking, the Janitors were already unloading the Humvees. Tom and Holly had accessed the front gate and the entrance door to the Joint and had blocked both gates and the door with a box of the paper material. Soon the procession was a well-run operation.

The general had the weapons, including the nuclear satchels, put in one of the trucks, and the hard drives put in the other. He then told the officer in charge of each truck where to take the material in his respective truck. That done, he started helping the Janitors carry the remainder into the Joint, while his driver stood guard at the front gate.

Just as the last of it was being picked up by Billy and Tom, an Air Force pick-up truck pulled up and Hector got out. Jim, who had walked out with Billy and Tom to make sure they had everything, asked, "Hi, Hec. How are you?"

"Broken ribs. Four…looks like each bullet broke two. Sore as hell, but I'll live. They gave me some pain pills—which aren't doing much—but I just took one before coming back here."

"Glad that's all it is," said Jim as he and Hector followed Billy and Tom through the first gate, where he picked up the box blocking it, and let it close.

Hector looked at the other box and Jim said, "No, leave it. Somebody else can come back for it."

Hector grunted, ignored Jim, and picked up the box with a degree of pain and followed him into the Joint. As they walked by, Billy returned and got the box holding the door open and said, "Nice to see you're as dumb as ever, Hector."

"Shut up, Indian."

While the last boxes were being brought in, General Bradley said, "Guess I better hit the road. I'll give you the word on where to send the information on the discs as soon as I get back to the White House. When is Schiller due in, Jim?"

"Soon, would be my guess."

Billy looked at the general and grinned. "General, for an Army guy, you did a nice job of arranging our flights

and air cover. Those Air Force guys did one helluva job.
Thanks."

General Bradley grunted.   "Coming from a
jarhead, I'll take that as a compliment."

Hector groaned as he glanced at Jim.   "Hey,
amigo, you gonna let him talk about the Marines that way?
He's surrounded by Marines and has nerve enough to come
out with that crap."

"And Air Force," joked Drew.

Hector tilted his head. "Come again?"

Drew grinned. "He's surrounded by Marines *and*
Air Force. I was Air Force Intelligence before going over
to CIA. Didn't Jim ever tell you that, Hec?"

Hector sighed.   "Naw.   He treats me like a
mushroom…you know, keeps me in the dark and feeds me
horseshit."

General Bradley laughed at that, and then looked
at Drew. "Isn't 'Air Force Intelligence' an oxymoron?"

Drew shook his head. "No. You're thinking of
'Senate Intelligence,' as in the Senate Intelligence
Committee."

General Bradley smiled. "As a member of the
Administration, I didn't hear that…in spite of how much I
might agree."

After the general left, Jim said, "Okay, gang, let's
try to organize this. For now, we'll put the tapes in even
piles at seven of our computers. The paper mess, let's just
put in stacks around some of the worktables. I guess we
better pour over that stuff first—except you, Tom. You
start on the discs."

Soon the chaos of the material started to become
piles upon piles of work in front of the Janitors. Jim and
Holly were two of the best linguists in America, both
speaking over twelve languages fluently and able to read
and think in those languages. All of the main Mideast
languages were included in the twelve. In addition to those
twelve, they could speak and understand several others, just

less fluently. Hector and Billy were both fluent in Arabic, the language that all the material was written in; however, they read it less well than Jim or Holly. Boris was fluent in the language, and read it rather well, while Drew was also fluent, but read it on a par with Hector and Billy. Tom was hopeless with languages.

The reason he had been assigned the task of starting on the discs was that all ten of the computers in the Joint had translating capabilities. While Arabic did not always translate into English well—and sometimes not at all—Tom could still pick out highlights and ask questions on what he couldn't decipher or understand.

While everyone on the team was tired, they all felt an eagerness to get started. As they started to actually study what they had, the phone rang and Jim answered.

Ben Schiller said, "Hi, Jim. I'm here."

"Okay, come on out to Andrews. I'll have you met at the front gate and driven to our place."

"Roger."

When Ben arrived, Jim and Holly got him into the facility and, after greeting everyone (who all knew him), Holly gave Ben a fast tour of the Joint.

After complimenting Jim on the facility, Ben asked, "Do you want to tell me about your nukes?"

Jim answered, "Small, portable, and in suitcase-type carrying cases."

"Yeah, we did some like those. I better see them. Let's hope they're fixed."

"Agreed," replied Jim before he called General Bradley to find out where the weapons had been taken.

After being told and being assured that access to the location would be arranged for Jim and Ben, Jim called for and was granted use of an Air Force car with driver. Jim was not surprised in the least to find General Bradley waiting on them. Ben took one look at the nuclear weapons and said, "Sorry. We fixed some in the same mold as these, but none just like them. I'm afraid you have usable ones."

"Damn," said General Bradley, then asked, "Ben, have you ever been in the White House?"

"No, sir."

Later in the White House, General Bradley, Jim, and Ben entered the Oval Office and, after greetings and Ben's introduction to the President, the latter said, "From what Jim has told me, we owe you a great deal of thanks for the help you have given him in some of his past adventures."

"Thank you, sir," replied Ben.

"Now," continued the President, "about these nuclear weapons…"

Ben said, "We did not tamper with these particular weapons. So one is to assume that they are in working order."

The President looked at Jim and asked, "We have no idea where the fourth one is?"

"None, sir. Since it is possible that it is headed toward Israel, I thought it only fair to inform them of the potential danger. I do think, however, that we are the more likely targets, in light of recent events."

The President nodded his head and asked, "General, do you concur?"

"Yes, sir."

The President looked at Ben and asked, "Do you make it unanimous?"

"Yes, sir. We will, of course, step up security, but since—from what Jim has told me—this was an al-Qaida operation he busted up, I'd bet on you being the target. Maybe somewhere in Europe…but probably not."

"I agree," said the President, "Ben, you may naturally tell your Prime Minister about this and then whoever else in your Government who really needs to know. However, I do *not* want this to become public knowledge. If and when we discover any hard intelligence, the public will be told, if necessary. At that point, we will share what we have with you. In the meantime, I do not want to cause panic—especially with a populace that has had to deal with what ours has recently. I know you have had to deal with this type of problem a lot longer than we have, and may or may not agree. However, I stress that I want the lid kept on this. That includes your allies, and ours."

Ben nodded his head and replied, "Fully understood, sir, and agreed with."

"All right," said the President, "let's all get back to work."

General Bradley showed Ben and Jim out. Jim had the Air Force driver drop Ben off and then returned to the Joint. Once back there, the work on studying and categorizing the intelligence from the raid went on. At various times, each of the members of the team took brief naps, but for the most part they worked through the night and the next day.

Early the following evening, Jim said, "Okay, guys, time for a break. Let's have a good meal, get a good night's sleep, and then tackle this in the morning. As tired as we're all getting, we may miss something if we don't get some proper rest."

He received no argument, but by 5:00 am the next morning, Jim had showered, eaten breakfast, and was back at it. By 7:00, everyone was hard at it. It took another two days to sort out and go over all the paper information. When what they wanted was copied, Jim called General Bradley and told him to send someone over to pick up that material.

Then the task of the mountain of computer discs commenced in earnest. In addition to the discs, from time to time information taken from the hard drives was forwarded to them. Early in the third day, Jim said (to no one in particular), "We need another person with good computer skills to help out."

Drew chuckled and asked, "What, we aren't fast enough for you?"

"Drew, let's face it. None of you is as experienced on computers as I am. Holly, Hector, and Billy are good and getting better, but I need help with trying to tie all these loose ends together. We have a hell of a lot of information, but it's a piece here and a piece there. What I've been doing—without as much success as I'd like—is to get all this stuff in chronological order."

Tom said, "Jim, Jessica is a whiz on computers. She wouldn't have much knowledge of what we're working on, but then neither do I."

"What about the training school?"

"About a month ago, Jess hired a gal, Elizabeth Crowley, to help out in the office. She's doing real well. If Jessie or I flew out every two weeks or so and were available on the phone for questions, I think she could handle it. I can call and ask Jessie what she thinks."

"We'd have to get her vetted…you know, White House stuff and all that. I could call the general and get him to hurry it along. He likes giving the FBI shit."

"Or," Holly interjected, "I could call John Engle. He likes me."

Jim chuckled and said, "He just likes your big…"

"Stanley James, don't say it," interrupted Holly.

"…tits. However, you do have a good idea. Tom, call Jessie and see if she's willing. If so, get her Social Security number and any information you can about her before you knew her. The more information we can pass on to John, the quicker we can get her vetted. As far as the Joint, if she's willing, get her on a plane. Better yet, I'll have the general get her a ride from the Air Force right here to Andrews."

Tom nodded and placed the call. When Jessica answered, he said, "Hi, babe."

"Hello, darling," answered Jessica.

"Honey, we're real pressed for time here so I'll get right to the point. Jim could use some help on the computers here. I nominated you. Do you think Beth can handle things there if we drop in every couple of weeks or so, and were available on the phone for her?"

"You mean come back there and be one of your Janitors?"

"Well…help out at least."

"I'd love to. And yes, I'm sure Beth can handle things. Do I get to know about all the good intelligence stuff?"

"Yes. Speaking of that, we have to get security clearance for you so you can get into the various intelligence places and the White House…"

"White House!!! Oh, my God. I'd get to go to the White House?"

Tom laughed outright and answered, "Yes, honey. From time to time we have to hand-carry stuff over there. Knowing Jim, he'd probably even get you into the Oval Office to meet the President."

"No way. For real?"

"For real. Now, I'm going to put Holly on the line in a minute and I want you to give her all the information you can about yourself. The more you give her, the quicker we can get you the security clearance."

"Tom, I'm so excited I could shit. Thank you so much for recommending me."

Tom laughed again. "You're welcome, darling. Now here's Holly."

Holly took the information and called John Engle with it. Engle was the Director of the FBI and knew Holly well. In fact, his name had been brought to the attention of the President for the FBI post from none other than Holly Hollins (before she became Holly Scott).

7.

Jessica Wilson arrived the next day, all smiles. Tom kissed her and everyone else greeted her one way or the other—including Boris, who walked over, took her in his arms, and kissed her deeply. Jessica enjoyed the kiss and remembered Boris trying to lick her tonsils on her wedding day. She knew she should probably be upset, but figured that was probably just normal for Russians. Tom just chuckled and soon went back to work.

Greetings out of the way, Jim had Hector get her set up on the retina and palm print portion of the security system and showed her how to use it. Then he asked Holly to show her around the facility and where to put her things in Tom's room. When she saw the plush bedroom and attached bath, she whistled. "Here I was worrying about Tom being cooped up in a hole in the wall on a cot. God, this place is magnificent."

After eating the snack offered by Holly, Jessica was ready for work. Within an hour, she had mastered just exactly what Jim wanted done and was working away.

At one point, Jessica asked, "Where in the world did all this data come from?"

"Iraq," answered Jim.

"How?"

"We, the Janitors, went there and took it away from the bad guys, who are happily all dead," Jim answered with a smile.

Jessica looked down to the computer Tom was working on and asked, "Did you go there?"

"Yes."

"And didn't tell me."

"Couldn't, sorry. Couldn't even tell you when we got back, the old open-line business. It was a piece of cake, really."

"Did you get shot at?"

Holly answered for Tom, "Yes, and he shot back—with better results. You can be proud of your man."

Later in the day, Drew suddenly said, "Hey, anybody run across anything on this guy Yasin Al-Sharif? I've seen his name three or four times, but nothing about him."

When he got no response, Drew continued, "I wonder why his name pops up but nothing about him. Jessica, would you mind tapping into the CIA and checking their known terrorists list for him?"

Jim went over to Jessica's computer and showed her how to access the CIA. She then got the list of known terrorists and scanned it for Drew. She said, "There are three Al-Sharifs, but no Yasin. The three I found all have known relatives listed, and none named Yasin either."

"Damn. Thanks, Jessica."

Jessica was beside herself with excitement. She had just tapped into the CIA computer and gotten information from it. She was so proud that Tom had thought enough of her to suggest her to Jim, and now she was actually helping and getting in on many secrets of the government.

About an hour later, Hector said, "Drew, got something on your Yasin Al-Sharif. He's Saudi. Riyadh is mentioned a bit later on. Probably where he's from. You're right, though, not much else here. Strange…like you said, his name keeps popping up, but with no information."

Drew said, "That does it. Hey, old man…want to take a trip to Saudi Arabia?"

Boris nodded and answered, "Yes. We're of little use on these computers. Jim, one thing before Drew takes me away. I've noticed quite a bit of information on al-Qaida helping the Chechen rebels. Do you think we could get the information about that to my former bosses?"

"Yes, I think so. I've been thinking for the last hour that a trip to see the boss might not be a bad idea."

Jim then picked up the phone and called General Bradley. When he had him on the line, he asked, "Any chance of getting in to see 'himself'?"

"Anything in particular on your mind?"

"A few things. I'd like to get some guidance from both of you."

"Well, since you're the hero of the moment—with all the stuff you brought back—I'm sure he'll see you. The CIA, FBI, and all the rest are falling all over themselves. Hold on a second while I check his schedule."

General Bradley was soon back on the line and said, "Okay…anytime in the next forty-five minutes."

"Thanks. Ah, I'd like to bring someone with me who isn't vetted yet."

"Jessica Wilson?"

"Yes. How'd you know?"

"She is…vetted, that is. John Engle called me a while ago. Her credentials are already with the Marines at the gate. Engle said something about Holly calling him. In addition, he said he has grown to trust your judgment."

"Great. See you soon."

"So long."

Jim then called and arranged for an Air Force car and driver. A few minutes later he glanced at the large bank of monitors from the cameras that covered the exterior of the Joint and saw the car pull up. He stood up and said, "Come, Jessie."

Jessica stood up also and asked, "Come where?"

"The White House."

Jessica was spellbound and just followed along, turning part way toward the front entrance to weakly wave to Tom, who was smiling.

On the trip Jessica said nothing, partly from excitement and partly from fear. She wondered how she looked, worried about her hair, and doubted if she would even be able to talk.

Once there, Jim got Jessica's credentials and explained the procedure for entering the White House. General Bradley was there and grinned as Jim handed his silenced Walther to the Marine guard who had taken the weapon on more than one occasion, but still wondered about the silenced and very illegal gun.

They followed the general through the White House, directly to the Oval Office. Inside, Jim introduced Jessica to the President. "Mr. President, I'd like you to meet Jessica Wilson, the newest member of the Janitors."

The President shook her offered hand and said, "Nice to meet you, Jessica."

"My pleasure, Mr. President."

The President then said, "Good job in Iraq, Jim…it would seem that you've brought back a gold mine of intelligence information. What do you have on your mind?"

"Two things. One, I think we should share the information I brought back with the Russians."

"*All* of it?"

"Yes, sir. I'm sure parts of it are already on the way to some of our allies. I just thought it would be a good gesture to share it with Moscow. Boris wanted to send them the stuff on the Chechen situation, but I really think all of it would please your counterpart there. I know you are trying to improve relations with them, and I feel in the long run they will become one of our best allies."

The President looked at the ceiling, looked at Jim, and asked, "You sure you wouldn't like that State Department job I offered you in January?"

Jim grinned.   "No, sir.   Thanks for the compliment, though."

"I agree with your judgment. We'll send it all. What was the other item?"

"Sir, there is so much information there, and so much to follow up on, I'd like to concentrate on the missing nuke. Before I get all wrapped up in that, I just wanted to make sure you and General Bradley didn't have any other plans for us."

The President looked at General Bradley, who just shook his head slightly, and said, "Everyone is going to be looking for that nuke. Do you plan to coordinate with the other agencies?"

"No, sir. Thought we'd go it alone. If we stumble onto something we need help with, I'll ask."

The President thought for a few seconds, then said, "Go get the darn thing for me, Jim. Make that, for *us*."

"Thank you, sir. See you later."

"Good hunting, Jim. Nice to meet you, Jessica."

Jessica barely stammered out, "Same here, sir."

In the hall, Jim arranged with General Bradley for a military plane to take Drew and Boris to Saudi Arabia. When he first asked for the plane, General Bradley had asked, "You onto something there?"

"No, sir. Drew Hollins just had one of those tickling sensations we spooks get from time to time. A guy's name kept showing up with no information about his involvement. Drew wants to check it out."

As they walked through the White House to leave, Jessica could hardly put one foot in front of the other. She had just met the President of the United States, in the Oval Office, and had actually shaken hands with him! A hand that would be a long time getting washed. She also was a Janitor…Jim had said so!

Back at the Joint, Jim informed Drew that General Bradley would be calling about the arrangements for a flight to Saudi Arabia. Then he said to Holly, "Honey, when I checked my gun in at the White House, I had a thought. From time to time, Jessica may be here alone. How about taking her downstairs and giving her a few pointers on the use of a Walther."

Holly said, "Good idea. Come on, Jessie."

Jessica, who had kissed her husband on returning to the Joint, now gave him another limp wave as she followed Holly. The basement floor of the Joint had a 50-yard, three-lane swimming pool, a work-out area, and a hundred-foot-long target range.

Out of a gun case, Holly got a silenced Walther, identical to the ones used by all the Janitors, and handed it to Jessica. She asked, "Have you ever fired a gun?"

"No."

Holly then showed Jessica how to load and unload the gun. She also showed her the safety switch. She then said, "One thing. Silenced guns are illegal. So don't go waving that around in public. We would eventually get you out of jail, but it might slow down whatever you were supposed to be doing.

"Now then, in a minute or two I'll bring that target down there up to about ten feet. My idea is for you to shoot at it from a close distance, then we'll move it out to further distances. When you start missing, that will give you your starting point for practice. For now, I just want you to get comfortable firing it. So take the safety off and have at it."

Jessica did as told, turned to the target, and fired. Then she fired again, and again. Finally, when the clip was empty, Holly, who was standing there in disbelief, pushed the switch to pull the target up to where they stood. She looked at the target, looked at Jessica, and asked, "You sure you never fired a gun before?"

"Nope. First time."

The heart area of the target was blown away. Calmly, Holly took the target off the sliding rack and put another one up. Just left of the heart area on the target was a very small circle, another circle of the same size was painted on between the eyes. Holly said, "Okay, this time I want two shots at the head target, and two at the heart spot…those two little circles."

"Got it."

Holly handed Jessica a new clip and said, "Go to it."

Jessica re-loaded the gun, turned, and fired four times. Holly brought the target up, looked closely at it, and said, "This isn't possible. Come with me."

Up the stairs they went. When they reached the computer room, Holly walked over to Jim, handed it to him and said, "From a hundred feet, four shots. Buster, you may have met your match when it comes to shooting. I wouldn't have believed this if I hadn't watched her do it."

Hearing Holly, the others gathered around and one after the other looked at the target. Drew, who had only glanced at it, said, "Not bad, three out of four."

"Look again, dad."

Drew did and saw that the hole in the center of the head shot circle was just slightly larger that it should have been. He said, "I stand corrected. Jessica, I never want to get into a gunfight with you."

Jessica was standing there dumbfounded. She had no idea that her shooting feat was so spectacular. Tom gave her a squeeze and said, "Honey, you may not know it, but Jim is the only one here that could have equaled what you just did. I can barely hit the damn target from a hundred feet."

As Jessica was basking in that bit of glory, Holly handed the first target to Jim and said, "Full clip...not a miss in the bunch."

•

Generals Al-Shahristani and Al-Majeed surveyed the wreckage that had once been a very expensive facility with dismay. As crews worked, diligently trying to uncover anything of value, it became quite apparent that little of use would be uncovered. Body parts, pieces of various items such as dishwashers, stoves, and bed frames, were being found. From the computer pod, only a few scraps of monitors, printers, and radios had been unearthed.

Deciding that little of value would ever be found, the two generals headed back to Baghdad. General Al-Shahristani again had the sensation of an image of Jim Scott pass through his entire body and he shivered. His plan to eliminate Scott to date had born little fruit.

That plan had been to send four top intelligence types to America to find a way to deal with the man who had killed Saddam. Not as revenge, because both generals were quite happy to be in charge of Iraq and, in a way, thankful to Scott for killing Saddam to make it so. Their reason for doing away with Scott was the threat he had made on them. He had warned them that a continuation of Saddam's policies would result in their death. They had continued those policies.

Two teams had been dispatched to America. A team of two former KGB agents, hired by Saddam after the fall of the USSR, and a team of two intelligence agents of the former East Germany were supposed to be coming up with a plan to kill Scott. The Russians, they had given up on. The Germans were still sending in reports that it could be done, but they had not yet determined the best way to approach it.

The Russian team had found Jim's Montana retreat and home, after much digging and legwork. They had even spied on Jim and Holly, from a very safe distance, and were developing a plan when Boris Telman came to visit with Drew Hollins. Drew, they didn't recognize; Boris, they did. He had trained both men in the KGB and had treated them well—much better than anyone else in the old intelligence network. Love might have been a stretch, but their feelings of regard for the man ran deep. On seeing Boris welcomed warmly by the Scotts, both men had left the area, never to return. They didn't leave empty-handed, however. Deciding they wouldn't be too welcome back in Iraq, they hatched a plan. They notified General Al-Shahristani that Scott could be eliminated, but that it would take a much better marksman than either of the Russians.

They also said they knew the perfect man for the job, had contacted him, and he was willing to do the job, but wanted six million dollars—half up front, paid into a numbered account. The general agreed and had the money transferred into the account. The account belonged to one of the Russians and was in a false name…a trick he had learned from Boris Telman.

The two men and the three million dollars disappeared forever.

The two Germans tracked Jim in Washington and discovered the Joint. They managed to rent an apartment not too far from Andrews Air Force base. Using a powerful telescope, they were able to watch the comings and goings at the Joint. The problem they faced was where to try for Scott. His movements were so irregular—and so often were to and from the base via aircraft—that they had decided they would have to make their try on the Joint itself. The rub, of course, was that they had seen the security system. With recent events, they felt certain that Scott would be at the facility for some time to come, so they contacted General Al-Shahristani and requested six additional men. Those men had been in place in Washington for a few days. Now it was a matter of figuring a way onto the base. As to the Joint, they had decided a daylight raid, full bore through the gates and front door, would be the only way to complete the job assigned them. Their escape from the base and Washington would also take some planning.

To say General Al-Shahristani was getting impatient was a gross understatement. He wanted Scott dead! The more he thought of it, the more he became convinced that Scott had been involved in the Hit fiasco—however irrational that thought might be.

•

The morning after Jessica's visit to the White House saw Boris and Drew in the air, heading for Saudi Arabia.

After they left, Jim said, "Fellas, it's going to take Jessica and me about three days to get this mess in some semblance of order. Until then, this would be a good time to take care of other things. Tom, you and Hector head for LA. You can spend a couple of days making sure things are okay with your business. Hector, same for you…and give you a chance to see Rosa and the kids.

"Billy, you may as well go home and get reacquainted with Sally. I know you three would like to keep pouring over this stuff, but if Jessie and I can get it ready for proper review, we can all dig into it then. Any grunt work I need done for the next few days can be done by Holly."

"Thanks a lot," joked Holly.

Billy said, "I could use the break. I'm getting damn tired of looking at all sorts of disjointed stuff. You want me to ride with the guys?"

"No, take the Gulfstream. If something should come up of an urgent nature, I can borrow something from the Air Force. If I need any or all of you, I know where you live."

Everyone laughed at that. Then the other three men besides Jim went to pack up for the trip home. After they had gone, Jim took the time to make sure Jessica understood the security system.

After they had gone over it twice, Jim said, "Please remember that if you should be here alone, you are not—repeat, not—to open either the security gate or the front door of the facility. To do so, you would have to go out, get whoever it is through the gate, then use your normal entry procedure to get back in here. If that someone isn't what they seem, they could breach the Joint, and that would be a very bad thing."

Jessica nodded her head and smiled. "Got it."

"Jess, this is important. If you're alone here and someone comes along wanting in, simply press the button that flashes a sign at the first gate that says, 'access denied'."

Jessica asked, "What if it's someone like General Bradley."

"He'll just have to come back. If it's the President, 'access denied'."

"Oh, sure. I'm going to deny access to the President of the United States. Oh, sure I will."

"You can bet if the President shows up here, he'll call ahead…or have someone call for him. If not, he would be under duress, and I'd bet a fat pig against a piece of bacon that will not happen."

"Okay, I understand…I think."

"Now then," Jim continued, as he handed Jessica a silenced Walther, "this is your gun. Since you've shown you know how to use it…"

"Didn't before Holly showed me how."

"…keep it near you at all times. As you can no doubt guess, we, the Janitors, have made a few enemies over a period of time. Most particularly, me…so if somebody comes gunning for me any time in the foreseeable future, this is about the only place to get me. Now if I have you sufficiently paranoid, let's get back to work."

8.

Early the next morning, Jim received a call from the CIA Director, Amos Longley. Jim answered on the first ring and the Director said, "Good morning, Jim. Amos here."

"Good morning, sir. What can I do for you?"

"Come over for a visit…and bring your wife with you. Our in-house linguists are having a disagreement about the translation process from Arabic to English on the Intel you brought back to us…thank you very much for that, by the way."

"You're welcome. Does it have to be both of us? We have a new team member, Jessica Wilson, Tom's wife. If Holly and I both leave, that would leave Jessica here by herself. Not that there is any great worry in that, but I'd like to avoid it if necessary."

"I guess we could get by with just one of you, but I had in mind to have you work with one of the warring factions, Holly with the other. I'm reasonably sure that if both groups are brought to the same spot by two different people—especially two people as highly regarded as linguists as the two of you—we just might come up with a happy group of campers. The problem we have is causing a slowdown in raw data getting to where it should be getting—namely, our field people. In addition, Director Engle is going to be here with some of his people and he suggested Holly, rather firmly."

"Oh, all right. But it seems like you should just sit your people down and give them a big talking to. There are just some Arabic words that do *not* translate."

"I know that, Jim. However, you can pick up the gist of a subject matter and create an English translation. From what I understand, Holly is your equal in that regard."

"Better. We'll both come. When?"

"Now."

"Of course."

•

One of those quirks of fate that has bedeviled mankind since the beginning of time found the two former German intelligence officers giving a final briefing to the six men supplied to them by General Al-Shahristani as Jim and Holly drove away from the Joint in the requested Air Force car.

After eight days of 24-hour-a-day surveillance of the Joint, they missed their target by that briefest moment. Their plan was simplicity itself. They knew that an occasional delivery was made, and that General Bradley had taken material from there. With long-range listening devices, they had learned the names of everyone coming and going from the Joint. They had learned that the military guards at the entrance of the base called the Joint "the Scott Facility."

Knowing that Scott was in the facility with only two women, they felt the time would never be better than now. So, after briefing their men, they all got into a Marine 6 x 6 covered truck they had managed to acquire and headed for the gate. All were dressed in authentic Marine uniforms and had authentic, but false, Marine identity cards. The six recent arrivals were in the rear of the truck. They were only minutes away and drove up to the gate as Jim and Holly were passing through it in the other direction.

At the gate, they announced that they had a delivery from the White House for the Scott Facility. They were passed through with surprising ease. With growing confidence, the eight assassins drove up to the security gates at the Joint. Only Hans Kruger, one of the two Germans, got out and approached the gate. Once there, he pushed a button on the intercom located there and said, "We have a delivery from General Bradley for Jim Scott."

Jessica, who was working away on her computer, looked up at the large security screen that showed the front gate area and, remembering Jim's instructions, got up and walked over to the security console and pushed the button that displayed the words, "Access denied" on the screen at the gate entrance.

Hans pushed the button again and said, "What am I supposed to do with this stuff?"

Though tempted to tell the Marine that she was alone and couldn't let them in by herself, Jessica again remembered Jim's stern warning not to talk and again pushed the message button. Again "Access denied" showed on the screen at the gate.

Flustered, Hans turned toward the truck and said, "We'll have to force our way in—hurry up, everyone."

Instantly the six men in the rear of the truck piled out, as did the other German in the front of the truck. They brought pre-rigged wads of C-4 explosive with them. Quickly one of the charges was placed on the locking mechanism on the outer gate. They stood back as it exploded. Through that gate, they did the same thing at the other one.

Jessica watched dumbfounded. But when the men poured in through the second gate, she tried to remain calm and follow the instructions Jim had given her earlier. When all eight men had passed through the gate, she raised a red cover on the console and pressed the button. That button was connected to six claymore mines. They exploded with a horrific explosion and literally tore six men to shreds. The other two men, the Germans who had rushed in first, had made it to the deeply recessed entrance foyer and, though hit, they were still upright and able to carry on. Had they stopped to think, they could have possibly made good an escape. Days before, they had placed explosives on the perimeter fence of the base, which could be detonated by a remote control, located in the truck. That had been their planned escape route.

However, adrenalin took over and they put another charge on the door. Meanwhile, Jessica had picked up a phone and placed a call to Ted Kuntz. She called him because it was a number she had for some reason remembered, while forgetting Jim's cell phone number and the base security office number. She was in luck. Ted answered on the first ring, and Jessica, a surprisingly small amount of stress in her voice, said, "This is Jessica Wilson calling from the Joint. I'm under attack by men dressed as Marines. Please help."

Before Ted could reply, there was another loud explosion. On the monitor covering the front entrance, Jessica could see the two men rush in. She dropped the phone and ran to her computer, where she had left her gun. As the two men came in through the foyer, Jessica raised the gun and fired twice. Both Germans fell to the floor with nice neat holes right between their eyes.

Ted acted quickly. He called base security—where they had heard all of the explosions and already had men on the way—and told them that men dressed as Marines were attacking the Scott Facility. Then he called Jim on his cell phone, and when Jim answered, he said, "Jim, Jessica Wilson is under attack at the Joint."

Not taking time to answer Ted, Jim told the driver to return to the base at once.

General Bradley walked into Ted's office as Ted was picking up the phone connected to Jessica and heard only eerie quiet. He asked, "Jessica, are you there?"

When he received no answer, he said to his secretary, "Arrange a police escort with lights flashing. I'm going to Andrews…emergency!"

General Bradley asked, "What's up?"

Ted raced out of his office and said on his way past the General, "Attack on the Joint."

General Bradley followed Ted without comment and they were soon speeding toward the Air Force base.

At the base, the Air Force security team arrived first. They piled out of their vehicles and the captain in charge took one look at the carnage on the Joint grounds and raced to and through the open front door of the building. As he rounded the corner, he stopped dead in his tracks. Jessica was pointing a gun at him and said, "I think you're supposed to wait outside until someone arrives who belongs here."

He replied, "Yes, ma'am," as he glanced down at the two dead men at his feet, before backing out of the building.

Once outside, he again looked at the blown apart bodies. The effect of six claymore mines at point-blank range was more than just devastating. The captain could hardly stand to look at the mess of what had once been six men.

He didn't know exactly what to do, but said to the man who had followed him as far as the doorway, "Go on back to the gate and post a guard. I'd bet Scott is on his way back. I'll just stay here for now."

Jim and Holly arrived at the Joint a few minutes ahead of Ted and General Bradley. Jim jumped out of the Air Force car and raced inside, Holly just a few paces behind him. When he got inside and saw Jessica still standing there holding the gun, he let out a sigh of relief and hurried over to her. Jim gently took the gun from Jessica and asked, "Are you alright?"

Jessica just dumbly nodded her head. Jim took her in his arms and could feel her trembling. Soon tears started to flow. After a few moments, Jessica said, "Jim, I'm going to be sick."

He stepped back and she threw up on the floor between them. When Jessica had finished retching, Jim looked at Holly, tilted his head toward Jessica, and got out of the way as Holly rushed forward and led Jessica off.

Just as Jim was getting ready to get something to clean up the vomit, Ted and the general arrived. Ted rushed inside. The general took time to stop and look at the bloody remains on the Joint grounds. Having seen the effects of claymore mines, he knew what he was looking at. He approached the captain and said, "Clean up this mess, please. For a body count, try belt buckles."

As the general headed inside, the captain said, "Yes, sir."

With the general approaching from behind, Ted turned over one of the Germans, who had fallen face down. He saw the two neat holes that had been fatal to the two men, looked at Jim, and raised his eyebrows.

Jim said, "No, not me. Jessica. Holly just taught her how to shoot yesterday."

Ted looked down again and then back at Jim and said, "I need Holly to teach me how to shoot."

"Holly said she's a natural. Gave her a gun and told her to fire off a few rounds, just to get the feel of the weapon. At 100 feet, she emptied the clip in an area as big as my fist, dead center. Then Holly had her try one-inch circles on another target. Two in one circle, two in the other."

"Wow," said Ted, before asking, "I wonder who these guys are?"

Holly, who had just come back into the room, went over and looked at the two men and said, "East Germans, working for Iraqi intelligence."

Jim got a funny look on his face and asked, "How do you know that? And why aren't you with Jessica?"

"I helped her clean up, then held her for a while and thought I'd let her be for ten or fifteen minutes, then go back in to her. She's pretty shook up. As to those two, they tried to pick me up the first time we went to Iraq. Told them I was diseased and they left me alone."

Jim didn't press the issue, but knew at some later time he was going to hear the rest of *that* story. Letting it pass for the moment, he said, "Ted, I'd appreciate it if you would get those two out of here."

Then, as he rewound the security tape and watched the whole episode that had taken place outside, he asked, "General, how many outside? Our monitor shows six guys"

"Who the hell knows. I told that Air Force Captain to count belt buckles. He didn't know if I was being funny or not. How many claymores?"

"Six. Set to go off one-a-second for six seconds. Probably sounded like one big bang, but wanted them spaced for maximum effect."

"Well, you sure as hell got that," the general said. "You probably killed all six of them with the first one. Jim, since Holly said these two were working for Iraq, who do you think…Shahristani and Majeed?"

"Be my guess. General, could you get all these guys disposed of on the quiet? I'd like whoever sent them to squirm a bit, not hearing from them and not knowing what happened to them."

"Consider it done. Well, Ted, if you have nothing else here, let's go. I've got another one of those meetings to attend. Damn bin Laden all to hell. His crap has had me in meetings until I think that's all there is to life."

After Ted and the general left, Holly returned to Jessica and Jim called Tom. When he had Tom on the line, he said, "Hi, Tom. I need you to come back here. Jessica is fine, but we were attacked here at the Joint. Or, I should say, Jessica was. She was here alone. Killed eight men: six with the claymores, two she shot…right between the eyes."

"Jesus. How's she holding up?"

"Took it pretty hard. Holly's with her now, but I think having you here will help a great deal. Call Hector. Tell him what happened and see if he wants to come back with you—or have Billy pick him up when Billy comes back."

"Can I talk to Jessica?"

"Sure, hold on a second."

        Jim put Tom on hold and pushed the intercom button for Tom and Jessica's room and said, "Jessie, Tom's on line one for you."

        While Tom and Jessica talked, Jim used another line and called his nearest neighbor in Montana, George Bostich. George and his daughter Peggy looked after his home while he was out of town. When he had George on the line, Jim said, "Hi, George. We had an incident here in Washington today. Someone after my hide. I do *not* want Peggy going to my place until further notice. When you go to look after the dogs and horses, please take a couple of your hands along…armed."

        "That serious?"

        "Afraid so. Hate to put this on your shoulders, but I really am needed here."

        "No problem, Jim. I fully understand. Don't know what you do for the government, but damn proud to help out any way I can."

        "Thanks."

        Jim's next call was to Billy. After filling him in on what happened, Billy said he would take another day or two and head back. When that call was over, Billy at once headed for Jim's ranch. Later that day he called back and said, "Jim, there are traces of someone having spied on you here. But it's been a while. They were pretty far out…my guess would be that they decided to try for you in Washington. Why, I can't imagine. Hell, if I wanted you, I'd just potshot you from about where they were. From what I found, I'd say they were here about two, maybe three weeks before the attack on New York and Washington."

        "I agree it doesn't make sense. Thanks for thinking to scout my place out. Good work."

                                •

        Drew and Boris flew into Saudi Arabia, unaware of the events at the Joint. Before they left, Drew had called an old friend at the CIA and found out that the CIA Station

Chief in Riyadh was Justin Walker. Walker was a former protégé of Drew's, so there was no trouble getting in to see him, and Drew knew he could count on any help he needed.

After being shown into Walker's office, Drew said, "Justin, I'd like you to meet Boris Telman. Boris, this is Justin Walker."

As the two men shook hands, Justin asked, "Are you the former KGB Telman?"

"One and the same," answered Boris.

As Justin and Drew shook hands, both Boris and Drew noted the coolness toward Boris. As the three men sat down, Drew said, "Justin, Boris is with us now. He and I are part of Jim Scott's team."

The beginning of a thaw came over Justin as he asked, "Did you fellas assist in the recovery of all this great stuff I've been getting from home?"

"Yes," answered Drew. "We were both there and did our share of dispatching al-Qaida soldiers to their forty virgins. At the rate al-Qaida is losing help these days, there aren't going to be many virgins left. Boris joined up with us in January. Justin, have you ever been to the Oval Office?"

"Not hardly."

"Well, Boris has...and the President personally authorized his green card and helped enlist him into our group. Russia is aware of that, and we have passed on a good deal of information to them, partially as a result of Boris. I am certain this relationship has helped forge the stronger ties between our two nations. I hasten to add that Boris has only *requested* information be passed along. The President has agreed in every case."

The thaw complete, Justin said, "Okay, I'm sold. Just seems strange to see you come in here with KGB."

"Former KGB," joked Boris.

Before Justin could reply, Drew asked, "What do you know about a guy by the name of Yasin Al-Sharif?"

Recognizing that the time for small talk had passed, Justin answered, "Close ties to the Royal Family. Importer, exporter. We have an interest in him, but nothing on him. I noticed his name a few times in the Intel we got from stateside. That why you're here?"

"Yes. I have that itching feeling about this guy. Boris came along to keep me out of trouble."

"Boris, I heard you were one hell of an operative, but this task may be too much—even for you."

Boris smiled and replied, "He's getting too old to get into trouble."

Drew grunted and asked, "What type of surveillance do you have on him?"

"None, or at least very little. As I said, he is close to the Royal Family, so great care in observing him is necessary."

"What kind of security systems does he have?"

"Not much at his home, that I'm aware of. His office had a pretty good system, but nothing a pro would have any problem with. I've got the specs in a file around here somewhere, with blueprints. You planning something?"

"We didn't come all this way to get hot in your lovely desert outpost. Since you have some stuff on file, I take it you have at least *considered* a more active interest."

"Yeah."

"Okay, Boris and I'll go in and place the bugs. You can monitor and give us *all* the yield. Before you bring it up, your ass is covered. Just consider this one done on Presidential orders."

"If you say so."

Late that night, Drew and Boris paid visits to both the home and office of Yasin Al-Sharif. When they left Riyadh the following morning, they carried with them a file containing all the information Justin Walker had on Al-Sharif.

On the long flight, they both read the entire file. After setting it aside and catching a nap, Drew re-read the file and said, "Old man, I see something in here that seems strange."

"What would that be, older man?"

"One of Al-Sharif's sons, Ibrahim, is going to school at the University of Missouri. A fine school, make no mistake, but with his father's money he could have gone anywhere. All those crap-ass liberal Ivy League schools would fall all over themselves to have him enrolled with them. So why is he getting his schooling in the middle of the country, in a small college town, when the education rankings and glitter of the East Coast beckon?"

"I don't know enough about your college system to appraise your analysis. From what you say—and the way you said it—I think we should, perhaps, learn more about this youth."

9.

When Drew and Boris landed at Andrews and were driven to the Joint, they noticed at once that something was not right. A team of Air Force security guards was stationed outside the front gate, which—with a good portion of the fence itself—was under repair.

Jim saw them drive up on the security monitor covering that area and came out to see them through the gate area. As they walked to and through the now-repaired front door, Drew asked, "What happened? Someone try an attack?"

"Yes," answered Jim, "and all are now quite dead…thanks to Jessica."

As they walked into the computer area, Jessica looked up from her computer, smiled, and waved. Jessica had recovered nicely from the shock of what happened and was diligently back at work.

After everyone there greeted Boris and Drew, Jim told the two the full details of what had transpired. Then Drew told Jim about their trip and his desire to further check on Ibrahim Al-Sharif.

Jim listened intently, then said, "I agree. He *should* be looked at."

Then to Jessica he said, "Jessie, please check the name Ibrahim Al-Sharif."

By the time Jessica had run everything in their now-much-better-organized system, Boris and Drew had gotten themselves some coffee. When they returned, Jessica said, "Nothing on Ibrahim. However, we have three references to 'Al-Sharif,' no first name used. They're printing out now, if you'd like to look at them."

Drew, Boris, and Jim read the printouts together and Boris said, "From what I remember of our earlier information, I don't think this sounds like the father. Not necessarily the son, but now I agree even more that this boy takes some looking into."

Jim nodded and asked, "Drew, do you and Boris want to go check him out?"

"Yes, as soon as we get some sleep. We're getting too old for all this flying."

"Speak for yourself, old man," joked Boris.

•

The next morning Billy arrived from Montana before Drew and Boris had left for Columbia, Missouri, home of the University of Missouri. With his entire team now back together, Jim called a general meeting in the dining area.

After everyone had coffee in front of them, Jim said, "Okay, here's the plan. Wait a second. Jessica, are you going to be okay if I send Tom off with Drew and Boris?"

"Yes, Jim. Thanks for asking. I'm okay now, though I'll miss my bedmate."

Jim smiled. "Okay, back to what I have in mind. Holly and I have an interrupted meeting with some of the CIA and FBI folks, where we were headed when the Joint got raided. Drew, you may as well come along and get the equipment you'll need in Columbia. We don't have enough hard information to get a legal phone-tap, so you or Boris will have to pull some spook stuff and set up your own tap.

"Tom, since you aren't the best in the world at what we'll be doing—going over this intelligence data— you can fly Drew and Boris to Missouri and be their leg man. The rest of us will see what we can see from our data.

"Okay, on to a matter we *haven't* discussed. I transferred over two hundred seventy million from al-Qaida accounts to mine. Everyone except Holly and I will get five million each of that money. Jessica, Tom, since you both work here, that's ten mil for the two of you. I will pull some for expenses, keep some in a contingency fund, and the rest will go to some good cause, when I figure out what good cause to spend it on. Any suggestions in that regard would be appreciated."

"How about the re-election of the President in three plus years?" joked Drew.

Jim smiled and replied, "I don't think so. The last time we got a bundle of money, he specifically told me that none of it was to wind up in his re-election fund. Speaking of which—the President, that is—I better let him and the general know we hit bin Laden hard in his wallet. Okay, does anyone have anything to add or ask?"

When no one did, the meeting broke up and everyone went about their business.

Jessica was stunned with the casual manner in which Jim offered, and everyone there accepted, the largess of five million dollars. Later, she would ask Tom about it. His answer was simple, "That's the way Jim does things."

•

After doing their best to explain the nuances of translating Arabic to English, Jim and Holly returned to the Joint with Drew. Jim and Holly helped Drew carry in the boxes of eavesdropping equipment he had gotten from his old employers at the CIA.

Later that day, Tom flew Drew and Boris to Missouri. When they reached Columbia, the three men went in search of a place to rent near the address they had for Ibrahim Al-Sharif. Al-Sharif had purchased a house more than ten miles from the university campus. It was in a wooded area of plush homes. As the men drove through the area, Drew said, "This isn't going to be easy. This is an upscale neighborhood."

Just as he said that, another of those quirks of fate came about, as they passed a "For Sale" sign across the street from Al-Sharif's house. Drew stopped the car, backed up, then pulled into the drive. With Tom and Boris following him, Drew walked up and rang the doorbell. The owner answered and Drew said, "I'd like to buy your house."

Stunned, the owner said, "You'll have to contact the real estate broker."

"Will you call him, or her, while we wait, please?"

Not sure what to do, the owner said, "I guess I could. Would you like to come in? Please, have a seat."

Twenty minutes later the real estate agent arrived and came in, after being met at the door by the owner. She was a young woman in her late twenties, without much experience. What happened next probably set her career back years, as she would expect things like this really happened.

Drew asked, "What's the asking price?"

"Four hundred sixty-two thousand," answered the agent.

"With or without furnishings?"

"Without."

Drew looked at the owner. "What do you think your furnishings are worth?"

The man thought a few seconds and said, "I guess about ten or twenty thousand."

Drew nodded and asked, "How many bedrooms?"

"Four."

"Is there a direct entry from your garage into the house?"

"Yes."

"Okay, as my son-in-law likes to say, here's the deal. If I have six hundred thousand wired into your account in the next ten minutes, can we move in today?"

Stunned, the owner looked at the agent, the agent looked at the owner, and the owner said, "Hell, yes!"

"One caveat. You both must keep this to yourselves. This is a matter of national security," Drew said, as he flashed his CIA identification (which was still valid).

To the owner, Drew asked, "Are you married?"

"Yes. My wife and kids are living in Lawrence, Kansas. That's where I now work. We have bought a house there, but haven't closed on it yet. We have a furnished apartment there, three-month lease. I was assistant dean here, now a dean there. I was just back here to pick up a few personal things and, hopefully, manage to sell this place before going back."

"Okay, dean, do we have a deal? You can move your personal things out as you wish. Keep a key until everything is out. For that matter, you can continue to stay here if you want."

"Yes, we do have a deal. And thank you."

The real estate agent had simply stood mute through all this. Now she asked, "I have a question, about this national security stuff. What do you mean, exactly?"

"Are you aware this nation has recently been attacked?"

"Yes, of course. I'm sorry."

"Now I have a question."

"Yes, dean."

"Are my tax dollars buying my home?"

"No. However, that's all I'm going to say on that subject. The money will come from my personal account," Drew said. Then, as an afterthought, he said to the agent, "You can re-sell this place for me when I'm done with it. Should be no more than a few weeks, at most."

"I'll never be able to get what you paid for it."

"I need a tax write off. After the dean has verified that the money is in his account, you can do whatever is necessary as to paperwork, but do *not* record the deed until I tell you to. Oh, and as I think of it, when you leave, please put a 'Sold' sign up on the 'For Sale' sign."

The dean coughed and said, "You sure are trusting. I could just take your money and…well I don't know exactly what."

Drew looked him hard in the eyes and said, "I don't think that would be a good idea."

The temperature in the room seemed to drop about ten degrees, and the real estate agent soon left...but not before Drew gave her his name for the deed and told her she was only to say that she had made the sale to a man who desperately needed a home for his family and had greatly overpaid for the house. He also told her that if he found out she talked out of school, he would have her arrested as a material witness and placed in confinement until the war on terrorism was over, which would probably be years. She believed him—though the lie had been a total bluff on Drew's part, as he had no authority to have her arrested.

After she left, Drew said, "As you heard, my name is Drew. That old fella over there is Boris, the youngster is Tom. What's your name?"

The owner suddenly realized he had just sold his home for over $100,000.00 above the asking price to a man who didn't even know his name. He could not help laughing. "Roland Wheeler, nice to meet all of you gentlemen. May I ask what this is all about?"

Drew answered, "You may. The fella across the street *may* be more than just a student at the university. We are here to find out if that is the case. If you ever mention any of this to anyone, including your wife, I'll have to kill you."

As Roland Wheeler swallowed, Drew smiled and added, "Actually, if we are wrong, you can tell your family, but please ask them to keep it to themselves. If we are correct, you'll have to keep it under your hat for a month or two, okay?"

"Uh, sure."

Drew then said, "While I make this call, write down your bank account number and the bank you use."

He then took out his cell phone and called Jim. When he had him on the line, Drew said, "Hi, Jim...Drew here. I need you to wire transfer six hundred thousand into an account that I'm going to give you shortly. I just bought a house in Columbia. Take the money from my Hit swag."

"Near Al-Sharif, I presume."

"Across the street."

"God, you're lucky."

"Sure am. Have the best damn daughter and son-in-law in existence."

Drew then gave Roland's name, bank, and account number to Jim. That taken care of, he said, "Tom, please pull the car into the garage."

As Tom got up to do that, Drew asked, "Roland, do we have any food in this place?"

Roland laughed and said, "Not much."

Drew took the money clip he always carried, peeled off five one hundred dollar bills, and handed them to Roland. He then asked, "Would you mind terribly doing some shopping for us?"

"Don't forget vodka," joked Boris.

•

Back in the Joint, Jim told Holly what her father had done and then made the wire transfer as requested by Drew. That done, he made sure things were going smoothly on the intelligence front and left for the White House, after calling General Bradley and making sure he could get in to see the President.

When he arrived, he and General Bradley went into the Oval Office. After an exchange of pleasantries, the President asked, "What's on your mind, Jim?"

"Money. During our raid in Iraq, I managed to lift some money from al-Qaida accounts and transfer it into my account."

The President rolled his eyes. "How much this time?"

"Two hundred seventy million...and some change."

"Oh, very well done, Jim," General Bradley put in.

"I'll say," agreed the President before he asked, "and where is this money going to end up?"

"Most of it in the Treasury. My thought is to increase the lease on my lot over at Andrews to one hundred million. The lease would be fully paid with that amount and be good until the Janitors are no longer needed or wanted...then the government gets a nice intelligence shack. Also, we've been using military aircraft and vehicles quite liberally and I was thinking that we should pay about a hundred million for past and future uses of both."

"Nice thought," said the President, "but I'm not sure just how to go about the paperwork on either of those ideas. Or even if they are legal—though I guess the lease could be worked out."

"I looked into it, sir, and the lease is no problem. Just amend the one we have now. The equipment use, we can call this a deposit for past, as yet unbilled, and future billing—just like when you use Air Force One for private use, or something of the sort."

The President replied, "We'll try. I'll talk to Treasuary and see what they say. I imagine the Secretary can come up with some way to take the money. Whether he can or not, thank you. The gesture is greatly appreciated. Also, if Congress ever gets to nosing around your operation, this would shut them up in one big hurry. And one thing you *didn't* think of, IRS will somehow be instructed to leave you alone."

•

Later that evening in Columbia, Roland Wheeler was having steak and baked potato with the three new occupants of his former home. He asked, "How do you go about spying on my neighbor?"

Drew answered, "About two o'clock in the morning, Boris and I will break into his house, place listening devices all over the place, then listen to everything he does and says. Before you ask, that *is* strictly illegal. Under ordinary circumstances, we would do no such thing in this country. However, these are not 'ordinary circumstances.' Not with a missing nuke floating around."

Roland almost choked on a piece of meat in his mouth before asking, "Nuclear weapon? Here?"

Drew smiled and answered, "Probably not here. However, my suspicion is that lad across the street just might know where it is. If he does, we hope to find that out from him and take it away from whoever has it. Now, Roland, obviously this information is for your ears only. Unless the President tells you personally that you can discuss the nuclear part of our investigation, please don't. The only reason I'm even telling you of this possibility is that with you staying here, you will be able to hear our conversations and listen in to the goings on across the street. If young Al-Sharif was to suddenly say something about blowing up some place or the other, I wouldn't want you to have a stroke. In addition, I trust you. Based on what, you may ask? Years of judging people."

"Thank you, Drew. I'm flattered. I think the last person that came right out and told me they trusted me was my wife…and I got her pregnant."

Everyone at the table laughed at that. Then they finished supper and went to bed. At 1:00 am, Drew's alarm went off and he got up, brushed his teeth, washed up, dressed in solid black, and went downstairs to make coffee.

Boris was in the kitchen, dressed the same as Drew, and with coffee already made. He said, "Good morning, old man. Have trouble waking up?"

"Funny, Russian."

Coffee consumed, the two men gathered the items they wanted to take and slipped out the back door, wearing light-enhancing night-vision goggles. As they crossed both yards and the street, they stayed in the darkest places they could find. The only area of concern was a streetlight on the far end of the Al-Sharif property.

When they reached the target house, Drew found and soon deactivated the alarm system. Boris had left Drew to his task and gone in search of the best place to gain entry to the house. He settled on the back door and waited for Drew. When Drew turned the corner of the house, Boris got to work on the lock and dead bolt on the door in front of him.

They were soon inside and went into each room on the first floor, leaving listening devices behind as they went. The three phones on the first floor and a cell phone lying on a table also were bugged. Roland had told them that three people lived in the house: Al-Sharif, another man, and a woman. Assuming there would be four or five bedrooms on the second floor, they crept up the steps to find four, two empty. They went into the first empty bedroom, bugged it, and the phone there. Next they bugged the adjoining bathroom, then went on through the bathroom to another bedroom, which adjoined the bath on the other end of it. In this room they found a man snoring softly. With great care, they bugged the room, phone in it, and cell phone in the pocket of the man's pants, which were haphazardly tossed on a chair.

They left the way they had entered, returning through the bath and empty bedroom. They repeated the same process in the other two bedrooms and adjoining bath. This time, they found two people in the occupied bedroom. While Drew bugged the room, phone, and another cell phone, Boris stood nearby with his silenced Walther drawn.

As they eased out of the room into the bath, the female occupant of the room stirred, but didn't seem to wake. On their way out of the house, Boris went into the garage, bugged both cars there, placed homing devices on them, and left the house to join Drew, who was preparing to re-activate the alarm system. Soon thereafter, the two men arrived at their own backdoor and entered Drew's new house. As they took off their night-vision goggles, Roland came into the kitchen and asked, "Did you do what you went to do?"

As he turned on a light, Drew chuckled to himself at Roland being up, smiled, and answered, "Yes, mission accomplished. The only slight difficulty was restoring their alarm system on the way out. I stripped one of the wires too much when deactivating it. However, it will take close inspection by someone who knows what he's doing to ever tell."

Roland swallowed. "Ah, may I ask a question?"

Drew nodded and Roland asked, "I thought—from what I see in the movies and on TV—that you guys had new-fangled stuff that you could just point at their building and hear what they were saying, without risking going in doing what you did, and if so why not use it?"

Drew smiled. "We do have such gear. But if they have detection gear—which I actually doubt—it would point right back here. Also, these bugs really give us a clearer sound pattern to listen to. The trick is not to get caught…which we didn't."

Boris groaned, stretched, and said, "I'm for bed."

"I agree," Drew said. "We can set up the receiving gear in the morning."

After no more than three hours sleep, Drew was back downstairs setting up the various receiving units. One was honed in on all the bugs planted in various rooms. Two others were rigged to cover the phone taps. They were set up in a way to allow simultaneous recording of any phone calls. The Janitors could listen to the call of their choice, if more than one call was made at a time. The devices placed in and on the cars had separate receivers.

Just as Drew was finishing up, Tom came down and asked, "Everything go okay last night?"

Drew laughed slightly and answered, "Yes, sleepyhead, just fine. Get yourself something to eat and then get in here. As of right now, we are on them twenty-four hours a day."

Roland and Boris appeared before Tom came back in and Drew said, "You fellas may as well get something to eat. Uh, Roland, wait just a minute. How long did you plan on staying here in Columbia before heading back to your family?"

"Three, maybe four days. I planned to get a moving van to haul some of our things, and hopefully sell the house."

"How long before you have to be back in Kansas?"

"I could stay as long as two weeks."

"Would you like to help us for a few days?"

"I'd love it."

"All right, later in the day, please call your wife and tell her you've sold the house. For now, just tell her you got a *'few'* thousand more than the asking price. Same story as your agent…'a guy in a hurry didn't want to quibble over price.' Then for the next two or three days— until I can get more help in here—I'd appreciate it if you would drive Tom around when time comes for following those guys across the street. We put direction finders on both their cars, but it's a lot easier to use them if one person is on the computer-generated screen and one is driving.

"We pre-programmed a map of the Columbia area into the systems, so following from a distance is no problem. However, as I said, two men make it easier. If they leave in separate cars, I'll follow the second one by myself. We have to keep someone here at all times to monitor this equipment. That way, if they use their cell phones away from the house, we can still listen in here."

"Question."

"Sure."

"Is it hard to tamper with a cell phone? I mean, I've seen movies of how to do it to a phone, but a cell phone?"

"Not easy, but done. Boris and I are old hands at things of this nature. Now, back to your situation. The moving van you planned on getting will have to wait a few days. Then you can go ahead and arrange it, and pack up any of the furnishings you or your wife are partial to."

After Tom relieved Drew at the bank of receiving equipment, everyone else finished eating and the listening began in earnest.

10.

In Baghdad, Generals Al-Shahristani and Al-Majeed were starting to get an idea of just how much damage the Janitors had done. They were getting feedback that indicated a massive breakdown in the funding of various al-Qaida operations. Not only was the central funding operation, which had been located at the Hit, fully interrupted, now it appeared vast sums of money had simply vanished.

While General Al-Shahristani had no knowledge of Jim's capabilities regarding the use of computers and money handling, he nonetheless had that sickening feeling again—that Jim Scott was responsible. He was further worried about the lack of contact by his German hit-squad leaders. They normally checked in on a fairly regular basis. General Al-Majeed was also getting on Al-Shahristani's nerves. He constantly questioned the advisability of having such a large al-Qaida operation within the borders of Iraq, and openly wondered if sending hit teams after Jim Scott was a wise idea.

Therefore, as the major war against terrorism moved forward, a disgruntled and slightly disorganized regime was leading Iraq. They, of course, knew of the nuclear weapon on its way to the United States. They did not have exact details, but at least General Al-Shahristani had no doubts that if that weapon was ever tied directly to Iraq, the consequences could be quite severe.

General Al-Shahristani grimly faced the fact that Iraq was not going to be a major player in the events ahead, unless it was in a *very* negative way. These unhappy thoughts brought him to the conclusion that no matter what else may happen, Jim Scott had to die. Accordingly, without consulting General Al-Majeed, he contacted the head of Iraqi intelligence and had another hit team dispatched to America. This one consisted of two more former East

German intelligence officers and another former KGB agent.

•

At the Joint, repairs had been completed on the front door, the building itself, the fence, and the two gates. Inside the facility, work was pressing forward in the sorting out of the intelligence data obtained from the Hit raid.

Just as Jim was scratching his head over some bits and pieces that didn't seem to have any rhyme or reason, Holly said, "Honey, I just took a call from CIA with a question about an 'it' that has popped up a few times. I noticed the same thing. There are a few references to 'it' in some of the later stuff I've been going over. You know, like 'it' is moving, or 'it' is on schedule."

"Hmm," replied Jim, "let me see what you have."

While Holly and Jim were looking at the references Holly had found and that the CIA had pointed out, the phone rang. It was Drew calling for Jim.

"Yes, Drew, how are things in Columbia?"

"Fine. Jim, the reason I'm calling is three different times our boy here has referred to an 'it.' I don't know if his 'it' is what we're looking for, but I have a feeling it's not something we're going to be very happy about."

"Funny how these things work out sometimes. Holly and I were just looking over some strange 'it' stuff of our own. Some references that Holly found, and some the CIA found. Tell me about yours."

"First time, Al-Sharif said to one of his houseguests that 'it' was due in sometime next week. Then he got a call and, during the conversation, was told 'it' was on schedule. Then he told his companions that when 'it' arrived, they would have to be ready to move in a hurry. Now, this may not be our 'it,' but I think we better stay on this lad like glue.

"Also, he has called a number in St. Louis on three different occasions. No reference to 'it' yet, but I called the agency and had them run the number. It's in a north county suburb called Bellefontaine Neighbors. I know it; it's up by 270 and 367. Close to the river…Mississippi, that is."

"Yeah, I know it. Once had a girlfriend up there, when I was in college. Your recommendation?"

"Maybe you should get somebody to check out whoever's there."

"You think we should keep this in-house, or bring in the FBI?"

"In-house. At least until we know if we really have something, and maybe even if we do."

"I agree, just wanted your input. Okay, I'll fly out with Billy and Hector…get them set up in a surveillance mode and then come on back here."

Drew gave Jim the address and rang off. Jim then said, "Billy, Hector, we're on a trip. Honey, you and Jessica keep at the job. I'll be back in a day or two. Billy, you check out the Gulfstream. Hector, come with me. We're going to raid CIA for some more eavesdropping equipment."

"Sure, Jim. But why don't we get our own stuff?"

Jim looked at Hector and smiled. "On the way, pal. Ordered it a couple of days ago. Should be here in a few weeks. Until then, we use CIA as our eavesdropping warehouse."

•

After talking to Jim, Drew took his turn at the bank of receivers in the living room of Roland's former home. While listening to a phone call made by Al-Sharif to his bank, Drew smiled as he realized that there was a very real possibility that the Janitors raid on Hit had borne fruit in one more regard. Al-Sharif was perplexed that money he was expecting to come in by wire transfer had not arrived.

Boris walked into the room and asked, "Anything new?"

"Yes, my friend, I believe there is. Our boy is—and has been—expecting money to hit his bank and it hasn't. We are quite aware that Jim's money robbing operation had to have repercussions somewhere along the line. I'd say we now have a real inkling that this boy may be naughty. We know his daddy has more money than God…now why do you imagine that he hasn't asked daddy for help? Because, old chap, the paymasters in Hit are supposed to be making tidy additions to his account."

"A normal person would say that you are reaching. Not being normal either, I quite agree with your analysis. Mr. Ibrahim Al-Sharif has no way of knowing that we took away much of al-Qaida's operating money, so he must be quite perplexed. I would venture a guess that a similar scene is being played out around the world. Can you just see in your mind's eye all the naughty boys around the world waiting on their operating money, and none is to be found?"

"Yes…and I love it. I think this information is worthy of passing on to my son-in-law."

With that, Drew placed a call to the Joint, to find out Jim was airborne. Having the number on the plane, Drew called that number. When Jim was on the line, Drew said, "Your Robin Hood efforts in Hit may be the first real chink in young Al-Sharif's armor. He is expecting money to arrive at his bank. Said money is past due."

"Me thinks," replied Jim, "that you are onto something with this fella. We'll be in St. Louis in about an hour. If anything else comes up, try my cell phone, if you can't get me on the plane."

"Right. Will do."

Less than ten minutes later, Al-Sharif placed another call; this one to the number in St. Louis. During that brief call, he told the person on the other end that money was becoming a problem and that he would get back to him.

Drew immediately called Jim with that information and then went back to monitoring the house across the street.

Jim landed his plane at Spirit of St. Louis airport. Spirit was a small-plane airport located in St. Louis County. After arranging for a rental car, Jim, Billy, and Hector set out for Bellefontaine Neighbors. Once there, they drove around the neighborhood where the target house was located.

After getting the lay of the land, Jim drove to the small police station, led his two companions inside, and asked for the chief. The chief was in and the three men were shown to his office. Inside, Jim produced authentic (but falsified) FBI credentials, and said, "I'm Jim Scott— out of the Washington office. These two fellas with me are Hector Garcia, with CIA, and Billy Longbow, with INS."

Both men produced authentic credentials, which were also falsified. After handshakes all around, the chief asked, "What can I do for you gentlemen?"

Jim answered, "We're here on a matter of vital national security and need some help."

"Do what I can to help."

Jim handed the chief a piece of paper and said, "Good, thank you. There are four addresses there. The odd-numbered house is occupied by what we believe to be potential terrorists. The three even-numbered houses are across the street. We need to get into one of them to set up surveillance. In that neighborhood, any long-term outside surveillance, such as a repair truck or something of the sort, will stick out like a sore thumb. As you no doubt know, the CIA can't conduct activities within the borders of the U.S. Agent Garcia is just here for identification purposes. He knows one of the men we believe to be in that house by sight. Agent Longbow is along because, if we are correct as to who is living there, he is in the country illegally, and if worse comes to worse, Agent Longbow can make an INS arrest.

"Now, what I'd like you to do is give us a rundown on who lives in the other three houses and give us some help in contacting the people in the one we agree would be the best to ask for assistance."

The chief looked at the piece of paper, paused, then rooted through some papers on his desk. After finding what he was looking for, he said, "You may be in luck. The owners of the middle house of these three are on vacation and I have a number where they can be reached. We could call them and probably get their permission to use their home in their absence."

Jim nodded and said, "We can keep that open as a possibility, but I would prefer one with the owners present, for two reasons. First off, if we handle this by phone, the owners may find it hard to keep what they would find out from us to themselves. I'd rather meet face-to-face with whomever we select, so I can stress the absolute importance of total silence on this matter.

"Secondly, if our bad guys know those people are on vacation and spot any type of activity in the supposedly empty home, they will surely get suspicious. Do you happen to know anything about the owners of the other two homes?"

"No, not off the top of my head. I do see your point about not using the empty house. So let me check with some of my men about the other two. Why don't you three gentlemen have a seat while I try to find something out from a couple of my patrol officers?"

Jim, who had seen the excitement level rising in the chief, said, "Fine, thank you. Please be careful in what you say to your men, however. I want what we're up to kept just between the four of us and whomever we contact for use of their home. I'd just as soon you mentioned this to no one…not even your wife."

The chief nodded and replied, "I understand," and left the office.

About forty-five minutes later he returned, shut the door to his office, and said, "Got the information you wanted. One of the homes is occupied by two older ladies, in their eighties or nineties. The other one also has older people—a couple in their late fifties or early sixties and two dogs, one of the officers said. One officer is pretty sure the wife works, sees her leave early and come home in mid-afternoon. He also knows the husband slightly. Has seen him work out at our recreation center. I've got names and phone numbers of each."

Jim replied, "Let's try the second one, the couple. What I'd like you to do is call him and get him to come up and see you. Let's think up some reason for you to ask him here without alarming him. How about the dogs? You could tell him you have had a complaint and want to talk to him personally before deciding on what action, if any, to take."

The chief reached for the phone, stopped, and asked, "I meant to ask you a while ago, are you perhaps related to Walter Scott?"

"Yes, my father. But please don't mention anything about this to him or anyone else. This operation is strictly on a need-to-know basis."

Jim's father had retired from the St. Louis County Police after serving four years on the St. Louis Department. He was now a police chief of another St. Louis suburb. The chief said, "I know him well. He has spoken of you often. Proud father stuff, but I thought you were in the Marine Corps and then went into intelligence—though he never said specifically which intelligence branch you were with."

"CIA, after the Marine Corps. When the Cold War was winding down, there were big cutbacks at the CIA and I was single and rather well off from investing in the stock market over the years. So I left the agency in hopes of saving the job of someone who might be married and need the job. Then I went over to the FBI."

The chief nodded, picked up his phone, and called the number he had for Gary and Betty Holmes. Mr. Holmes answered on the second ring and the chief ran the story about the dogs by him. Gary Holmes was not overjoyed that one of his neighbors would complain about either of his dogs, but agreed to come up and see the chief.

When he arrived, he was told which office belonged to the chief and knocked on the door. Jim opened it and the chief said, "Please come in, Mr. Holmes."

As he entered, he looked at the other three men in the room, noticed the door quickly shut behind him, and said, "Hello, I'm Gary Holmes."

The chief introduced himself and the other three men, then Jim said, "Mr. Holmes, we asked the chief to get you up here on the ruse of a complaint about your dogs. In reality, we have a far different matter to discuss with you. It involves national security, of the highest priority."

"Does this involve my wife?"

"No, not at all. Why do you ask?"

"She works at Boeing, in parts procurement."

"No, has nothing to do with her," Jim assured him, before telling him approximately the same story he had told the chief.

When Jim finished, Gary Holmes thought for a few seconds and asked, "I take it you want to move into our home?"

"Yes. We'll pay the food bill during our stay and try to be as little bother as possible."

"Boy, oh, boy! My wife will freak out about terrorists living across the street. But she's a good citizen, never misses voting, and is behind the President one hundred percent. I'll have to ask her, of course, when she gets home from work, but she'll go along. As for me, I'm proud to help out any way I can."

"Thank you," replied Jim, "I have a few things to point out. No one except your wife is to know about this. Not children, neighbors—especially neighbors—not anyone. When this matter is resolved, I will tell what you can and can't tell anyone about. Is that understood and okay with you?"

"Sure, I understand. What do you want me to do?"

Jim reached in his pocket, pulled out a wad of money, pealed off five hundred dollars, and said, "On your way home, do some grocery shopping. Don't overdo it for now...I don't want your neighbors seeing you bringing in enough to feed an army. You'll have to make subtle daily food runs for us. We obviously can't be seen. Then tonight...what time do you normally go to bed?"

"A little before ten, most nights."

"Okay, about nine-thirty, turn off all the lights in the rear of your home and be sure the drapes are closed all around the house. When we scoped out your neighborhood, we saw that you have a fence in the rear of your lot, where it adjoins the house behind you. We'll come over the fence and in the back door. It would help if you were near the door and, when you see us, you can just open it up and we'll come on in."

"All right, but I better warn you...that neighbor behind us has dogs, too. Like mine, they aren't big or vicious, but, like mine, quite noisy when it comes to anybody being around."

"Thanks for the warning. We'll bring steaks for their dogs," Jim joked.

Feeling he had made all the arrangements with Gary Holmes that he wanted to at the present time, Jim bid him goodbye with thanks. Then he thanked the chief, again reminded him to keep utter silence on the matter, and left with Billy and Hector. Once in their rental car, Hector said, "Amigo, you didn't tell that poor chief one damn thing that was true. Well, almost nothing."

Billy joked, "White man sure speak with forked tongue."

"Guys, if I told him the truth, we would have wound up having to call General Bradley to vouch for us. Probably would've had to get the President on the line to tell him it was okay to help us. As it is, he thinks he's helping the FBI and can live on in bliss. Though I'm going to have to call my dad—or better yet, go see him—and fill him in a bit. For now, I better call Drew and see if he has anything new."

Drew had nothing to report, except that Ibrahim Al-Sharif was getting more and more worried about money and called his bank twice more to see if money had arrived in his account.

•

At 9:20 that evening, Jim, Billy, and Hector, all dressed in black, parked their car in a school parking lot five houses down from Gary Holmes' backyard neighbor and walked up the street carrying three satchels full of espionage equipment. Good to his word (almost), Jim carried half a pound of raw hamburger with him. When they went down the side of the backyard neighbor's house and reached his fence, Jim looked over it, saw nothing, and was quickly over with Billy and Hector close behind. With no wasted motion, they also hopped the Holmes' fence and raced for the back door. As they reached it, Gary Holmes opened the door and his three houseguests came in.

His wife stood a few feet back from the door, and as Gary closed it, he said, "Honey, these are the men I told you about."

Jim held out his hand. "Nice to meet you, Mrs. Holmes…."

"Betty, please."

"…thank you, Betty. I'm Jim…Jim Scott. The short fella is Hector Garcia; the ugly one is Billy Longbow."

Gary said, "You guys may as well call me Gary, since we're going to be living together."

Jim replied, "Thanks, Gary. Now we have a few things to discuss. First off, the story you got in front of the police chief is not entirely accurate or complete. Since you will be able to hear the same things we do with the gear we'll set up, and since we may well have to speak openly in front of you, I'm going to give you the true and full story.

"We think the people across the street and down one house are al-Qaida terrorists. There is a nuclear satchel bomb floating around somewhere, and these fellas may just be involved with it."

As Betty sucked in her breath and looked frightened, Jim held up his hand and added, "Please don't be too alarmed. We are rather certain they don't have it at this time. Even if they do, they sure aren't going to waste it on a residential neighborhood. More like downtown St. Louis, if at all in this part of the country. We have another team monitoring another suspect in the case in Columbia…ah, Missouri…and from phone intercepts there, it would appear that the nuke is in transit. To where, we don't know. That is what we hope to find out.

"Again, I must stress absolute secrecy about this matter. Even if we are successful and recover the bomb, only the President can make the decision to inform the public. My guess is he wouldn't because he wouldn't want the enemy to know what happened. A confused enemy is a good enemy. If we get the bomb and al-Qaida has no idea what happened, we'll have them rushing around chasing their tails for nothing."

"That makes sense," said Gary.

"Now a few questions. How are you on beds, Gary?"

"Well, happily, Betty and I sleep together in our bedroom. The dogs, which you can hear quite well, sleep on a queen-sized bed in what we call their room. The back bedroom doesn't have a bed. You're welcome to their bed. They can sleep with us. They do half the time, anyhow.

So two of you could use that bed, and our couch is rather large, so one of you could use it."

Jim said, "I won't be staying. After I do a little bit of spook work, I'm leaving. These two guys will monitor your neighbors."

"Sure glad you said that," joked Hector. "If you remember Iraq, Billy snores like crazy and I have no desire to sleep with him."

That drew a round of chuckles, but at the puzzled look on Gary's face, Jim said, "We were in Desert Storm together…the three of us and some others. Hector is right…Billy does snore more than a normal person should."

"You people come to my land, steal it, and now pick on the red man for no good reason," joked Billy.

Jim held up his hand, "Enough, fellas. I don't want to hear how the white man stole California from the Mexicans, the rest of America from the Indians, and all that other stuff. We've got work to do. Gary, why not let your dogs out of their room? We may as well meet them."

Gary did as asked and two mid-sized dogs bounded down the hall barking. Gary soon had them calmed down, and Jim had two friends for life, as he divided up the hamburger he still had between the suddenly quite happy dogs. After he washed his hands in the kitchen sink, Jim, followed by Hector and Billy, all carried their satchels into the living room.

Jim did his best to explain each piece of equipment as they unpacked them. When everything was organized, Jim said, "Okay, Gary, Betty…here's what's going to happen. About midnight or one o'clock, I'm going to sneak out the back door, hop the fence alongside your home, and do my best stealth act as I try to bug our friends' house. Uh, Gary, do they have dogs?"

"Not that I ever saw."

"Good. Oh, Gary, I forgot to ask you what you do…for a living, that is?"

"CPA. Work out of my basement. Come and go quite a bit as I call on my clients. Have mostly corporate accounts and go to their offices to monitor the computer systems I set up for them."

"Okay, good. Would you mind doing any leg work Billy and Hector need done?"

"Not at all."

"Thanks. If it's getting close to your bedtime, you may as well hit the sack. It'll be two or three hours before I do my thing."

Gary asked, "Are you kidding me? I wouldn't miss this for anything."

Betty shook her head and said, "Well, I'm for bed. Good night. Nice to meet you all. I'm counting on you to do what you do correctly, so my city doesn't get blown up."

•

As Betty Holmes was walking down her hall toward the bathroom to prepare for bed, Sergey Terekhov and the two Germans with him were landing at the airport in Billings, Montana. Sergey was in charge of the operation to eliminate Jim Scott. He left no doubt as to who was running the show, even though he had known both men before the Soviet empire crumbled. The master of all master spies had trained him, and he considered the two Germans to be far less than his equal.

From the reports received in Iraq from the two previous hit teams sent after Scott, Sergey knew there were two prime locations to hunt down the target. While he felt sure that, at least for the near future, Scott would more than likely be in Washington, his plan was to booby trap his Montana home, then head to Washington to determine the best way to eliminate the man.

After the three had rented a car and checked into a motel, Sergey sent the other two to meet their contact, who would supply arms and explosives. While the Germans were gone, Sergey surveyed the map he had of Montana and decided it was best to wait until morning to set out for the Scott property.

•

In Columbia, Ibrahim Al-Sharif finally ran out of patience and placed a call to his father. When his father answered the phone, Ibrahim said, "Hello. I have a problem. My funding has ceased for some reason and I have immediate need of funds."

Yasin Al-Sharif answered, "My son, this phone call is quite inappropriate. You know better than to discuss things other than family matters on the phone."

"Yes, father, but this borders on an emergency. '*It*' is due in soon and I do not have funds enough to carry out my mission."

"*IBRAHIM, please*…not on the phone."

"Father, you worry too much. Just please send me some money at once."

"That I will do. Now, goodbye."

"Have you heard anything about money problems?"

"Yes, but that is all I will say. Except I have been contacted by others seeking money. However, they at least used proper procedures. Now, goodbye," Yasin said as he hung up the phone abruptly.

•

Across the street, Drew yelled, "Bingo!"

He said it so loudly that the other three men in the house heard him, got out of their beds, and came running downstairs to see what had Drew so excited.

He called Jim just as his son-in-law and Billy were about to leave on their bug-planting mission. Jim answered and Drew said, "Got him! Silly young fool just called his father for money. And, you'll be happy to know, he said way more than he should have. So did the father in a moment of additional stupidity. The father confirmed, without knowing he was doing so, that our little trip to Iraq and your money removal efforts have borne fruit. Young Al-Sharif is not the only one looking for money. But the topper is the young fool not only stressed 'it' in his conversation, but also stated that he needed money to carry out his mission."

"Oh, good job, Drew! That itchy spook feeling about Al-Sharif the elder paid off! To bring you up-to-date on this end, I'm about to bug these guys here. Then, if nothing else comes up, I'm going to run out to my place. I've decided to bring Lady and Bowser back to Washington, and move my horses over to George's place. I keep having my own itchy feeling that Al-Shahristani will try again and I'd be sick if anything happened to George or Peggy because of it. George is an old Navy guy and can handle himself, but not against guys like us."

"Good idea. Also, it'll be nice to have Lady and Bowser around. They'll liven up the place, and Lady is the best detection system we have."

Jim chuckled. "You're probably right. Okay, I'm off. Call me on the Gulfstream, or my cell phone, if you need me."

"Right."

Within minutes after Jim told the others about his conversation with Drew, he was over the fence, across the street, and over a fence at the suspect's house. Billy was right behind him, to act as his backup. Both had night-vision goggles. As Jim deactivated the alarm system, Billy whispered, "What happens if we wake somebody up?"

"We don't. Let's just hope they don't have a guard posted. If so, we'll play it by ear."

Billy grunted as Jim went to the back door and picked the two locks on it. Then they eased into the kitchen of the house and Jim placed a listening device there and one in the phone. Unlike Drew, Jim went from the kitchen into the garage first. There he put homing devices on, and bugs in, the car he found there and also a delivery-type truck. Next, he went into the living room and bugged it and the phone there. While there he saw a number of papers on a coffee table and investigated. As he looked them over, he noticed quite a large amount of information on train schedules from Alton, Illinois to downtown St. Louis. Satisfied that he had all the information he needed, he next went on to the three bedrooms. Each had someone sleeping in it, so Jim was very careful as he bugged each of those rooms, the three cell phones he found, and the regular phones in each room.

After the two bathrooms were also equipped with listening devices, Jim tried the door leading down from the kitchen to the basement. One of the stairs squeaked slightly and he froze. After a few moments, he went on down the stairs, until he was about halfway down. From there he could see most of the basement. He stopped, placed a bug on an exposed beam near a water pipe and parallel wire running through the beam, then quickly retraced his steps, being careful to miss the squeaking step.

He signaled Billy and they quickly left the house. Jim reactivated the alarm system and both men headed back over the fence, across the street, and over the Holmes' fence. Gary was waiting for them at the door.

Once inside, Jim said, "God Almighty. They've got at least fifteen men in the basement sleeping on cots. Damn guys sure are sloppy...no one awake. Guess they figure they're so sly, nobody would even think they may be bad guys."

Billy said, "Yeah—glad they feel that way. But, we're sure onto *something* here. Maybe not the nuke, but damn sure something."

Jim nodded and said, "Okay, I'm off. You know where to reach me if you need me."

•

Drew's cell phone rang. "Hollins."

"Drew, Justin Walker here. Your friend Yasin Al-Sharif just got a call from his son that I think you'd be quite interested in."

Drew laughed. "I heard it from this end. Thanks for the heads up, though."

"Uh, Drew…never mind, I won't ask."

"Thank you. Have a nice day, Justin."

"You, too. Good luck. I think you've hit pay dirt this time old friend."

"Yes, I believe we have."

After Drew hung up, Boris raised an eyebrow. Drew grinned, "My man Justin is playing by the rules. Keeping me up-to-date on what our bugs on Al-Sharif elder turned up."

Boris just nodded his approval.

11.

After the flight to Montana, Jim used an SUV he always left at the local small-plane airport and drove the twenty minutes to his home. Once there, Lady, his large German shepherd, and Bowser, his part beagle/part basset hound, greeted him warmly. When he felt they had enough loving, he went into his kitchen and put on coffee.

Then he called George Bostich. "George, I'm home for a day or so. I'm going to take Lady and Bowser back to Washington with me. We're going to be there quite awhile."

"I can imagine."

"If you have room, I'd like to move my horses to your place. As you know, since we sold off most of our stock last summer, we're down to only four and I'd just as soon you stayed away from my place."

"Still worried about what you were the last time we spoke?"

"Yes."

"Give me a few minutes to hook up my four-horse trailer and I'll be right over."

"Thanks, George."

•

Long before Jim and George talked, Sergey Terekhov and his two companions were driving toward Jim's home. Sergey found a place of some concealment about a mile north of the large car park at the bottom of the curving driveway up to Jim and Holly's home. He parked the car, got out, and said, "We'll walk from here. Bring the bags."

The bags Sergey referred to were two duffel-type bags that contained explosives and other items needed to rig booby traps in the target house. Each man had already armed himself with pistols that had been in the bags.

From studying the map he had, and remembering the information supplied by the first team that had come here, Sergey was confident he could find the Scott house, after the cross-country trek in front of them. Despite some grumbling from his companions, they finally had Jim's house in view.

Sergey told his men to hunker down while he went forward with field glasses to get a better look. What he saw surprised him. Jim came out to greet George. Sergey had long studied photos of Jim, so he was sure of what he saw. He watched as George and Jim shook hands and chatted in front of the house for a few minutes. Then he watched as the horse trailer was pulled around to the barn and four horses were loaded up.

After George left with the horses and Jim had gone back inside the house, Sergey went back to his men and said, "We're in luck. Scott is here. We'll wait until dark, and then go down and place our explosives all around his house and blow him to hell. From what I have heard of him, it is better to do it that way than to try a frontal assault."

•

In Columbia, Drew was listening in as Ibrahim Al-Sharif said, "The money has arrived in my account. Now all we have to do is wait for word that 'it' has arrived."

Drew smiled and called Jim to report. After he did so, Jim said, "Okay, looks like I still have some time, so I think I'll sleep here tonight. I'm getting pretty tired."

"Not as young as you once were, son-in-law?"

"No, but I never was real good at going long without sleep. Talk to you tomorrow, unless something comes up."

After hanging up, Jim called Holly and filled her in on what had happened since he left the Joint, and let her know that he would be spending the night in their home. He also asked her to have Jessica check on train schedules between Alton, Illinois and St. Louis, covering a period over the next several days. He then put food out for the dogs, ate a snack, and decided on a nap.

As he slept, Sergey and friends made bombs. Then they too napped. As dusk approached, Sergey woke his two companions and they ate the sandwiches they had brought.

While they ate, Jim was up after his nap and busy disposing of the food in the refrigerator that had or would spoil. Next he made something to eat for himself, then sat down at his computer and wrote a long love letter to Holly and e-mailed it to the Joint.

As darkness approached, Jim flipped a switch that turned the front windows across the front of his home into one-way mirrors. There was a space between two separate panes that were gas-filled and, though Jim could see out easily, anyone on the outside was unable to look in, as the outside pane was specially treated to react to the gas.

Sergey saw the change in the windows and, though he had heard of such windows, he had never actually seen them in operation. He informed his men that they would start on the end of the building nearest them, work around the back, then rig the far end of the building. He felt that three sides of the house rigged to explode at once would be sufficient to do the job, and he didn't want to risk being seen by Scott. He also decided to wait until after 10:00 pm to give Scott a chance to settle in for the night.

His idea would have probably worked, except for two things. One was Lady; the other was permanent sensors Jim had installed after an abortive attempt on his life staged some nine months earlier by a large Iraqi hit team, who all now laid dead in the bottom of a nearby abandoned mine shaft.

As the time for the attack neared, the three assassins moved forward slowly. Sergey and the two Germans were less than halfway to the house from their hiding place when Lady raised her head and uttered a low, menacing growl. Jim knew that Lady didn't growl at small animals passing by the house and instantly jumped up and walked over to the screen that displayed any data from the sensors. In a few minutes, there was a low beep from the speaker next to the screen, then three blips appeared.

Jim told Lady to stay and raced upstairs. The second floor of his home had a veranda that circled the entire house. He went into his well-supplied armament room, grabbed a climbing rope with grappling hook attached, and put a leather glove on his left hand. He put on night-vision goggles, took out his silenced Walther, and slipped out a door to the veranda.

Moving silently but quickly, Jim went to the end of the house where he had seen the three blips. By the time he reached that end of the house, the two Germans were busy placing charges, while Sergey stood back a few feet to watch. Jim couldn't see the Germans, but could see Sergey and could figure out where the other two were by the direction Sergey was looking.

Without urgency, Jim calmly placed the grappling hook under the base of the solid two-foot high wall, which had a gap between the floor and wall, and wrapped the rope around his left hand. He jumped over the wall and headed downward. On the way he spotted the two Germans, fired two shots, then landed and turned toward Sergey, who was raising his gun. Jim shot the gun out of his hand, then shot him in the upper thigh. Sergey yelped at the searing pain in the palm of his hand where the bullet disarming him had ricocheted and the developing pain in his leg.

Jim glanced at the two Germans who were down and said to Sergey, "Don't even think about moving."

He quickly backed over to the other two, checked them, and found both dead from direct hits to their heads. Then he walked over to Sergey. "Please don't give me any reason to kill you. If I wanted you dead, you would already be in hell with your two friends. You're going to be a good boy and tell me all I want to know, aren't you?"

"Nyet."

"Oh, Russian, are you?"   Jim said in that language.

Jim then kicked Sergey's weapon away and quickly frisked him. He went back to one of the Germans, removed his jacket, tore his shirt off, and into strips, then did his best to stem the flow of blood from Sergey's two wounds.

Next he herded Sergey inside the house and told him to sit down in a wooden chair. When Sergey was in the chair, Jim took the man's belt off and secured one arm to the chair and said, "You are going to tell me everything I want to know, or you'll tell a friend of mine. He's quite good at interrogation. You may know him…fella by the name of Boris Telman."

The mention of Boris had an immediate impact on Sergey. Jim saw the recognition on the face of Sergey…and something else. It wasn't fear, and Jim couldn't quite figure out what it was. He asked, "How do you know Boris?"

Sergey looked at Jim for a few seconds, then answered, "Boris was my mentor in the KGB. I will tell you anything you want to know."

"I take it that you rather like Mr. Telman."

"More than like…he was like a father to me. Treated me, and others, better than anyone else there. He was a demanding taskmaster, but fair and honest with all who responded to him in a like manner."

"Who sent you, Al-Shahristani?"

"Yes."

"Any others, besides you three?"

"Yes. Two Russians, who have disappeared. Two Germans, along with six men sent to help them, have also failed to report on schedule."

"The last eight are dead. My secretary killed them. Now tell me about the two Russians."

Sergey smiled in spite of himself. "Even your secretary is a killing machine. How upsetting that piece of information would be to Al-Shahristani. The two Russians were here, at your home…had you under surveillance and reported that they needed an expert marksman. Claimed to have found one and arranged for funds to be sent to his account as a down payment on his fee for killing you. Now I have a question for you. Did Boris happen to visit here about a month ago?"

Jim laughed and the same thought ran through his mind as he answered, "Yes. I bet those two also knew Boris and felt of him as you do and decided to leave the Iraqi Foreign Legion behind."

"So you know of the Foreign Legion. Well, you're right…those two did know Boris, quite well."

The so-called Foreign Legion was a group of ex-patriot intelligence officers from various segments of the collapsed Soviet Empire, suddenly out of work, who had been approached and hired by Saddam Hussein to join his intelligence apparatus.

Jim smiled and replied, "Yes, I know about the Foreign Legion. My wife told me all about them after my secretary killed those two Germans. She knew them from Iraq."

Sergey raised an eyebrow, but said nothing.

Jim said, "Long story, I'll tell you about it sometime. For now, I have a question for you. Would you like to switch sides? We are fighting al-Qaida on all fronts, and need all the help we can get. Thanks to some help from Boris, we even got quite a bit of information about their activities in Chechnya. That information, along with everything else we have developed, is routinely being passed on to your former motherland. By the way, what the hell's your name?"

"Sergey Terekhov. Do you mean you want me to work with Boris again? Against this al-Qaida terror network?"

"Yes."

"Yes, it would be an honor. I certainly cannot go back to Iraq…and I never much cared for that al-Qaida scum."

"Fine," replied Jim, as he walked over and undid the belt from Sergey's arm. Then he walked over to the bar and poured two drinks—vodka for Sergey.

As he handed the drink to Sergey, he said, "Let me make a phone call so we can get you some proper care, and then we'll go see Boris—or at least, for now, talk to him on the phone."

Jim walked over to his phone and called the White House and asked for General Bradley. When told the General wasn't in, he asked for Ted Kuntz. On learning that Ted also was not in, the nighttime secretary in the General's office asked if there was a message or if one of the two men should be awoken. Jim answered, "No. This is Jim Scott. Leave a message for both of them that I decided to give them a break and wake up someone else."

He then turned on his computer and pulled up a program with phone numbers. He put in his personal code and got the home number of FBI Director John Engle. He then called Director Engle and said, "Good morning, John. Jim Scott here."

"Do you know what time it is?"

"Sure do…just after midnight your time. I need some help."

Now more awake and sensing a midnight call from Jim Scott would be of importance, John said, "Closer to one, but what can I do for you?"

"I've got a wounded man at my place in Montana. I wonder if you could have your Billings office get a reliable doctor up here by chopper. My local doctor is a fine fellow, but he talks too much."

"How did he get wounded?"

"I shot him."

"And he's still alive? You drunk or something?"

Jim chuckled. "I shot to wound. I wanted somebody to talk to. Holly's in Washington."

"Did he talk?"

"Oh, yes. More than that, he has decided to leave the Iraqis and join forces with us. The fact that he knows and respects Boris had more to do with that than anything I said or did."

"All right, hold on while I use my other line to get a doctor on the way. Wait, how will they find you?"

"I'll emit a homing signal on your emergency frequency two, and put my outside floodlights on."

"You know about that, do you?"

"EF2? Yes, I know."

John sighed. "Okay, hold on."

A few minutes later, John was back on the line and said, "Help is on the way. Anybody else shot up there?"

"Do you really want to know?"

"Not if the bodies disappear…forever."

"They will, right on top of some Iraqis who made an attempt on me last January."

"Okay. How are things going on the nuke hunt? Bradley mentioned that Drew Hollins might be onto something in Missouri."

"Actually, we may have found the right person to home in on. It looks like the damn thing is headed for St. Louis. We don't know, yet, if St. Louis is the intended target, or just a way station. Either way, we'll let you know when we know something for sure. You might alert your office there to be ready to help. However, you know how this stuff always happens…never time to do anything but act."

"I'll call the St. Louis office first thing in the morning and tell them to offer any assistance you need. Think I'll tell them to put an extra man or two on the night shift. Anything else?"

"No, thanks. Talk to you later, John."

"So long."

Off the phone, Jim went to the room containing his radio equipment and set up the homing device. Then he put on the floodlights outside his home and said, "Sergey, the booze is over at the bar—help yourself. Not much food left in the kitchen, but feel free to eat whatever you can find. Lady, he's okay."

Sergey just nodded, as Jim left to go take care of the bodies outside. Once alone—except for the two dogs, the big one having been ready to eat him alive, he was sure, until her master called her off—he got up and hobbled over to the bar and re-filled his glass with more of the brand of vodka that Boris Telman was partial to. Sergey pondered the turn of events that had just transpired. He knew he was alive only because Jim Scott chose it to be so. He had seen the two shots to the back of the Germans' heads while Jim had been dangling from a rope. Now, he had been left alone in the man's home and knew there would be other weapons around, if he decided to find them and lay in wait for Jim's return.

He almost choked on his vodka at that thought, sure that even if he was so inclined, he would somehow wind up dead. He also wondered just how Boris had come to be aligned with this man.

While Sergey pondered, Jim was disposing of bodies. After making sure that no identification was on either body, he loaded them into his SUV and drove to the abandoned mine shaft that held nineteen dead Iraqis. The Germans were soon added to the pile at the bottom of the shaft. On top of the bodies went the two satchels full of explosives. Jim had no use for those items, but he did pick up all three guns to add to his collection of arms.

Back inside, Jim tossed Sergey his gun and asked, "What about your transportation here and identification?"

Sergey told Jim where the car was parked and told him that identification for all three men was hidden nearby.

Jim just nodded and went in search of something to eat. Sergey joined him in the kitchen and the men talked little as they awaited the FBI helicopter. When it arrived, the doctor on board tended to Sergey, while Jim told an agent where to find the rental car and identification for the three men. He offered the use of his SUV, which was accepted with thanks.

A while later, two agents returned, one driving Jim's vehicle and the other the rental car. Jim retrieved Sergey's identification—false, of course—and handed it to the now-patched-up Russian. To the lead agent, Jim said, "Please have one of your men turn the car in," and handed the agent three hundred dollars, sure that would be more than sufficient. Neither agent asked about the two extra sets of identification, having been told by their Director not to ask questions of Jim Scott.

After one agent left in the rental car, and the helicopter took off, Sergey said, "At some point I should thank you for my life. So, thank you."

Jim smiled and replied, "You're welcome. Now, we're out of here. I'd planned to sleep here tonight, but I napped this afternoon and am wide awake now, so we'll just go."

Jim closed up the house as Sergey and the dogs got into the SUV. They then drove to the airport where the Gulfstream had been left and were soon airborne toward Missouri. After setting his course, Jim asked, "Do you happen to fly?"

"No."

"Pity."

As they flew eastward, Billy called the plane phone. Jim answered, "Jim."

"Hi, Jim. Billy here. Wasn't sure just what your schedule was, but figured if you answered this phone, I wouldn't be waking you."

Jim joked, "Actually, you did."

"White man make joke. The reason I'm calling is we had a little incident earlier tonight. Well, not really. Because we knew what was coming. Anyhow, they went out in their delivery truck and bought pizzas, about fifteen of them. The more I thought about it, the more I wondered just what in the hell Hector and I would do if they took off on business. My thought was to ask Gary—but hell, Jim. He's not experienced, and besides which, if I got his ass shot off, I'd feel awful."

"So you were sitting there with the early morning shift with nothing to do and figured you'd just give me a call and give me something else to deal with," joked Jim.

"Yeah, something like that."

"I agree with you. The way things are going, we need to make you mobile. Until I get you some wheels, you'll just have to rely on Gary. However, I think I'll get Drew there as fast as I can. I've got a new recruit—name's Sergey Terekhov. I'll stop in Columbia and trade him for Drew. He and Boris are old friends."

"Where'd he come from?"

"Tried to blow up my home. Didn't work."

"Oh. I won't ask more…I know you."

"Good, bye."

Jim flew on to Columbia, landed, rented a car in the early morning, and drove to the address Drew had given him. On the way, he called ahead and got Drew on the phone. "Drew, I'm on my way to your new house. Is there a garage I can just pull into?"

"I'll make it so."

"See ya."

Tom was up to relieve Drew on the monitoring equipment and Drew said, "Tom, go out and put our car in the drive. Leave the garage door open. Jim's on the way and wants to pull right on in."

"Gotcha."

When Jim arrived, he pulled into the garage and Drew was there to meet him. Drew pushed the garage door opener button to shut the door as Jim and Sergey got out. Jim introduced the two men and Drew said, "I've heard of you."

"Oh?" Sergey uttered with raised eyebrow.

"Boris Telman told me about you."

Sergey just nodded and the three men went into the house, where Jim introduced Sergey to Tom, before asking, "Where's Boris?"

"Just behind you," Boris said as he came down the stairs. "With all the noise you made coming in, you woke me."

As Boris finished that sentence, he saw Sergey and rushed forward and gave the man a big hug. Before long the story of how Sergey happened to be there was told. At that point, Boris said, "Sergey, you are a *very* lucky man to be still alive."

"I'm well aware of that fact."

Jim then said, "Okay, here's the plan. I'm taking Drew-the-housebuyer with me and leaving Sergey with you. Boris, you three will continue to monitor things here. If young Al-Sharif leaves town, follow him."

With little further conversation, Jim and Drew left.

12.

Sa'd Kahdi was quite an unhappy man. The plan had been so simple. He was to take the suitcase atom bomb up the Euphrates River to Syria, where the Syrians would give him diplomatic papers. From there he would go to Berlin, where he would be met by an al-Qaida cell who would have him on a plane with different identification (which he already had) to Toronto, Canada. In Toronto, he would be met by another al-Qaida cell that would help him onto a plane for Chicago, Illinois.

At Chicago, he would rent a car and, on the way to St. Louis, Missouri, would use the cell phone he had—which was the only phone he was to use on his mission—to call Ibrahim Al-Sharif, to be met in St. Louis.

The overall plan of al-Qaida was the strike on New York and Washington, which had been three fourths successful. Then a tractor-trailer bomb attack on the West Coast movie industry was the second phase; however, that had *not* happened. Next would be the first of four atom bombs, set off as steps three through six.

That plan had started off well, with the successful attacks on the East Coast. Kahdi was to leave Hit on the day of the second strike. The second strike never happened because the members of the al-Qaida cell in Los Angeles were all dead or in prison, thanks to the intervention of Jim Scott in an unrelated incident. Jim busted up an Iraqi drug ring in the early stages of his mission to eliminate Saddam Hussein. That fact, however, was unknown to the leadership of al-Qaida.

Five days after the Los Angeles attack was to have happened, it was decided to send Kahdi on his way. The first snag was in Syria, where the Syrians had become nervous. Though they didn't know Kahdi carried a nuclear device with him, they knew he was al-Qaida. It took two days there for the Syrians to garner enough nerve to send him on, as a low-level Syrian diplomat, with diplomatic immunity.

On reaching Berlin, he wasn't contacted as had been planned. Unknown to him, the al-Qaida cell there had been arrested by the German authorities, on information supplied as a result of the Janitors' raid on Hit. After three days of waiting, Sa'd Kahdi decided to take a chance. Even though the papers he had showed him assigned to the Berlin embassy, he hoped the diplomatic passport would discourage a close examination of the other papers. Using those papers, he bought a ticket for Toronto, checked his two pieces of luggage, and held his breath. The second piece of luggage he carried had been carefully selected to be very similar in looks, though smaller, to the one containing the bomb. The bomb wasn't detected, and Kahdi had an uneventful flight to Canada.

At Canadian customs, he was the only passenger flying with diplomatic papers, so there was no line at the customs' counter assigned to diplomats. He boldly carried his two pieces of luggage to the counter and presented his papers. Even as he tried to remain calm, he could feel sweat forming under his arms. The customs' agent looked at the papers, at Kahdi, at his two pieces of luggage, and waved him through without comment. He nearly fainted with relief as he slowly took the offered papers and passport, then picked up his luggage and was on his way.

The next problem he faced, however, was he had no idea how to contact the Toronto cell. That information was to have been supplied to him by the Berlin cell. Now already three days past his planned arrival time in St. Louis, he did what he was supposed to do only in emergencies. He called a man in Madrid, Spain, using the cell phone. That man was a cutout with knowledge of the three cells involved: those in Berlin, Toronto, and Missouri.

Kahdi said, "My friends in Berlin were not in and now I cannot contact my friends here in Toronto, either."

The man in Madrid understood at once and asked, "Where are you?"

Kahdi told him the name of the hotel he had checked into and was told that he would be contacted.

After ending that conversation, Kahdi decided to let the Missouri connection know he was running late, but was still on the way. He called Ibrahim Al-Sharif and said, "I have been delayed. I will visit you in five to seven days."

Ibrahim, who by now was getting quite nervous at the delay, said, "It's about time you called. We are anxious to receive 'it'."

Kahdi thought, *"Idiot,"* but said, "Be patient. Goodbye."

The Janitors, in the person of Boris Telman, of course were listening to that second phone call made by Kahdi. Boris immediately called the airborne Jim and reported what he had heard.

Jim replied, "Thanks, Boris. I'm sure we now have little doubt that 'it' is the bomb and is on its way. At least we have a few days to get ready, and I may have time to take care of a pain in my side…Al-Shahristani."

"Planning a little side trip to Iraq, are you?"

"Yes. Should be able to take care of that little bit of business in a day or two…if I can get the help I hope I can."

"Good luck."

•

In Madrid, the man there feared the phone call just received might have jeopardized him, so he packed up and left for Paris. He was correct in his fears. His name had been found in the volumes of data collected by the Janitors in Hit and his phone was under surveillance by the Spanish. As he drove down the street away from his residence, the Spanish authorities drove up, missing him by less than a minute. The Spanish decided to stake out his home and wait. That allowed him to make good his escape to France.

Once in Paris, he called the Toronto cell and informed them of Kahdi's predicament. He told them to proceed with caution. That call completed, he decided that Europe was no place for him and booked a flight home to Saudi Arabia.

•

After a day of waiting outside the empty house, the Spanish authorities finally had the thought to contact the Canadians about the man in their midst. They didn't know his name, but were able to tell them where he was located. That proved to be of little help to the Canadian authorities because Sa'd Kahdi had checked into a hotel of some size, which was frequented by a large number of Mideastern types. The best they could do was to put a plainclothes detail in the lobby, hoping to spot a suspicious-looking person and comb through the files of recent arrivals. What they found there were thirty-seven people of Mideastern descent who had checked in during the past seven days. Further checking proved that none of those thirty-seven had placed a call to Spain in the last two days.

Sa'd Kahdi had been picked for this assignment because he was familiar with Canada and the United States, having traveled to both countries on numerous occasions. During those trips, he came to the conclusion that North American police forces more or less left people alone if they acted in a normal and relaxed way. Now, as he walked through the lobby of the hotel after having eaten, he was forced to put that conclusion to the test, as he spotted what had to be police officers in plainclothes.

Calmly he walked to the bank of elevators, pushed the button, went to his floor, and into his room. Only when inside did he exhale fully. Kahdi wondered what to do. The police being present might have nothing to do with him. But instinct told him otherwise. Yet, if he left the hotel he would never make contact with the Toronto cell. And that cell was vital because they could get his luggage aboard the flight he would take to America and bypass customs in Chicago. The experience of customs on arrival in Canada had been harrowing, even though it had gone well. He knew a closer inspection of his papers might arouse suspicion—suspicion that would easily turn up the fact that he had no business being in Canada *or* the United States.

He felt he had used up all the luck he was entitled to. The Americans would not be so lax—especially not now. Just as he was about to decide to leave the hotel and take his chances on another method to reach America, the phone rang. The voice said, "Check out now. Leave the hotel, turn right, and wait at the corner for a red sedan to pick you up."

Kahdi hung up the phone, gathered his things, went to the lobby, and checked out. He did his best not to look at the police officers he had spotted earlier, as he calmly walked from the hotel. At the corner, the red car pulled up in front of him. Without haste he opened the door, put his bags in the back, and rode off with a young woman at the wheel.

Around the corner and driving with a pace to match traffic, the woman said, "You are Kahdi. No need for you to know my name. We cannot get you out of Canada and into the United States by airline. Our man in Chicago has been detained by the authorities for questioning."

"How can I get into America then?"

"We have ways. Right now, however, we have some difficulty. Something has happened to our funding. We are quite short of money to operate with."

"I have some money, but most of it I will need. I could let you have about one thousand dollars, American, if that will help."

"It will. With what we have available, it might be enough to arrange things to get you across the border. For now, I am taking you to my home, an apartment. You will have to stay there until arrangements can be made."

"How long do you think it will take? I am already past due for my arrival in Missouri and the contact there is having a fit of nerves."

"Perhaps three days. I didn't know you were going to Missouri. What is there?"

"I spoke out of turn. Sorry."

"I understand. The less we know the better. We don't even know what your mission is. The only thing we know is that it is important and we must not fail in getting you into America."

•

While Sa'd Kahdi had been busy trying to recover from his setbacks, Jim had been busy, also. After leaving Columbia, he had landed in St. Louis and rented a car after taking the dogs for a walk and letting them relieve themselves before placing them back on the plane. He drove Drew through the neighborhood where Billy and Hector were staked out. He pointed out the house they were located in and the house of the terrorists.

That done, he drove back to the airport, gave Drew the keys, and said, "Good luck house hunting."

Drew just grinned and patted Jim on the back, as his son-in-law left him for the plane. Back aboard, Jim flew on to Andrews, arranged a ride for himself and the two dogs, and arrived at the Joint, ready for sleep but realizing that would have to wait.

He had called Ben Schiller while in flight from St. Louis. With Ben on the line and pleasantries out of the way (after making sure Ben's phone was a secure line), Jim asked, "Ben, old friend, I need help. Is Sid Spillman back in Iraq?"

"No. We viewed that as too dangerous after your escapades there with him. We have another man in place, however."

"Okay, here's the deal. I want to take out Al-Shahristani. He's becoming a big pain in the ass. He's sent three hit teams after me. The first is, I hope, neutralized; the second is wiped out; and the one man left from the third has been turned…working with us now."

"Name?"

"Sergey Terekhov."

"Never heard of him. Which means exactly nothing, except he might be good."

"Trained by Boris, who thinks of him as a son."

"Probably good, then. What's your plan?"

"I think I'll drive in from Jordan, with Jordanian papers prepared by my good friends the Mossad."

"Of course."

"Then if I could get the same apartment to shoot from that I used when taking out Saddam, it would make life easier. I know it…how to find it…and could just go there and wait my chance, then drive away. I'd never have to meet your new man in Baghdad or expose him in any way. Well, wait a minute…"

"Here it comes."

"…there is one thing he could do for me. I'd like to get a note to Al-Majeed, telling him he's next."

"We can figure something out. Come on to Tel Aviv. We'll put the final touches on it when you get here."

"No checking with the bosses?"

"They'll go along. They love you."

"Nice to be loved."

•

Meanwhile, Drew's house-hunting skills were little changed from Columbia. This time, however, the house was empty and two blocks away. He called the real estate company name on the "For Sale" sign and waited twenty minutes for the agent to show up. When the agent arrived, Drew was shown through the house. Then he asked, "How much?"

"Listed at seventy-two five."

"Sold. I'll have the money wire-transferred into the account you tell me to use. I want the keys now. I'll give you my address in Belleville to mail the deed to."

"Moving here from Belleville?"

"No, needed a summer home up north."

The agent looked at Drew with a funny look. He realized that the twenty-mile distance from Belleville to Bellefontaine Neighbors would make little difference in climate and that he had just been told to mind his own business. Deciding not to look a gift horse in the mouth, the agent gave Drew the account information he had requested and got Drew's name, Belleville address, and cell phone number (if he had any questions).

Then, with the man still standing there, Drew called Jim and said, "I now own a house in Bellefontaine Neighbors—or will as soon as I give you the information on where to wire seventy-two thousand five hundred dollars."

Jim just chuckled and waited for the information. When Drew finished, Jim said, "Nice work."

After Drew hung up, the agent said, "The utilities are on, but you'll have to change the accounts over to your name."

Drew thought a second, reached in his pocket, took out a wad of bills, and counted out ten one-hundred dollar bills. He handed them to the agent. "Please take care of that for me. Keep what's left over for yourself…a little bonus for being so helpful."

As he tried to calculate how much of a bonus he'd just "made," the agent took the money and handed Drew the keys. "I really shouldn't give you the keys yet, but I guess it'll be okay. By the way, Bellefontaine Neighbors has a residency permit law."

"Fine, thank you. Good day."

Minutes after the agent left, Drew did also and went in search of furniture. He found a store that would deliver the same day and bought a bed, kitchen table (with chairs), a sofa, two easy chairs, and a coffee table. He told them to deliver even if he wasn't home; the front door was open and please to leave it that way when leaving. Next, he bought a refrigerator and stove that could be delivered that day and gave that store the same instructions.

After buying bedding and towels and making a visit to a grocery store, Drew was ready to set up housekeeping until needed by Billy and Hector, who he called to report readiness.

In the Joint, Jim hugged and kissed Holly, hugged Jessica, and introduced her to Lady and Bowser. After Holly had finished spoiling the dogs, Jim started to say something, but Lady uttered a low growl and Jim looked up at the security monitor just as the signal announcing someone at the gate went off. It was Ted Kuntz.

Jim noticed the way Jessica was looking at Lady and said, "She's well trained. Trained to not much care for strangers, and she doesn't know Ted."

As Ted came in, Jim said, "Your timing couldn't have been better. I was just getting ready to tell Jessica about Lady and was going to work with the two of them so they can get along. May as well include you in that. The dogs will probably be here for some time, and if you come waltzing in here when no one is in this area, Lady might just eat you."

"I'm all for avoiding that," joked Ted.

"Before we start this training exercise, what brings you here?"

"Some design data and so forth on the nukes you brought back. The engineers, with help from our Russian allies, have it all down on paper for you."

"Good. Billy and Hector are two of the best demolition guys around. It'll be nice to have this stuff in their hands. Speaking of which, how would you like a trip to St. Louis?"

"Why?"

"To take a copy of this stuff to them to study. Actually, you can take it to Drew and he can get it to them. I've got the address of the new house he just bought."

Ted—who knew about the Columbia operation—jokingly asked, "Another one?"

"Yeah, he's collecting houses these days. This time we have him set up near Billy and Hector, in case they need some help with the monitoring job they're doing on that al-Qaida cell in St. Louis."

"Sure, I'll be glad to help out. Get me out of the White House for a day—well, most of a day, at least. The President's busting balls over there—nicely, politely—but busting balls, nonetheless. This guy doesn't make excuses and doesn't accept them. Hell of a man, our President."

"I agree, and he knows what the definition of 'is' is. Let's get on with dog training."

Within an hour, Jim had Lady taking orders from both Jessica and Ted, and was sure that the big dog would do as told by either. That accomplished, Jim said, "Honey, pack an overnight bag. We're off to Tel Aviv."

Holly looked at Jim and asked, "Do I get to know why?"

"Sure, and since Ted's here he can let the general and President know. I'm going to blow Al-Shahristani's ass off. He made another attempt on me when I was home."

At that piece of news, Holly raised an eyebrow and Jim told the story of the ill-fated attack and the new recruit in the war against terrorism. When he finished, Holly asked, "How are you planning to get General Al-Shahristani?"

"With luck, the same way I got Saddam. If that apartment is still available, I thought I'd just wait for a clear shot, take it, and come home."

"I'm going with you?"

"Only to Tel Aviv. I need you to fly, so I can get some sleep."

"Jeez! From his lover to his wife to his personal pilot—straight downhill."

That brought a laugh from everyone. Then Jim rubbed his chin, had a thought, and looked at Ted. "Got an idea, Ted. While Holly and I are gone, how about finding the time—one side or the other of your trip to St. Louis—to show Jessica how to shoot a rifle?"

"Be glad to. If she's half as good with a rifle as she is with a handgun, she'll be dynamite."

Ted left soon thereafter, and while Holly packed, Jim got his personal favorite sniper rifle, a Crosswhite, made by Charles Crosswhite, a master craftsman of the gun-making art. The gun was a twin to the one that Jim used to kill Saddam Hussein. That one was in the proud possession of the emir of Kuwait, who received it from Jim hours after the deed had been done.

Before Holly and Jim left, he asked, "Jessie, are you going to be okay here by yourself?"

"Sure. Especially with Lady here."

Holly joked, "If you don't want company in bed, close your door. Now that they both know you, there'll be a wild scramble to see who gets in bed with you first."

"Just like most of the men she's known," Jim said, before receiving a poke in the ribs from his wife.

Jessica said, "It'll be nice to have a bedmate, since Jim insists on keeping my man away from me."

Holly joked, "If I want my man, I'll have to put the plane on auto-pilot on the way over the pond."

Then, turning more serious, she asked, "Honey, are you sure you don't want me to come to Iraq with you?"

"No, love. Fast in and out. Should be a piece of cake. They don't know I'm coming this time. Sergey is going to call Al-Shahristani and tell him he has me under surveillance and is working on a plan to take me out."

An hour later, Holly and Jim were on their way to Israel, with Holly doing the flying and Jim sleeping.

•

In Baghdad, General Al-Shahristani had received the call from Sergey, telling him all was going well. After cautioning Sergey to be careful and hanging up, he said, "We should have sent Terekhov in the first place. He's the best of our Foreign Legion."

General Al-Majeed, who had only been informed of Sergey's mission after it had been started, looked over the top of his reading glasses and replied, "Maybe we should never have sent anyone after Scott. Did Terekhov say anything about the others we have sent? Has he seen any of them?"

"No. He said nothing of them."

"I suspect that we never will hear from any of them again. If Terekhov fails, I think we can expect a visit from Scott. I think we may have just grabbed a vicious tiger by the tail. Alas, there is now no way to turn the tiger loose."

"No, but we can kill the tiger."

"I would not count on it, my friend. He has been here at least twice and, including Hit, probably three times, and has accomplished what he set out to do each time."

"You worry too much."

"Or you not enough."

•

In Canada, Sa'd Kahdi, while not happy with his overall circumstances, was very happy as he lay exhausted with the woman, whose name he still didn't know, laying next to him. "I always like to please the brave men of our cause," she said throatily.

"Consider me pleased. Your charms are vast; your talents in bed equally so. However, I would also be extremely pleased to learn that you have found a way to get me across the border."

"That I cannot do at this time. Sorry. Would you like further attention, or would you like to sleep now?"

"I slept most of the day while you were gone. But first I best make a call to my idiot contact in Missouri. This will be brief, then we can go back to more enjoyable things."

As he said that, Kahdi reached for his cell phone and called Ibrahim Al-Sharif. When the man answered, Kahdi said, "I've been further delayed. I will contact you when I know more," and hung up before Al-Sharif had time to answer.

Listening in, Boris said, "That same voice. I bet young Al-Sharif will be quite upset."

Sergey smiled and they both listened in as Ibrahim was saying to his companions, "What could have possibly gone wrong? The whole plan was so simple. Delayed? How delayed? I wish he would give more information, so I know how to plan."

Those with Al-Sharif said nothing, but the more he went on, the less respect they had for him. A true warrior of the faith would simply be patient and keep his mouth shut.

Boris and Sergey thought much the same, and Sergey said, "This boy is not right for this job. Which should make our job all the more easy. Are you going to pass this information along?"

"No, no reason to. Jim is probably on his way to Iraq by now, and has ample time to take care of business and get back. It would appear that he now has even more time."

"Do you think he will be able to get at Al-Shahristani?"

"Could you?"

"Yes."

"Then you have answered your own question."

•

After clearing his trip to St. Louis with General Bradley, and making arrangements for a flight, Ted called Jessica and asked if she was in the mood to learn how to shoot a rifle. She eagerly agreed, and not too long after that they were on a Marine rifle range outside Washington. Ted knew the type of sniper rifles the Janitors used, so that was the weapon he used to instruct Jessica.

After going through all the routine items—like how to assemble and load the gun—Ted explained its features to Jessica. When he was satisfied that she had absorbed that information, he pointed downrange. "We'll start with that nearest target. It's a hundred yards out. You take the one on the right, I'll take the one on the left. I may as well get in some practice, just in case Jim ever lets me go on a mission with you guys. We'll start with five shots apiece—each fired from a different position. Don't miss and make me look bad to Holly-the-super-gun-trainer."

Jessica smiled and fired five rounds from the varying positions as instructed. Ted did the same. All ten shots were bull's-eyes, in the silver dollar-sized center bull's-eyes. When that fact was relayed by the range master, Ted nodded his approval. "Well done, Jess. I've known Marines in boot camp who couldn't even hit the target first time out. This time we'll go for the next targets out…they're at two hundred fifty yards. Five rounds again."

When the results were the same at two hundred fifty yards, they moved out to five hundred. All bull's-eyes again. When the report came in on those shots, Ted smiled and looked approvingly at Jessica. "Do you ever miss?"

"I hope not."

At a thousand yards and out, they fired only three times. One of Jessica's three shots only creased the center bull's-eye. At a mile, only one of her shots hit the bull's-eye, the other two were in the target circle next to it. At a mile and a quarter, all three of her shots hit the target, but no bull's-eyes.

As they disassembled the guns, Ted said, "Jessica, with practice, you'll be just fine. Excellent, I'd say. You may not realize it, but that was some fancy shootin' you just did."

"Thanks. But not as good as you. You never missed once."

"Fox Team members had to hit a grapefruit at a mile—every time. If any of us missed, we had to buy drinks for the team, and we had to get ten straight hits to leave the range. At times we hated Jim because he *never* misses—never. But when we got to Iraq, behind enemy lines during the Storm, each of us would have happily kissed his rosy rear-end in thanks for the training. Ten of us went in, ten of us came out, and we left over a thousand dead Iraqis behind, just from our rifle shots. So every chance you get, come out here and practice. Jim or Tom or somebody's life may depend on it at some point, if Jim takes you into the field with the team."

Jessica was dumbfounded at what she'd just heard. "Wow. I'll be out here all the time."

Then she chuckled. "When Jim lets me get away from the computers. How do I get out here without you along to clear the way for me?"

"I'll arrange it. Jim get you one of those White House passes yet?"

"Yeah. But I shake every time I even think about it. I still can't believe I saw the President and got to talk to him."

Ted laughed. "Takes some getting used to. Anyhow, since you have that pass, I'll set it up so all you have to do is show that."

"Good, thanks. I really appreciate you showing me how to shoot."

"As Holly found out, it's a piece of cake with you. You're one of those rare birds—like Jim—who's a natural. The rest of us have to work at it."

13.

When they were about half an hour out of Israel, Holly woke Jim and he called ahead to Ben Schiller, who was waiting at the airport after arranging clearance for them to land. As Holly taxied the plane to the area indicated, Ben walked up, waited for them to stop and open the door, then he went aboard. "Good to see my favorite assassins again."

Jim shook his hand and, as Holly hugged Ben, said, "Good to see you, pal."

Ben turned, headed out of the plane, and said, "Follow me, I have a car waiting to take you to your 'lovers' bungalow.'"

The building Ben spoke of was a Mossad safe house on the grounds of a government compound. It had been in that structure that Jim had proposed to Holly on the first of two previous times they stayed there.

On the trip, the three old friends engaged in small talk. When they arrived, Ben turned to the matter at hand. "Are you going along this time also, Holly?"

"Nope. I'm just a pilot on this trip. Jim's getting too old to fly himself."

"I didn't think you were…or Jim would have said something about getting papers for you. Yours are ready, by the way, Jim. Just need to get your picture after you do whatever to your appearance you plan to do."

"Just some of your famous body dye, contacts to turn my blue eyes brown, black hair coloring, and false mustache to match."

"About what I figured. The dye, contacts, and hair coloring are in the bedroom you used last time. Some clothes bought in Amman that should fit you are laid out on the bed, with Jordanian and Iraqi currency in the pants pockets. There are three mustaches there, also. Pick the one you like best…or the one Holly likes best."

"Nice to see you've figured out that Holly's the boss."

"You guys are full of it."

Ben laughed and said, "I'll give you an hour to get organized, then I'll come around with your car. I'm going as far as Amman with you. You can drop me there, then you're on your own."

"Okay. See you later."

Alone, Jim said, "Come on, honey. You can help me with the body dye."

The dye referred to was of a color to match the predominant skin coloring of people of the Mideast. Both Jim and Holly had used it before they went after Saddam in January.

Holly followed Jim into the bedroom and, as he started to strip so that his entire body could be covered with the dye, she did likewise. Jim just grinned and opened his arms. Later, their lovemaking complete, Holly helped Jim with the skin dye and his hair coloring. Then, with much teasing from Jim, picked the mustache she felt looked best on him.

They had only been finished a few minutes when Ben returned. The time in Tel Aviv was 9:00 p.m. and Jim had nearly twelve hours of driving in front of him. With that in mind, Ben said, "We better get going. Let me take a fast picture, then finish your papers."

When that was completed, Ben said, "If you leave now, your arrival in Baghdad will be just about right."

Jim nodded. "I've got a Crosswhite in its case and a long-range mike, with trusty recorder, in case I hear anything of interest before popping Shahristani."

"Good idea. The car I've got for you has a false bottom in the rear seat for those items. I also have a sample case for you to toss in the back with a suitcase full of clothes. You're papered as a Jordanian dental supply salesman. In the sample kit are three sets of false teeth. They are mini-bombs, just in case you need a diversion at some point. Just pull the bottom, back left molar to use them…you'll have thirty seconds."

Jim nodded, kissed Holly, picked up his two cases, and followed Ben out to the car. After they stowed those in the false bottom, they got in and drove away, with Holly standing at the front door waving.

Ben glanced at her, then at Jim. "You've got a good one there, pal."

"Don't I know it."

Jim drove (at Ben's suggestion) to become familiar with the car. On the trip Ben said, "Our crossing into Jordan has been arranged. You must return by the same route, in the same car, as your re-entry into Israel is also arranged."

Jim asked no questions, feeling that had Ben wanted him to know about the "arrangements," he would have told him. However, he did ask, "Do you happen to have a map for me?"

Ben laughed. "Sure do. In the glove box. Jim, you know I'd like to come all the way with you, but I've been to Iraq a few too many times. And as I have risen in the Mossad, my time in Arab lands has been greatly reduced."

"I fully understand, Ben. I just appreciate the help you've given me. Speaking of which—Iraq that is—what about the apartment?"

"All set. I talked to Sid and he told me he had the new man keep it. So all you have to do is drive straight to the building, park, and go up. The door is open. You can leave your note for Al-Majeed there. My man will see that it gets to him."

"Thank you. As always, I can depend on you when I need help."

"I may not have mentioned it, but you are doing us a favor, also. Al-Shahristani was in charge of Iraq's Scud missile program during Desert Storm. We owe the bastard."

•

In Canada, Sa'd Kahdi was alone in the woman's apartment, wondering if he ever would get to Missouri. He also wondered if St. Louis had to be the target. He thought, *"Why not blow up Toronto? Let the Canadians in on the fun."*

Actually, he knew the answer. St. Louis was the "Gateway to the West" and therefore a symbolic target. What he didn't know was that St. Louis was really no more than a test site. The leaders of al-Qaida wanted to see firsthand how much damage the bomb would do. They would analyze the damage and, from that, determine the proper placement of the last three satchel nuclear weapons, which were intended for Seattle, Denver, and Atlanta.

The problem faced by Al-Qaida was that they got the bombs and instructions on how to arm them, but very little additional information. They really didn't know how much damage they would do, and if it would be better to place them in a structure rather than in open space, as was planned in St. Louis.

About the time Kahdi had reached the conclusion that he would just have to exercise patience, the woman returned. "We have made arrangements. In three days, a load of automobile parts will cross into the United States for delivery in Detroit, Michigan. You will be hidden in the rear of the tractor-trailer hauling them. In Detroit, you will be met and given a properly registered car. You will drive the car to Chicago and park it at an address given to you. From there, you will take a taxi to the car rental (already arranged for you) and pick up the car you will use for the trip to Missouri."

"About time. Thank you. How long will the trip from Detroit to Chicago take me?"

"I'm not sure, but I think ten or twelve hours."

"I've been told the trip from Chicago to St. Louis will take about eight hours. So in less than four days, I should be there. I better call the idiot and let him know, before he wets himself."

As the woman started undoing his belt buckle, Kahdi was ringing Ibrahim Al-Sharif. When the latter answered, Kahdi said, "In about four days, I plan to visit you. I will call when I am near to arriving."

For once, Al-Sharif showed good phone technique…said, "Thank you," and hung up.

Tom was on the monitoring equipment when the call was made. Roland was in the room with him and Tom asked, "Will you go get Boris up, please?"

Minutes later Boris was downstairs and listening to a replay of the call. Without saying anything, he got out his cell phone and called the Joint. After a few rings, Jessica answered and was informed that the new timetable on the "package" was four days. Boris also told her he would let St. Louis know.

His next call was to Drew. After giving him the information, Boris added, "I sure hope Jim's trip doesn't cause him to miss the fun."

"I wouldn't think so. He gave me a pretty detailed run-down on his plan. If things go well—and they always seem to for him—he should be back in forty-eight hours."

•

After dropping Ben off in Amman, Jim drove to the Iraqi border. There he met with only a small amount of trouble. The Iraqi border guard was bored and, while not really hassling Jim, poked around and asked needless questions. Finally, Jim rudely said, in the perfect Arabic he spoke, "Look, I have a long drive in front of me. The minister I'm supposed to meet is already in a foul mood, since one of his false teeth has broken and 'makes me look like an oaf,' according to him. Which he probably does."

The guard grunted and waved Jim on. He drove on through the night at very high speeds and arrived in Baghdad by 8:30 a.m. local time. As planned, he drove directly to the apartment building containing the unit he planned to use, parked, then carried all four pieces of luggage up and into the fifth floor apartment.

Once safely there, he realized he was getting tired, but thought, *"Not as tired as I'm going to be."*

He found a note, which read, "Coffee and some food in the kitchen. Good luck."

Jim smiled as he went into the kitchen and made coffee. Then he wrote his note to General Al-Majeed. It simply read, "You're next," and was signed, "Jim Scott."

After addressing the envelope and leaving the note on the kitchen table—unsealed, so Ben's man could read it if he chose—Jim headed into the room where he would shoot from. There, he pulled back the drapes just enough to be able to see. After opening the window, he pointed the long-range listening device in the direction of the Presidential Palace, opened his gun case, and put the Crosswhite together in three simple movements. He loaded the gun, then went back for some of the coffee he had made.

After eating a sandwich and pouring a second cup of coffee, Jim headed back into the bedroom containing the listening device and gun. He pulled up a chair, picked up a pair of binoculars that fit nicely into the listening device case, and looked the Palace over. Across the front of the Palace was a veranda, attached to three rooms facing Jim's direction. All had drapes that covered the windows. The end room nearest Jim was the room Saddam Hussein had been in when Jim had killed him. The drapes in that room were parted, and on the listening device Jim could hear conversation.

He soon identified those talking as being Generals Al-Majeed and Al-Shahristani, plus the voice of the fake Saddam. Jim thought to himself, *"Guess these guys aren't superstitious, using the same room where their great leader met his proper end."*

With the binoculars, he was able to see all three men clearly. They were all seated in large, comfortable-looking chairs and were drinking something out of cups. Seeing that, Jim looked at his now-empty cup and went for a refill.

When he returned to the room, he heard General Al-Shahristani outlining to the fake Saddam what was expected of him that day. Once "Saddam" was on his way, the two generals sat and talked about a variety of things.

As Jim listened, he decided he would wait until General Al-Shahristani was alone before taking his shot, if possible. If it looked as though the man was about to leave the room, he would just have to take the shot with a witness around. That was not the best of plans, since he would be under pursuit right away. However, whoever was with the general would not know where the shot had come from, so he would have something of a head start. If roadblocks were set up, he would just have to bluff his way through them. With luck, even early detection of the general's death wouldn't prove too much of a problem.

When he had killed Saddam, Jim had traveled south to Kuwait. Since he had blown up a drug-processing plant on the way, and had spoken to many people along the way, he felt certain the generals knew how he had escaped. He was sure their follow-up investigation would have easily uncovered that fact. Assuming that was correct, he hoped that any search for him after taking out Al-Shahristani would concentrate in that direction, which is why he planned on the Jordanian route in the first place.

With all of that re-thought out, Jim sat, listened, and watched, waiting for his chance.

•

Back in Tel Aviv, Holly received a call on her cell phone from Jessica, who said, "Looks as though the package of underwear you ordered will arrive in about four days. They just called a while ago and said they were sorry for the delay."

Holly at once understood what Jessica was telling her and said, "That's fine. My boyfriend loves that kind of stuff. I'll probably see him tonight and tell him about it. Right now, he's off delivering a present to an old 'friend'."

Jessica understood that Jim and Holly would be heading home within a day or two. "How's the weather there?"

"Just fine. How about there?"

"Couldn't be better. Everyone seems to be in a good mood. Well, your dad is a bit grumpy. He had trouble getting the water and electricity turned on in his new house, but that's taken care of now."

Holly laughed. "Pity that man can't make up his mind where he wants to live. If you talk to him, tell him I love him and hope to see him in a day or two."

"Will do. Talk to you later."

"Bye."

"So," Holly thought, *"dad's hunch may be right. That damn bomb may be headed for Ibrahim Al-Sharif and St. Louis."*

●

Back in Washington, Jessica placed a call to Drew and informed him that Jim would be back within two days. Drew relayed the message to Boris and friends in Columbia, then called Billy and Hector with the same information. That done, Drew took a nap. As he napped, the others listened in on various conversations.

In Columbia, the four men there were eating snacks and listening in as Ibrahim Al-Sharif said to his two companions, "I can hardly wait to see the destruction we do to St. Louis."

Boris and Sergey looked at each other and shook their heads at the stupidity of young Al-Sharif. Across the street, the two people with Al-Sharif had much the same thought as Boris and Sergey, but said and did nothing.

Before he made calls to announce that they had just heard confirmation, Boris said, "That boy is dumb as a rock. Tom, you're new to this game, but you've seen me use that black box we have with our things to check this house on a daily basis. In addition, as you know we have set up another system to detect other types of eavesdropping equipment that might be aimed at us. Without those two toys, I wouldn't say anything to you but 'hello.' Those fools across the street obviously don't have similar equipment and haven't found the bugs Drew and I left all over their house. With any kind of sophistication, they would have found at least some of the bugs just by carefully looking.

"I point all this out to you for future reference, as part of your education in the art of spying. You know how careful we are on unsecured phone lines, and you know that we have several scrambled lines we talk on freely. But to just sit around and talk out of school, as that boy just did, is totally unacceptable."

Tom nodded his head. "I understand…and thanks for pointing this stuff out to me. Even though Jim has covered much of this with me previously, I must admit that seeing the results of loose lips in action and having you point out the dangers in it as it happened really helps."

Roland, who had taken in the conversation, said, "God, I'll never be able to talk freely to my wife again in my own home. This stuff is scary. I know, I know…this is necessary to combat these terrorists, but anybody who wanted to listen in on what I have to say could do so, and I don't like that one bit."

"Don't blame you," Boris said, "but you're right. Anybody who knows what he's doing can listen in to your every word. Happily, governments and those working with them try to only go after the bad guys. Unscrupulous individuals, however, can get the same basic technology. Now I must call and pass on this information."

His messages to St. Louis and Washington were simple. He simply said, "We have confirmed that 'it' is what we thought it was. The young man has a big mouth."

Boris had called Drew, who in turn called Billy and Hector with the message.

In Washington, Jessica thought a while about how to say what she had to say on an open line and then placed a call to Holly. When she had her on the line, she said, "Hi, Holly. I just got confirmation that your new panties are what we thought they were...pure silk. The delivery schedule is still the same."

"Great, thanks for calling. I was hoping they would be silk. Would you call Ted? I think he wanted to get some for his wife, if they were silk."

"Okay, will do. See you later."

"Okay. Bye bye."

Following the clear orders of Holly, Jessica next called Ted Kuntz at the White House. "Ted, Holly asked me to call you with confirmation that the 'it' talked about in Missouri is the missing nuclear weapon. From what Boris told me when he called, that fella they've been listening to in Columbia just said something he shouldn't have and let the cat out of the bag."

Ted replied, "Well, that is good and bad information. Obviously good, in that we have a line on the damn thing; bad, in that it's here in America, or soon will be. I'll pass the information on to the general. He's in a meeting with you-know-who right now, along with all the big shots. Sure is nice to talk to you when you aren't in the midst of a shootout at the O.K. Corral."

"Don't remind me. I might wet my pants."

"You didn't when the chips were down. Tom should be damn proud to be married to such a cool lady."

"Thank you, sir."

"You're welcome. While I have you on the line, you said Holly asked you to call me. Any word on Jim's progress?"

"No, just that Holly said they would be back 'in a day or two.' She indicated things were going as planned, as far as she knew."

"Good. Thanks."

After hanging up, Ted thought for a few minutes, then headed to the situation room, where the President was in conference with General Bradley and several other high-ranking members of the intelligence apparatus. He knocked, entered the room, and said, "Excuse the interruption, but thought I better get this information to you. The Janitors have confirmed that the 'it' we have heard so much about is, in fact, the nuke."

Amos Longley, one of those in attendance, said, "Well, it looks as if Drew Hollins had a good hunch."

The President nodded. "Thanks for coming down, Ted. At least we now have a firm lead on the thing. I trust Jim and his team to be right on top of things and know who to call if they need help—which I'm sure they probably won't."

Though none said so, everyone in the room agreed. A few heads did nod, however, as Ted left the room and went back up to his office. After he left, the President looked at John Engle. "Have you had much recent contact with Jim?"

"Not too much, sir. However, I did talk to him two…or was it three days ago. Anyway, he had just shot some guy who was trying to blow up his house and wanted me to send a doctor, which I did. From our conversation, I'd guess the fellow was Russian, because Jim told me that after learning Boris Telman was now working with Jim, the guy started talking and agreed to change sides. I guess by now he's a Janitor."

The President interjected, "I hope he doesn't find bin Laden…I'd hate it if he wound up a Janitor."

That brought a round of laughter, then John continued, "Jim did mention that it looked more and more like St. Louis was going to be the target, or the way station for the bomb."

Amos Longley said, "Mr. President, we do have the best spies of the last several years on the job tracking that bomb in Boris Telman, Drew Hollins, and Jim Scott. If anyone is going to find it, it will be those three. I still can't get over the fact we have the best of the old Soviet Union and our best working side by side."

The President smiled. "It is a comforting thought. All right, let's get back to our meeting. We have the man responsible for all this to deal with."

14.

In Baghdad, Jim was eating another sandwich and drinking still another cup of coffee as the two generals droned on. His interest picked up when he heard his name mentioned, as General Al-Majeed said, "The more I've thought about it, the more I have become convinced we should just leave Jim Scott alone. I think you should call Terekhov back."

"I have told you before that you worry too much. Terekhov is quite capable."

"As were the others we sent. What if Scott has turned them? You know we have information that Boris Telman is now working with Scott. The first two Russians knew Telman well, as does Terekhov. All the Germans at least knew of him. What if Scott is using Telman to turn our people?"

As Al-Majeed had spoken, Jim thought, *"Now I wonder how they know Boris is working with me?"*

General Al-Shahristani answered, "You are starting to irritate me with your whining. We don't *know* that Telman is working with Scott. Samohin said he 'thought' it likely, not that he actually knew."

"I'll be damned," thought Jim, *"that bastard Yuri Samohin is selling information to Iraq. I'll bet Boris has his ass when he hears of that."*

Yuri Samohin had been a top KGB operative and was now a top advisor to the Russian President. As such, he would be one of the few men in Russia to know about Boris Telman now working with Jim.

Jim listened on as General Al-Majeed said, "Yuri Samohin distinctly said, and I quote, 'Boris Telman is responsible for the information we are receiving from America…most of it developed by Scott.' Now don't give me crap about 'thought' he was working with Scott. It's as plain as the big nose on your fat face."

"My, my! Are you getting a little testy, my pint-sized friend? Don't you have some little girl to molest? Please leave me to my thoughts before I get really angry with you."

As soon as General Al-Shahristani said that, Jim picked up his rifle and used the scope on it in place of his binoculars.

"Better little girls than little boys," General Al-Majeed replied as he took his reading glasses off and got up to leave.

Jim watched him leave, then swung the gun toward General Al-Shahristani. He sighted in on the man's forehead, exhaled, and squeezed the trigger. The nearly silent shot found its target, as the back of General Al-Shahristani's head blew out and splattered the wall behind him.

With no wasted motion, Jim closed the window and drapes, then took the gun apart, and placed it in the gun case. Next he took the listening device apart and placed it, the small tape recorder, and binoculars in the other case. Very calmly Jim walked from the apartment, carrying all four pieces of luggage, and went to his car. After putting the two incriminating cases back in their secret compartment, he got in and turned the key. Nothing happened.

Jim thought, *"Well, at least it isn't the starter. Must be the battery."*

He looked around, trying to decide which nearby car to steal, when he remembered Ben's words about using the same car to cross back into Israel. That item remembered, he got out and opened the hood in hopes that, rather than a dead battery, he might just have a loose cable.

As he did that, a man walked up and asked, "Do you have a problem?"

Jim nodded and said, "It would seem that I have a dead battery."

"Just a moment. I believe I have what you need," the other man said as he walked away, got into his car, drove over near Jim's vehicle, and got out. After freeing the latch on his hood, the man walked around the front of his car, carrying a set of jumper cables.

Jim looked at the man, at the jumper cables, and thought *"How lucky can I get?"* and reached for the cables. In minutes, Jim's car was running, the cables were put away, both hoods were closed, and Jim said, "Thank you very much."

The man smiled and said, "You are more than welcome. Please tell Ben that I said 'hello'."

Before Jim could reply, the man got into his still-running car and backed up. When Jim pulled out and left, the man re-parked his car where it had been, got out, and went into the building. When he reached the fifth floor, he went into the apartment Jim had just vacated, picked up the note for General Al-Majeed, and left.

As Jim drove, he hummed a little tune and smiled happily. On the way back to Jordan, he stopped at a station he had used on the trip to Baghdad for gas. There he left the engine running until he asked the attendant if they happened to have batteries that would work in his car. When told they did have the correct battery, Jim asked to buy one, as well as a tank of gas.

Back on the highway to Jordan, Jim thought, *"With as much as has gone right so far on this trip, I wonder what kind of shit is yet to come?"*

As he drove down the highway, he tried to spot the area where the Hercules had picked up the Janitors. Soon he realized that he was doing anything to keep his mind occupied so he wouldn't fall asleep at the wheel. Twice he stopped and got out of the car to relieve himself and be refreshed by the cool desert air. Barely able to stay awake, he drove on with grim determination, until the Jordanian border appeared in the distance. Knowing danger could lurk there, he suddenly became more alert.

•

Long before Jim neared the border, many things had happened in Baghdad. With Jim two hours down the highway toward Jordan, General Al-Majeed and the fake Saddam walked into the room where General Al-Shahristani lay dead.

The reason for them being there was the note, which had been hand-delivered at the Palace gates. Ben Schiller's number one man in Baghdad had arranged for the note to be delivered, with the gate guard to be told it was from the Russian Embassy. Though the guard was a bit curious at the method of delivery, he had summoned someone to take the note to General Al-Majeed.

When the general got the note, he turned pale, and, on his way up to see General Al-Shahristani, had bumped into the fake Saddam, who followed along— uninvited but curious at the state of General Al-Majeed. Now one look told them that their former cohort was just that— former. He just stood pondering what to do, as he absently-mindedly handed the note from Jim to the Saddam look-alike.

"Saddam" read the note and walked over to the dead body of General Shahristani. He took the gun from the holster attached to the lifeless form, flipped off the safety, chambered in a round, turned, and fired at point-blank range into the face of General Al-Majeed.

Al-Majeed had watched the entire process, and only at the last moment did he realize what was afoot. Much too late to save his life, he just stood dumbfounded as the bullet ripped into him.

"Saddam" smiled and said to the fallen body, "Scott was right…you *were* next." Then, thinking quickly, he fired another shot—this one into the ceiling above.

As security guards raced into the room, he said, "Remove these traitors from my presence."

The guards looked at "Saddam," at the two dead generals, then sprang into action, doing as told, before the Baghdad Butcher decided to turn his weapon on them.

"Saddam" went over and sat in a comfortable chair and thought, *"You fools have served your purpose and were starting to get on my nerves."*

What the two generals had failed to know when rapidly hatching their plot was that at an early age, Saddam had noticed that one of his cousins looked almost exactly like him. That cousin may even have been Saddam's "half-brother." Only Saddam's father and the cousin's mother knew of their one-time affair. However, his father *thought* he might have sired the other boy, and the cousin's mother was *sure* she knew who the father was, but took that information to her grave with her.

As a young boy, the cousin (half-brother?) and his family moved to the northern town of Mosul. As Saddam started working his way up through the Baath Party, he ran into his cousin and became re-acquainted. Saddam noticed that his cousin could be his twin brother and realized that from time to time having "two" of himself might be useful.

Over the years that followed, Saddam on many occasions had his cousin stand in for him and he schooled him in the affairs of state, so that when the cousin was in his stead he'd know what to do.

Now, as the guards were taking care of the removal of the two dead general's, the extreme ruler of Iraq knew the experiment of letting the generals think they were running things was over and he had lost time to make up for. And he alone knew if he were the real Saddam or his cousin (half-brother?).

After the bodies were removed and the mess cleaned up, "Saddam" sent for his Foreign Minister.

When the Minister arrived, "Saddam" said, "I want you to arrange a visit to Iran. When there, do what you can to re-new closer ties with them. They support al-Qaida, just as we do. Point out that the Americans are common enemies, and that we can live in peace and work against that foe, without having to be close friends.

"When you have finished that task, go to Jordan and remind them to keep their place. Then go to Syria and tell them we expect their support when the Americans decide to pressure us. They too have given aid to al-Qaida and you may broadly hint that, if injured, we are not above letting the Americans know of that fact."

●

As Jim pulled to a stop at the border, he noticed that there seemed to be no unusual activity. He wondered if it was possible that Al-Shahristani's body still hadn't been found, and immediately dismissed that possibility from his mind.

After reaching the conclusion there was nothing to be gained worrying over the matter, he decided to be alert for any sign of trouble and handed his papers out the window of the car to an approaching border guard.

To his great relief, he was soon on his way from the border and headed toward his crossing point back into Israel. At that border he was waved through, without even showing his papers. As he started to proceed, he saw Ben, stopped, got out, and, as he circled the car, said, "You drive."

Ben smiled, got in on the driver's side, and, after Jim got in, drove off. As he did, he said, "I understand from my man that you got them both."

"What?"

"Both generals, Al-Shahristani and Al-Majeed."

"No, I only took out Shahristani. Left the note for your man to deliver, then got out. Well, got out after your man who, by the way, said to say 'hi,' gave me a helping hand. This fine car you gave me had a bad battery. Wouldn't start after I made the shot, but your man was 'Johnny on the spot' with a set of jumper cables."

"Bet you about filled your drawers when this thing wouldn't start."

"Nah, just tried to figure out which car to steal, until I remembered you said to cross back in this car. Was afraid another car might not work."

"We would have made it work, with me at the crossing, but glad it wasn't necessary."

"Well, anyhow, back to your guy. His having jumper cables handy was a blessing. I guess he knows your track record with cars and figured it might be needed."

"Funny, old friend. Actually, all Mossad field agents carry jumper cables."

"All right, now, about two dead generals instead of one. What's that all about?"

"They're both dead. About two hours or so after you left, my man observed, through binoculars, from a different location…obviously, both carcasses being carried away from the Palace. He said he was sure of his identification, but later checked somehow—and found out he was right."

"I'll be damned. See if you can find out what happened to Al-Majeed. Al-Shahristani died of one bullet through his head. In the front, out the back. No doubt he was dead. I kept my scope on him long enough to see his brains plastered on the wall behind him."

"See what I can find out."

"Back to your man, thanks. I guess you told him to keep an eye on me."

"Yeah. Asked him to keep in the shadows, but if you got your tit in a wringer, to do his best to get you out somehow."

Jim yawned for about the fifth time since getting back in the car and said, "I need a power nap, until we get to the safe house and I can get some real sleep."

Ben smiled and joked, "Sleep on, Prince Charming," then glanced over and realized he was talking to a sleeping man.

As they arrived at the safe house, Jim woke up immediately when the car stopped. When he got out, Holly ran up and kissed him, and gave him a big hug. Then she helped the two men carry in the four items from the car.

Once inside, she asked, "How did it go?"

Jim smiled and said, "With the exception of Ben's car, it went better than could really be expected."

Ben groaned. "I'm going to have to hear about that car the rest of my life."

Holly asked, "What happened?"

After Jim told her the story of the dead battery, he added, "By the way, Ben, you now have a new battery. Of course, I used your money to buy it. Mossad got to help the Iraqi economy. Now, if you two will excuse me, I'm for bed."

"Uh, Jim," Holly said with pity in her voice, "we better leave right away. You can sleep in the plane on the ride home."

Jim sighed and asked, "What's up?"

"In two or three days, the nuke will be in St. Louis."

Jim shook his head and sighed again. "Okay. Ben, how about a ride to the airport?"

•

In Toronto, arrangements were going forward for Sa'd Kahdi's trip to Detroit. A false parts box, big enough for him and his luggage, was being prepared, complete with custom stickers and stenciling showing it to be bumper assemblies. The problem for the al-Qaida operative at the plant was that when that box was removed from the truck at an unauthorized stop, the manifest for the entire shipment would no longer be accurate. The assumption would be that someone had stolen the bumper parts. The most likely someone would be the very man who was indeed responsible. In the end, it was decided that al-Qaida would have one less employed member of the Toronto cell.

Of course, the problem with that was that the cell was running low on operating funds, due to the raid on Hit. One less employed member of the group would just put that much more pressure on them in their efforts to be ready for any eventuality that might come their way.

The cell members discussed all of those matters in detail and decided they simply had to go ahead, because the mission of Kahdi had been dropped into their laps with a "most urgent" tag. The last time a mission had been so designated, two members of the air piracy team had been gotten into the United States when all other means had failed.

•

On the trip back from Israel, Holly piloted the plane and Jim slept. Ten minutes out of Andrews, Holly hollered back at Jim to wake up and come forward. As he slid in the right-hand seat, he muttered, "Not nearly enough sleep."

"What do you expect, buster? You go thirty-odd hours without sleep and it seems you never catch up. Next time, plan better, so you get some sleep."

"Before we were married, I would have gotten at least *some* sympathy."

"Bah."

After they landed and were driven to the Joint, Jim called Drew and said, "Holly and I'll be in St. Louis in the morning, unless something comes up."

"Has Al-Shahristani passed into history?"

"Yes, and so has Al-Majeed. Don't know what happened to him, though. It wasn't me. Ben told me his man in Baghdad saw both of their bodies hauled off from the Palace. Ben is going to try to find out what happened."

"Good…one less jackass to deal with down the road…which I'm sure will lead us directly to Baghdad."

"Wouldn't be a bit surprised. Let the others know my plans. For now, I'm going to call General Bradley and let him know the good news, then I'm off to bed."

At that pronouncement, Holly grinned, and groaned about being married to an old man while Jim placed his call to the general. When he had him on the line, he said, "Both General Al-Shahristani and General Al-Majeed are off to their promised land. I don't know what happened to Majeed, but I took out Shahristani."

"Interesting. I wonder what the deal with Al-Majeed is."

"So do I. I can't even venture a good guess, unless the fake Saddam decided to become the 'real' Saddam."

"That's a bit farfetched, don't you think?"

"Yeah…my attempt at humor when I can't keep my eyes open."

"Go get some sleep. I'd guess you haven't had much in the last thirty-six hours."

"Damn sure not enough."

After hanging up with the general, Jim headed down the hall to the bedroom he shared with Holly and started taking off his clothes. As he did, Holly came and said, "You've got some husbandly duties to perform before you go back to sleep. I'll wash your back in the shower."

"Who said I was going to shower?"

"I did."

•

In Columbia, Ibrahim Al-Sharif was beside himself with anticipation. He just couldn't bring himself to exercise any type of proper procedure as far as speaking out-of-turn was concerned. Boris, Sergey, and a better-informed Tom listened with growing disdain for their foe. Even Roland—who had been sleeping and hadn't met Jim when Drew left in favor of Sergey, and found he liked the new man a great deal also—was catching on that Al-Sharif's constant talking on the subject of the nuclear weapon was not sound procedure.

Al-Sharif's two housemates were becoming more and more concerned with their "leader," to the point that when he left—with Tom and Roland dutifully following—one said, "If we had access to the money, I'd like to quiet that fool…permanently."

The female member of the "team" said, "I agree, but, as you say, there is the money. I've been trying to think of a way to get it, but not only is it in his name, but if we run low, there is always his daddy to help out with more. This whole operation is set up wrong. What if he is killed in an auto accident? We would have no way to move forward."

Across the street, Sergey said, "Now *there*'s an idea."

Boris replied, "It certainly is.   A missing component to their plan might make the others involved a bit more careless."

"Yes, but with mister big mouth across the street, we have a steady source of information—so maybe it isn't such a good idea."

"True, but still worth thinking about.   We are hearing everything they're saying on both ends, so his free talk isn't really helping us that much. We know where and approximately when—and I'm not sure his continued existence is of much use to us—but his demise might just cause mistakes.   And, in addition, an under-funded operation, as we well know from our KGB days, makes life difficult."

"So should we take him out?"

"From what Drew said, Jim is going to be out of action until morning, trying to catch up on his sleep, so we'll just wait until then. I don't want to do anything like that without his approval. I've gained a great deal of respect for his judgment and leadership."

"You don't mind subjugating yourself to a much younger and less-experienced man?"

"Not at all. And don't downplay his experience. In the closing days of the Cold War, he was a worthy adversary. While I never had direct dealings against him then, I know others who did. They consistently came out second best—and in our business, second best is nowhere."

"I must say I totally underestimated him in Montana. Walked right into a trap without a clue."

"That, my young friend, was as much your fault as his."

"I agree, but his execution was flawless. I still can't believe those four shots he took in the span of less than ten seconds. Dangling from a rope, he killed the two men with me, landed, and, without blinking, hit me twice, just where he wanted to. He disarmed me *and* slowed me to a point of no resistance with less effort than it takes to pee."

"You make my point for me. I guarantee he had the whole thing planned out before he jumped off his veranda. We'll wait until morning before worrying about taking out young Mister Al-Sharif."

15.

Early the next morning—less than forty-eight hours before Sa'd Kahdi planned to arrive in St. Louis—Jim woke up, refreshed and ready for action. Holly had in mind a different kind of action that Jim did, not that he minded.

After they showered, at the end of another love-making session, Jim made breakfast for them and Jessica. Then all three went into the computer room and Jim called General Bradley. When the general was on the line, he said, "Good morning, sir. If you and the boss have nothing else in mind, I'll be heading for St. Louis with Holly shortly."

"The only thing the President and I have in mind for you is to get that damn nuke."

"Will do, sir. Talk to you later."

After he hung up, Jessica asked, "Do I get to go along with you?"

Jim looked into Jessica's eyes and saw neither fear nor glee. Satisfied he was being asked a legitimate "business" question, he answered, "Let me think on that for a bit."

Then, with Jessica still standing right there, he called the White House and asked for Ted Kuntz. When he had Ted on the line, he asked, "Can Jessie shoot a rifle?"

"I'll say. Up to five hundred yards, she was my *total* equal. At a thousand, she was nearly as good. A mile and beyond, she fell off some. May have just been tired, or the weight of the gun caused her to waver just a bit. But at a thousand and under, she can shoot the sweat off a bull's balls without ending his usefulness for breeding."

"Do a bull's balls sweat?"

"You know what I mean, Jim. I started her off at a hundred yards. Five shots from five different positions, all in the silver-dollar center bulls-eye. Same story at two-fifty.   At five hundred, I got the bright idea to make a contest out of it. I'd call it a tie, but I'm prejudiced."

"Okay, sold. Thanks for the input and thanks for taking her out to the range. Talk to you later."

"When are you leaving?"

"Soon. Have a couple of calls to make. May have to come see the President before we leave, so see if he'll be available for me."

"Will do."

To Jessica, Jim said, "You can go. But I want to talk to you more about this."

Jessica merely nodded her head, without saying anything, lest her excitement show.

Next, Jim called Drew to see if anything new was afoot in St. Louis. When told there wasn't, he then called Boris.   When he had Boris on the line, after talking to Sergey for a few minutes, he said, "Boris, old bean, I have some rather disturbing information for you."

"Which is?"

"Yuri Samohin is naughty. Been selling or giving info to Iraq. Got it straight from the horse's mouth, said horse being Al-Shahristani."

"The dead general?"

"The same. Before I sent him after his forty virgins, he had enough to say about Yuri that there's no doubt."

"You guys are sure hung up on that."

"On what?"

"The 'forty virgins' thing."

"Come again?"

"When Drew and I went to Saudi, he told that Walker fella the Janitors had been to Iraq and sent a bunch of al-Qaidas after their 'forty virgins'."

"Oh.   Well, anyhow, what do you want to do about Yuri?"

"Strangle him, if I could get my hands on him. You said you heard Al-Shahristani tie the can to Yuri's tail. You didn't perhaps tape that conversation, did you?"

"Sure did."

"Would it be possible to get that tape to Russia?"

"Yes. If I can get in to see the President in the next hour or so, I'll take care of it today. Otherwise, it'll have to keep until we've completed the nuke hunt."

"Good, thank you. Speaking of the nuke hunt, Sergey came up with an idea. What do you think about taking young Al-Sharif out of the game with an 'accident'?"

Jim thought for a few moments and answered, "It just might bollix up their planning and, with their money situation, it might put a strain on them that way, also. Especially if the money is in his name and the others can't get to it."

"That's the impression we have. His two housemates discussed the idea of doing him in themselves, but decided it would only hurt the operation, since they couldn't get their hands on any of the money."

"Do it. Make it look good, though."

"Maybe you should come do it for us. CIA is good at that type of thing. KGB never did anything like that."

"In a pig's ass. Goodbye."

The other three men had been in the room as Boris spoke to Jim. Now Boris looked at Sergey. "The next time Al-Sharif leaves, follow him and see that he has a believable accident."

The room grew very still as Roland looked at Tom, then Tom looked at Boris and Sergey. Sensing the sudden tension, Boris said, "Roland, if we eliminate Al-Sharif, we will, as you Americans say, 'throw a monkey-wrench' into al-Qaida's plans. In addition, we will further damage their situation by denying them their main source of funding.

"An enemy under-funded and leaderless is an enemy that just might make a mistake, or series of mistakes, which will make our efforts to find the nuclear weapon and take it away from them an easier proposition."

Roland thought for a few seconds and a picture of airliners being flown into tall buildings flashed through his mind. He replied, "I should, by all rights, object to the out-and-out murder of another human being. However, I have only this to say...I will never mention a word of this to anyone, not even my family. Oh, one more thing I have to say. I will be happy to help in any way I can."

Boris smiled. "Thank you. Now that you mention it, how would you like to donate your car to this mission? It is much heavier than our rental and, as such, would make Sergey's job all the more easy to accomplish."

"My car is your car. Drive the son-of-a-bitch off a bridge and into hell."

"Sergey, you better take Tom with you. He has official papers—FBI, right, Tom?"

"Correct. However, as you know, they aren't exactly kosher."

"Aah, but you also have the President's number and, if not his, at least General Bradley's...which is almost the same."

"True."

"Good, that is settled then. All we have to do is wait for young Al-Sharif to leave by himself and then we shall see what we shall see."

•

Back in Washington, Jim had made arrangements to see the President and was being shown into the Oval Office by General Bradley, as he said, "Hello, Mr. President. Here I am again."

The President grinned. "Nice to see you, Jim."

After the two men shook hands and Jim sat down at the President's invitation, General Bradley said, "Jim has found out some disturbing information that will have to be handled with care, Mr. President."

"Tell me about it, Jim."

"When I took my little side trip to Iraq to remove a thorn in my side, I listened in as Generals Al-Shahristani and Al-Majeed discussed Boris Telman working with me. During the course of that conversation—which I have on tape, by the way—they said that Yuri Samohin was the source of their information. I'm sure you're aware that Yuri is a top advisor to your counterpart in Russia."

"I am. Have met the man, as a matter of fact, during rather high-level discussions. I'm more than just a little dismayed at this piece information. What do you propose?"

"If there is a way you can call the Russian President and get him on the line without an interpreter listening in, you could broach the subject. Or you could just get him on the line, then hand me the phone, and I could talk to him in Russian and tell him what we have found out. I don't know if he speaks Arabic, but my guess is he has at least a working knowledge of the language…enough to understand what he hears if I play a tape of the conversation I overheard."

The President thought for a few seconds, then nodded. "Let's give it a try. He knows of you and, of course, knows that Boris works with you, so the mention of your name might be enough."

A few minutes later, the connection to Moscow was made and the President said, "Mr. President, I have Jim Scott here with me and he would like to speak with you."

After a slight pause, the Russian President's interpreter replied, "That will be fine."

The President handed the phone to Jim, who switched to Russian and said, "Mr. President, what I have to say is for your ears only. After you hear what I have to say, you can make up your own mind who in your government should know and who should not."

The Russian President came directly on the line and replied, "We are now speaking privately. Your Russian is quite excellent, much better than my English."

"Thank you, sir. The news I bring you, you are not going to like."

"In these days, there is little to like. I assume you have terrorist information for me."

"Not exactly, sir. Rather, you have a less-than-loyal person in your inner circle."

"Who?"

"Yuri Samohin."

The Russian President felt as though he had been kicked in the stomach. With a lump in his throat, he said, "I find that *very* hard to believe. He is a most-trusted aide, and an old friend."

"I'm aware, sir…as was Boris Telman when I told him what I had accidentally unearthed, and he suggested we somehow get the information to you at once."

"Do you have some sort of proof? And exactly what is Yuri accused of?"

"Yes, sir, I have proof of his complicity in passing information to Iraq. I just got back from there…took care of a little bit of business. While there, I had occasion to tape a conversation between Generals Al-Shahristani and Al-Majeed…"

"Both now dead. I have no doubt you're aware of that fact."

"I am. However, I was only responsible for Al-Shahristani…"

"According to my information, Saddam killed them both."

Jim thought quickly and realized that the Russian President had not been informed of Saddam's death before he replied, "That explains that."

"Excuse me?"

"When I got back to my jumping-off point from removing Al-Shahristani, the information that Al-Majeed was also dead greeted me. I was at a loss to figure out what had happened to him."

"Israel, I presume?"

"No comment, sir," Jim answered, knowing full well that he had just confirmed that Israel had been somehow involved.

"I understand and I don't blame them in the least for wishing Al-Shahristani dead and being willing to help the cause somehow. Now, back to Yuri, please," the Russian President said, as both men wondered silently just why "Saddam" had taken credit for killing both generals, when he had in fact killed only one.

As Jim started to speak, the light dawned that he had joked correctly about the situation—that the fake Saddam must have really decided to seize the opportunity to take full control of Iraq by eliminating the one other man there who knew he was an imposter. After a slight pause to digest that thought, Jim said, "Back to the conversation I overheard…and taped. During it, they discussed receiving the information that Boris Telman was working with me. They both clearly said that the information came from Yuri."

"I would like to hear the tape, if you don't mind."

"Not at all, sir. Do you speak Arabic?"

"Not that well, but I *can* understand it."

"Very well. Just give me a minute or two to get the tape in a machine here, and get to the point of the conversation that we just discussed."

"There is something earlier that you don't want me to hear?"

Jim laughed and lied, "No, sir. There are actually three tapes. Most of it idle conversation. I only brought the last one, which has the information in question. You are welcome to hear all three in their entirety if you wish."

"No, that will be all right. Just play what you feel I need to hear."

Jim sighed an inward sigh at his bluff having worked. He had no intention of letting the Russian President hear the earlier conversation when the two generals had given "Saddam" his orders for the day. If his President hadn't seen fit to pass on the information about the death of the real Saddam, Jim certainly wasn't going to do so.

When he had the tape to the portion where the conversation had turned to Yuri Samohin, Jim said, "All right, sir, I'm going to put the receiver down near the tape player."

When the tape reached the point of discussion about the sexual preferences of the two generals, Jim shut the player off and asked, "Were you able to hear that all right, sir?"

"Much too well, thank you. Will you give me a few minutes to set up a tape player on this end and then play it again?"

"Yes, sir."

After replaying the tape so that it could be copied in Moscow, Jim said, "I'm sorry to be the one to give you this information, sir."

"I won't thank you, because, as you can no doubt imagine, this is information that sickens me. However, again, Russia is in your debt."

"I understand, sir. While I have you on the line, may I ask about another matter?"

"Yes, of course."

"As you may or may not know, Sergey Terekhov has been working for Iraqi intelligence. However, he has now left them and joined up with my group. I've been thinking when we complete the operations we're working on, it might not be a bad idea to set up a shadow operation to ours here, with one in Moscow. That way, when information needs to be passed without going through official channels, it will be an easy matter for Sergey and me to contact one another, with information to be passed on to our respective presidents. I'd be willing to fund his operation—if you agree, that is."

"I think that is an excellent idea. Thank you. Again, Russia is in your debt."

"Thank you, sir. Now I guess I better let you get back to running your country. Goodbye."

Jim then recounted the conversation in English to the President and General Bradley. When he finished, the President said, "I like the idea about setting up a sister operation to yours in Moscow. And I'm thankful you didn't give out the information about Saddam. However, from what you were told about the fake Saddam, we may just have another one just like the original. All of which doesn't change my desire to bring about a regime change in Iraq. Saddam, no Saddam—it's all the same, as long as that group is running things there."

"I quite agree, sir. If you have nothing further for me, I'll go find us a nuke."

When both the President and General Bradley said there was nothing else, Jim left the White House and returned to the Joint. Once there, he called Ben Schiller and told him what had happened to General Al-Majeed.

•

In Canada, Sa'd Kahdi was being entertained by his female al-Qaida contact. Their sexual encounter complete, she rolled off him and said, "That was wonderful. Thank you."

Kahdi thought that his companion was just trying to boost his self-esteem for the task in front of him, but said nothing on the subject before asking, "What's our next step?"

"Tonight, late—actually, more like early morning, just after midnight—I will take you to the shipping center. There you will try out the box that has been prepared for you to make sure it is a comfortable fit. Then you will have to spend the remainder of the early morning in the box. At about six a.m., the box will be loaded onto the truck, a tractor-trailer, and about six or seven hours later, you'll be in Detroit."

"As enjoyable as my time with you has been, I'm anxious to get on with my assignment."

"I understand."

•

As that conversation was taking place, Ibrahim Al-Sharif had decided to go to his bank and make a sizable withdrawal in cash. Across the street, all four men were listening in. Boris said, "Sergey, this seems to be your cue. You and Tom get ready to follow. Look for the best spot, but don't force it. If you can't make an accident happen, let it go."

"Understood," replied Sergey. "Let's go, Tom."

Tom followed Sergey into the garage and they sat in the car until the blip on their monitoring screen started to move. Tom reached up and pushed the automatic garage door opener in the car as Sergey backed out of the garage.

When they were following at a safe distance, Tom said, "If he follows the same route he has used in other trips to his bank, he'll make a left-hand turn two blocks up. Then three blocks later, he'll make a right onto a two-lane rural highway. He'll stay on that highway for about five miles, and then get into more of a city setting. You'll almost have to try for him on the highway."

"How much traffic is usually on the highway?"

"Depends. This time of day, I'd say not much. The last time we followed him to the bank, it was a little later in the day…about an hour or so…and it wasn't bad. Only about—oh, I don't know—four or five other cars and a couple of trucks."

As Sergey made the first turn as predicted, he asked, "How is the highway? I mean is it straight, or have a number of bends?"

"Three or four straight-aways of maybe half a mile to three quarters long. At least half the time, you're in a no passing zone."

"Any bridges?"

"Just small ones, over creeks."

Sergey nodded his head and tried to visualize the route they would be taking. From Tom's description, he felt certain the highway they would be on was the one Jim had used when bringing him to Boris and the others. After doing his best to remember what he had seen during that trip and coupling it with what Tom had just told him, he knew he would probably have to make a spur-of-the-moment decision based on what he could see, and the traffic situation.

When they turned onto the highway, Sergey was able to get behind Al-Sharif, with no cars in between them. He followed at a normal distance and waited his chance. A few cars passed from the other direction, but the traffic was light. Suddenly, he saw a chance. Up ahead he could see the beginning of a bend to the left, which had a guardrail for quite a distance. Even better, there was a tractor-trailer just appearing around that bend in the road, heading toward them.

Sergey floored the accelerator and their car picked up speed rapidly as he pulled out to pass. Ibrahim Al-Sharif barely noticed and, if he had, he would have thought the trailing car had plenty of time to pass. However, Sergey eased off the gas as he drew up to Al-Sharif's vehicle, so that his front bumper was even with the rear door of the other car. His intent was to be in the blind area, where Al-Sharif wouldn't be able to see him without the effort of turning his head.

With the approaching truck getting closer and closer, Sergey knew his timing would have to be perfect and hoped that human instinct would prevail. He waited until the last possible moment, then swerved left, toward the far shoulder of the road. When he did that, the truck driver instinctively swung to his left to avoid Sergey. In so doing, he drove right into and over the car driven by Ibrahim Al-Sharif. Even though the truck driver realized his mistake almost as soon as he made it, he was far too late to save Al-Sharif. As one of the two first-arriving state troopers would say to the other, "Poor guy was smashed like a grape."

Sergey, meanwhile, nearly lost control of his car on the shoulder, then had to deal with two oncoming cars. He let the first one pass, and then swerved back up onto the highway and back into his original lane. Next he slammed on his brakes, spun the wheel, and accelerated, so that he was soon behind the second of those two cars, driving in the same direction as they and the truck had been heading. Without hesitation, he drove back onto the shoulder of the road and passed the two cars, which had both slowed and were stopping to avoid running into the back of the now-stopped truck.

As Sergey raced by on his right, before getting back on the driving surface and speeding away, the truck driver got on his CB radio and called for help. He was able to think well enough to get a description of Sergey's car, but unable to get a license plate number. After calling for help, the driver started trembling, and realized as he got out of his truck that what he was going to find would make him sick to his stomach.

Tom was having sick feelings of his own. When Sergey was speeding back down the shoulder on the roadway, Tom had looked over at the smashed wreck of Al-Sharif's car. While he was glad the event had gone well, the thought of what Ibrahim Al-Shrif must look like was unsettling—not to mention how close a call it had been for him and Sergey.

16.

When Jim returned to the Joint, he sat Jessica down and said, "Okay, Jessie, you can go with us, on one condition. Tom has to approve."

Jessica smiled and said, "He's my husband, not my daddy."

"Nonetheless, if he has an objection, you aren't going. Now, on to another matter. If you *do* go, it is on the understanding that you will do *exactly* what I say…nothing more…nothing less. Understood?"

"Yes."

"We, the Janitors, have done extensive training to work as a team…"

"I know. Tom fessed up that that was what he was doing on his 'business trips'."

"…and you haven't been a part of that. So if you go into the field with us, you will have to do *exactly* as told. No thinking allowed. If it seems like I'm overstressing this, it is for your own good and the good of the team. With your skills with both a pistol and a rifle, you may be of some real value. We can always use an expert shot. Now, I better call your husband."

"Tell him if he says 'no,' he can plan on a lot of sexless nights."

Holly laughed, Jim smiled, and he then called Boris on the secure line. When Boris answered, Jim said, "I need to talk to Tom."

Boris replied, "He's not here," and explained where Tom and Sergey were and what they were doing.

"Well, when he gets back, have him call me. If we're not here, we'll be airborne. However, I'd just as soon talk to him before we leave, so have him call me first thing."

•

As Jim and Boris talked, Sergey, who had slowed down after rounding the first bend in the road he came to, put on his left-hand blinker to make the turn leading back to the stake-out house. When he made the right turn onto the street leading back to the house, Sergey spoke for the first time since the event, asking, "Are you all right?"

"A bit shaken, but fine. Damn glad to be alive…you scared the shit out of me."

"Didn't do my nervous system much good either. Each time I survive one of these incidents, I wonder how many more I'll live through. One mistake in this business can be your last one. I'm only alive after the mistake I made in Montana because Jim wanted me alive to question.

"By the way—just so you don't think me a heartless rogue—I'm *very* glad the truck driver wasn't injured. One always hates to involve innocents in something like this. I saw in my rear-view mirror as we drove away that he seemed fine."

Just as Sergey said that, they arrived back at the house and he pulled into the garage, and then went on inside the house.

Boris asked, "Well?"

Sergey nodded and answered, "I believe we have put a crimp in al-Qaida's plans."

Then he explained what had taken place. When he finished, Boris said, "Well done. Tom. Call Jim."

As Tom walked over to the phone to make the call, Boris looked at Roland and said, "Your car better stay here for now…until we find out if it is being looked for."

Roland replied, "I hadn't thought of that."

Boris smiled. "Not your line of work."

After Jim got on the line, Tom asked, "Hi, Jim. What can I do for you?"

"Tell me how things went with Al-Sharif. But first, I have a question for you. Jessica wants to go into the field with us on the nuke thing, and I said okay as long as you approve."

"Was that a question?"

"Yeah."

"She's a big girl. If she wants to go and you feel she'll be okay, I don't really have the right to object."

"Glad you realize that. Just didn't want to cause any friction between the two of you…or between you and me. Now tell me about Al-Sharif."

Tom told Jim about the demise of Ibrahim Al-Sharif and how it came to pass. When he finished, Jim said, "Okay, Tom, here's what I want you to do. Get in the rental, go to the scene of the 'accident,' and make absolutely certain that he is dead. Use your FBI identification. Then, after finding out he is in fact dead, get the name of the truck driver. He is no doubt more than a bit upset. We'll have to do something for him. Find out if he owns the rig, or if he is just a driver."

"Sure, Jim, good idea. Sergey felt sort of bad about involving him and was happy the guy didn't get hurt."

"Tell Sergey I said 'nice job.' Also, tell Boris to stay on top of those other two there. My guess is when they find out their leader is dead, their conversations about what to do will be quite revealing."

After hanging up with Tom, Jim called John Engle and said, "John, Ibrahim Al-Sharif met with an unfortunate accident. He was run over by a tractor-trailer. I've sent one of my men to make sure he is in fact dead. Either way, this will cause confusion in the enemy camp and I'd like to put a bit more pressure on them."

"What do you have in mind?"

"As I told you, the ones in St. Louis had a bunch of train schedules laid out on a coffee table that I just happened to get a look at."

"I remember."

"Anyhow, I think it would be a good idea if all the train stations in and out of St. Louis were manned by extra security personnel. *Very* obvious and *very* visible security personnel. I'm betting they plan to board the train in Alton, Illinois with the bomb and either leave it there and jump off, or stay with it and go after their forty virgins."

John chuckled at the 'virgin' comment. "What if they see the extra security and change their plans?"

"What I'm hoping for. We're on them, all over them, and want them to be forced into changing their plans. That will take quite a bit of conversation—and conversation helps us, because we're hearing everything they're saying. Some of these guys—not the one who just got himself killed, but most of the rest—use pretty good phone and conversation procedures. I want to break them out of that posture, get them talking too much. The more information we have, the better chance we have of getting our hands on that damn nuke."

"I'm with you…makes perfect sense. Pretty good idea."

"Actually, the guy I shot in Montana came up with the original concept. He's proving himself to be quite valuable."

"You want me to tell you what the President said after I told him about that little incident?"

"John, you've got a big mouth. You learn that from Holly?"

That drew a poke in the ribs from Holly, as John replied, "Probably. Anyhow, the President indicated that you would probably make bin Laden a Janitor if you came face-to-face with him."

"Wonderful, you get a big mouth from her, and the President picks up her sick sense of humor."

Holly smiled demurely as John said, "Back to the situation at hand. What do you think…concentrate on Alton and St. Louis, and four or five stations up the line in both directions?"

"That should do it. You know, if you have the time, it might not be a bad idea for you to come to St. Louis for the next couple of days."

"I was just thinking along the same lines. For that damn bomb, I sure can find the time."

"You're welcome to fly with us."

"No thanks. I have some things to clear up here first. See you in St. Louis."

After hanging up, Jim told Holly and Jessica what the President had to say about bin Laden. Both thought that to be quite funny. Then Jessica joked, "If we ever do run into bin Laden, I get dibs on blowing his sick brains all over hell and gone."

•

Back in Columbia, Tom did as asked by Jim. He drove to the scene of the 'accident' and, on arriving at the end of the long line of traffic, drove up the shoulder of the road until stopped by a Missouri State Trooper. At that point, he flashed his FBI identification, said, "Official business," and was waved on, after being told to be careful driving on the shoulder.

When he arrived at the wreckage of Al-Sharif's car, it had been pulled off to the side by a tow truck. Paramedics were trying to extract the mangled remains of the terrorist, and one look by Tom confirmed that the man was indeed dead. Another State Trooper walked up and Tom showed him his FBI identification. As Tom looked across the highway to see the tractor-trailer pulled off on the opposite side shoulder, he said, "I'm just here to check out the results of this accident. We had that guy in the car under observation. He is…or was….a terrorist, al-Qaida. No great loss to mankind, but it would have been nice to interrogate him after he led us to others and we arrested him."

The Trooper grunted and said, "You should tell that to that poor truck driver. He's all broken up."

"Maybe I will," replied Tom. "I wanted to talk to him anyhow."

"He said another car was passing and, at the last second, drove off the road on his right and he swung left instinctively and ran over the guy you say is a terrorist."

"Guy in the car should get a medal—the truck driver, too. But that information is for your ears only…not to go into your report. We don't want al-Qaida to know we know what this guy really was. What kind of description did you get on the other car, the one that did the passing?"

"Not much. Black sedan, large. That's about it… No make and no plate number."

"Okay, thanks."

With that, Tom darted through the slow-moving traffic to the other side of the road, where the truck driver sat in the open back of an EMS vehicle. Tom walked up and flashed his FBI identification still again. "Hi, I'm Tom Wilson with the FBI. I'd like to talk to you," then, glancing at the nearby paramedic, added, "privately."

"Sure," replied the driver, as he followed Tom some fifteen feet away.

Tom turned, took out a notepad and pen, hoping to look FBI-like. "I'd like your full name, address, and Social Security number."

The driver gave Tom the information he wanted. Tom nodded. "What I'm about to tell you is absolutely top secret, do you understand?"

The driver, who had been feeling awful about the 'accident' and who was feeling more than just a little sorry for himself, suddenly came alert and answered, "Yes, I understand."

"That guy you ran over was a terrorist. We've been on him for a week, thanks to our new allies, the Russians. He not only wanted to do bad things here, he was connected with the Chechnya rebels. We believe, from what we have been able to piece together so far, that the man who caused you to swerve toward the terrorist was a Russian agent, bent on intentionally causing the 'accident.' I'm going to tell you the truth, but if you ever repeat a word of this to anyone, I'll deny it. I'm not going to look real hard for the Russian. Do you understand me?"

"Not exactly…except I feel like the weight of the world has just been lifted from my shoulders."

"All right, what I mean is we, the FBI, have a very good idea who caused this. Rather than look too hard for him, I, for one, would like to pin a medal on him. For national security reasons, I can't tell you what that slime bag you ran over was up to, but rest assured, it was not good for our country."

"Thanks…again. You've made it possible for me to live with myself."

"Good. Now I have a few questions for you. Do you own that rig or do you drive for someone else?"

"I own it."

"You married?"

"Yes, with two kids."

"Okay, as my boss likes to say, here's the deal. Your insurance company will be reimbursed for any costs to them, your record will be kept clean, and your out-of-pocket expenses will be covered. Oh, one more thing…any loss to the company you were hauling for will be covered. The one stipulation to all this is you keep your mouth closed…forever…to everyone, including you wife. Do we have a deal?"

"Hell, yes!"

"One other thing, don't go over and spit on that dead bastard. I'll do it for both of us."

Tom then walked back to the edge of the road, darted across when traffic allowed, and asked the State Trooper to help him get into the flow of traffic back the way he had come. As he drove away, Tom was quite pleased with himself and knew Jim would be also…even if he had just cost the Janitors a sizable sum of money.

•

In Washington, Jim and the two women were ready to travel. Jim packed a couple of bags with a number of different types of equipment and, in addition to their clothing, he took five cases containing sniper rifles. Before they left, Jim called Ted Kuntz and asked him to feed the dogs for a day or two. Ted readily agreed and wished them a successful journey.

Once airborne, Jim called both Drew and Boris to let them know he was Missouri-bound. Then he asked Jessica if Tom had shown her how to fly a Gulfstream. When told he had, Jim turned the plane over to her, closed the cockpit door on his way out, and said to Holly, "It seems to me that we've never done it while flying."

●

In St. Louis, Drew passed on the information to Billy and Hector that Jim was on the way, with Holly and Jessica. Billy raised an eyebrow at the news Jessica was coming into what promised to be a field operation. Hector teased him about it and, after talking it over, both men agreed her cool handling of the attack on the Joint had earned her the right to be a full-fledged member of the Janitors.

●

In Columbia, Tom returned and reported what he had found out and what he had done. When he finished, Boris said, "Roland, it looks like your car is clean. But, I'd still leave it here until you're ready to head for Kansas. If you run into any kind of trouble, I'll give you a number to call. Probably Drew's cell phone, but let me think about that."

"Sure. Thanks," replied Roland.

"Next," said Boris, "I better bring Jim up-to-date, then we'll just sit and wait for these two across the street to find out they are now leaderless…and short of funds."

Boris called the phone on the Gulfstream and, on getting Jessica, said, "Hi, this is Boris. May I speak to Jim, please?"

Jessica answered, "Sure, hold on a second. They're in the cabin."

Jessica already had the plane on autopilot, so she got up and went through the door separating the cockpit from the cabin. What she saw caused her to blush at first, then smile, before she cleared her throat.

Jim and Holly, both naked, had finished with their lovemaking, but were in an embrace, which soon ended as they pulled apart. Jim smiled. "Glad you didn't come back here a few minutes ago. What do you need?"

"Call for you…Boris…and I'm jealous that Tom isn't here so you two could take over in the cockpit."

Jim laughed as he and Holly scurried to get at least partially dressed. As Jessica turned and headed back into the cockpit, he said, "Tell Boris I'll be right there."

Holly giggled as Jim pulled on his pants and headed to the front with no shirt and wearing only socks on his feet. When he reached the cockpit, he slid into the right-hand seat and soon was on the line to Boris, who said, "Tom got the information about the driver, told him we'd cover the expenses from the wreck, and confirmed that young Al-Sharif is no longer amongst the living."

"Okay, good…now you guys better be alert for a rapid departure. Those other two may just panic and head for St. Louis."

"That's what I was thinking, also. However, they may not, because they seem more level-headed than Al-Sharif was—or at least the woman appears to be so."

"Very well. We'll carry on as planned and land in St. Louis. Now put Tom on the line so he can speak to his wife."

•

In Bellefontaine Neighbors, Billy and Hector listened in as Abdullah Mohamed, the leader of the terrorist cell across the street, said, "We better get the first of our rental cars. I don't want to get them all at once…it might raise questions."

Another of the terrorists replied, "As always, you're right. I'll take one of the Illinois observers and go get them their car."

Hector said, "That's the first we've heard of 'Illinois observers.' I wonder what the hell that's all about."

Billy just grunted as he placed a call to Drew. "Better get ready to rock-n-roll. Two of the guys are going after a rental. You might get lucky and be able to put a homing device on it before they ever drive it out."

"Right, on my way," replied Drew before he hung up and went outside to get in his car and make the short drive over to the terrorists' house.

He drove up the street in time to see two men leaving in their car, and followed them all the way to the car rental agency. After the two terrorists went inside, Drew held back, ostensibly looking at the available cars.

When he went inside, the two terrorists were well under way with their paperwork. Drew waited for an agent to be available, then said, "I'd like to check on renting a car for my daughter, when she comes into town later today."

As his paperwork was being completed, he listened in on the problems of the men he had followed. A clerk said, "I'm sorry, sir, but your credit card charge was refused as 'no funds available'."

The man was stunned, but recovered quickly, as he said, "My father assured me that funds would be forthcoming. I fear he may be upset at my most recent grades."

Drew almost laughed outright at the man's plight, as he was sure Jim's money pilfering was paying still more dividends.

Then the other man said, "I will pay for you," and handed over his card.

That card was accepted just as Drew finished with his arrangements. As the two men left, Drew followed. When their car was pulled around, Drew walked around it and muttered, "Maybe I should have gotten one like this for my daughter."

At one point in his inspection, he knelt down out of the line of sight of the two terrorists and quickly placed a homing device under the rear fender. Drew was standing there looking at the car and scratching his head as one of the men drove the car off, soon followed by the other one in the car they had arrived in.

Drew got in his car and noticed that the homing devices on both cars were working fine, as his monitor now showed two blips. He followed at a safe distance, until sure both cars were headed back to the house in Bellefontaine Neighbors. He took a parallel street and returned to his house.

Once there, he reported in to Billy and Hector, told them of the credit card problem, and then called Jim to let him know. Jim was still in the right seat, with Holly back in the left seat, as the call came in. After listening to what Drew had to say, he said, "Call Boris and let him know about the credit card situation. This could get interesting, if the two in Columbia have the same problem."

Drew did as asked, then kicked back to wait until he heard from Billy or Hector. That call was not long in coming. Billy was laughing as he said, "You should hear all the shit over that card. The guy with the bad one is swearing on his mother's moustache or something that he had not used the card since receiving it. Of course the others don't believe him, or they are just giving him a hard time. I'm not sure which."

Billy paused to listen in on more of the conversation, then said, "One of the guys is sharp enough to wonder if the bad card has anything to do with the money problems Al-Sharif had in Columbia. Little do these guys know that the great American remover of al-Qaida funds got to them for two hundred and seventy mil."

Hector, who had been listening in on the conversation across the street while trying to block out what Billy was saying, nudged Billy and indicated he wanted the phone. When he got it, he said to Drew, "They've decided to go after another car at a different agency."

Drew replied, "Well, if the same guy goes along, I can't get too close this time."

"Naw, sounds like the lead guy is going to take someone else for the next car."

"Are they going now?"

"Sounds like it."

"I better go into my following act again. I'll call Jim on the way and see how many cars he wants. I'd think at least one, maybe two more. Now that I think of it, probably only one. He'll pick one up when he lands."

17.

In Columbia, the two terrorists across the street from Boris and the others were about to find out they were leaderless. The State Trooper Tom had spoken to realized he might give something away after being told the dead man was a terrorist, so he sent another Trooper to give official notification of the death. He did, however, follow the other Trooper as far as the corner of a side street that intersected with the street where the terrorists lived.

As the Trooper sent to deliver the news pulled into the driveway, the two terrorists saw him. The male said, "Police! What do we do?"

"Answer the door when he knocks," replied the female calmly, "but have your gun ready in case it is trouble. I'll answer the door."

Which she did when the Trooper knocked. "May I help you?"

The Trooper asked, "Are you Mrs. Al-Sharif?"

"There is no Mrs. Al-Sharif. I'm a friend."

"Is there a relative of his living here?"

"No."

"Do you know how to contact his nearest relative?"

"Maybe. His father lives in Saudi Arabia. I'm not sure how to contact him, but I may be able to find out. May I ask what this is about?"

"He was killed in an auto accident with a big-rig truck."

"Oh. I will try to find out how to contact his father."

"Thank you," replied the Trooper, as he wondered at the strange reaction the girl had shown. No shock, no dismay, no tears. *Very* strange.

After the Trooper left, the female terrorist asked, "Now what do we do?"

"We better contact St. Louis and let them know. Then we better go there as fast as we can."

"No, I don't think we should do either. Kahdi will call here looking for Ibrahim; we should wait for that call. Also, if we call St. Louis with this news, what good will it do?"

"They should know."

"Why?"

After a pause, the question was answered, "I really don't know, but I still think we should."

"Well, I don't. Our immediate problem is money. How much do you have?"

"About two hundred dollars."

"I have three hundred, or close to it. I wonder how much they have in St. Louis?"

"Can't be much. Ibrahim was supposed to bring ten thousand dollars in cash with us. *That* is a reason to call them."

"You may be right, but let's wait until we hear from Kahdi."

Across the street, Boris said, "My guess is we now have the name of the bomb carrier, for all the good it will do us. We already know he's using false documentation…probably several different sets. I had the feeling that girl over there would be the sharper of the two."

Sergey nodded his head and replied, "It would seem you're right. However, even her past attention to sound procedure is slipping. Taking out Al-Sharif may pay big dividends."

"I agree," Boris said as he reached for the phone to call Jim with the latest bit of information.

In the Gulfstream, after hearing what Boris had to say, Jim replied, "Their money problems may be worse than they realize. One of the credit cards they tried to use to rent a car in St. Louis is no good. Drew said a charge on it was refused for 'lack of funds'."

"I wonder if the credit cards these two have will be any good?"

"No way of telling. We'll be landing in about ten minutes, so if you need me again, call me on my cell phone."

"Right."

•

As Jim and Boris spoke, Drew was quite pleased at what he was hearing. This time neither credit card of the two terrorists trying to rent a car was valid. Both had charges refused for lack of funds.

When the two terrorists left, Drew waited a while, told the clerk that he just wanted information on availability and wasn't ready to rent at that time, then followed the terrorists back to the neighborhood where they were holed up. As he drove back to his house, Drew called Hector (who answered their phone) and told him what had happened.

Hector replied, "I know all about it. Billy and I are listening in as they try to figure out what's going on. They're having a fit. Jimbo really kicked these guys in the balls, taking all their money. Here, have a listen," he added, as he put the phone receiver next to the speaker on the listening device.

Across the street, Mohamed was saying, "We're going to have to find out which cards are still good and which ones are bad."

Another terrorist said, "Maybe we can all go to drive-in ATM machines and try to get out some money, maybe fifty or a hundred. We can use any that work to rent cars with."

Mohamed said, "All right, good idea. Four at a time…use that nearby bank."

When that conversation ended, Hector put the phone back to his ear and asked, "You get all that?"

"Sure did. Don't think I'll bother following them this time. If they have any good cards, we can bug all the new cars they get late tonight. Jim should be landing soon, so I'll just wait to hear from him."

There were twenty men in the house. They already knew they had one good credit card and three bad ones; so four trips were made to the bank. Of the sixteen cards tried, thirteen were refused money due to "lack of funds."

When that alarming fact was discovered, Mohamed said, "We have two cars and the truck. I would like to avoid using the truck so, at a minimum, we are going to need at least three more cars. We've been to two rental places, so let's find three more and try to get cars."

Hector notified Drew of the latest information with great glee.

•

In Columbia, the female terrorist was using age-old methods to assert control over the male of the species. Across the street, Boris said, "While those two go at it, let's get things ready for a fast exit in the morning. I'm sure as soon as they get the word that 'Kahdi' is on the way, they'll head for St. Louis. Roland, if we have to leave in a hurry, please put all of this listening equipment in a closet before calling in the movers."

"After the deal on the house that Drew made with me, I feel sort of guilty taking *any* of the furnishings."

"Don't be silly," Tom said. "He told you to take what you want. I'm sure he wouldn't mind if you took it all—especially as much help as you've been."

"I don't think I've been all that much help."

"More than you realize," said Boris.

Sergey said, "Thanks for the willing use of your car."

"I wish I could have been with you when you used it."

"No, you don't," joked Tom, "he scared the shit out of me. If there's a funny odor in your car, that's what it is."

That brought a few chuckles before Boris said, "Back to our planning for tomorrow. Tom, be sure the monitoring system for the homing device is in our car. Do it now, so we don't forget if we're rushed."

Tom nodded, picked up the device, and headed for the garage. As he was leaving, Boris said, "Sergey, since you've been stealing clothes from Roland and me, you have nothing to pack, so while I get my things ready, you can listen to the sex show across the street. I think I'll shower and shave now and put on the clothes I'll wear for tomorrow. When I'm done with all that, we'll plan what each person is going to take to the car if we're rushed. You might make a list while I'm getting ready."

As Boris had finished what he was saying, Tom returned and Boris said to him, "You better pack, too. If you want to shower and shave and get out what you'll wear tomorrow, it'd be a good idea."

"Right," agreed Tom, as he headed up the stairs, followed by Boris.

•

After Holly landed the plane, Jim arranged for a rental car, drove it around to the plane, and helped the women load up the luggage and armaments. Then they drove to Bellefontaine Neighbors, to the latest of Drew's inventory of houses. As they walked in with their arms full, Holly said, "Nice place, Dad."

Drew grinned, kissed his daughter, and, as he followed them all back out to the car, said, "If you weren't married to such a rich man, I'd give it to you for a belated wedding gift."

"Less rich," said Jessica as she picked up the last bag in the car, "I forgot to tell you, Jim, but the new lease agreement and the use of military aircraft agreement came in. As soon as you sign them, you can send the government two hundred million."

As Drew shut the door behind them, Jim said, "Easy come, easy go."

Drew said, "You found a charity to give the money to, I see."

"Yeah. At least for the next eight years we won't be pissing money down the drain like we did the last eight, so I'm happy to help out."

Drew joked, "I'd say you're pretty confident our guy will be re-elected in three-plus years."

"I am. Aren't you?"

"Yes, I guess so…hope so."

Jim nodded, then asked, "Okay, where are we at?"

"The guy carrying the bomb is named 'Kahdi.' Our little nest of terrorists here in St. Louis has sixteen bad credit cards and four good ones. How much money they have left on the cards, I have no idea. Might be a good idea to find out."

Holly said, "I still have my FBI identification, which—unlike everyone else's around here—is probably still valid. If you remember, I tendered my resignation verbally to the President, and I'd bet big bucks that no paperwork was ever done on it. I bet, if I checked my old checking account, that I'm still getting paid."

Jim laughed. "I'd bet you're right. At the rate I'm giving money to the government, you better hang on to that. We may need it when the baby comes."

After Holly grinned, Jim continued, "I do see your point, and agree. I guess we better go around to all the car rental places, get their credit card numbers, and have John Engle do a fast check for us. Speaking of him—John, that is—he's coming to St. Louis later today, Drew."

"Good idea to have him close at hand, in case we need him," replied Drew, "but you won't need to go to all the rental agencies. They all went to the same ATM machine to see if their cards were any good. There's a bank about five blocks from here and I'd bet they went there. They all tried to take out fifty or a hundred, and there'll be thirteen rejects, so the sequence of card numbers'll be easy to find. Why don't we—me, Holly, and you, Jim—go check that out, then we can get the other car I've rented? The fourth valid number is there."

Jim nodded. "Okay. Jessie, you watch the shop here. Before we go, Drew, show her how everything works."

Drew had set up the same type of anti-bugging equipment that had been used in the Columbia house and in the home of Gary and Betty Holmes. He explained that as long as the equipment remained silent, it was safe to talk, but that if the monitor started humming, it was time to clam up. He then showed her the monitor for the homing devices on the truck and two cars of the terrorists, which had already been bugged.

Next he handed her the keys to his rental and said, "You shouldn't be needed by Billy and Hector, but if you are, just do what they tell you to do. Give Hector a call on his cell phone and tell him you're here in my place. If anybody—except your husband—calls from Columbia, tell them to call Jim on his cell phone."

"Gotcha," a smiling Jessica said as the other three prepared to leave.

At the nearby bank, Drew's guess turned out to be right. Holly, followed by Jim and Drew, went into the bank, showed her FBI identification, and asked for the manager. Soon the three of them were shown into the manager's office. Once seated at his invitation, Holly tossed a leather case containing her shield and identification card on the manager's desk and said, "I'm Special Agent Holly Hollins and we're here on a matter of national security. Earlier today we believe that a series of transactions were made at your ATM. We need a printout for," she paused, looked at Drew and, after he said "three hours," Holly continued, "the last three hours. And we need them now."

The bank manager swallowed and started to say something about normal procedure and warrants, checked himself, looked down at the FBI shield staring him in the face, and said, "Right away."

Fifteen minutes later he was back and watched as the three people in his office poured over the printout. Jim was the first to spot the sequence they were looking for and said, "Here it is," as he took out his pen and wrote down the three valid numbers in a sea of invalid ones.

Holly thanked the manager for his cooperation and was followed out of the building by her husband and father. In the car, Drew gave her directions to the first car rental agency tried by the terrorists. There they finished the paperwork for the car, and then Holly took out her FBI identification and said, "By the way, there is one other matter. When my father came in to arrange for my car, there were two gentlemen in here renting a car. One of them had his credit refused, so the other one put it on his card. I'd like that card number."

The young clerk looked at the FBI shield and then at Holly before she said, "I don't know if we can do that."

Jim flashed his false FBI identification and said, "You can either get it for us or spend the night in jail as a material witness. This is a matter of national security. Those two men are believed terrorists and they're not in St. Louis to visit the Arch." Even as the words left his mouth, Jim wondered if maybe the Arch *was* the target.

The clerk looked around for help, but she was the only employee of the rental agency in the office at that particular moment. She looked at Holly, at Jim, and at Drew, who at that moment flashed his CIA identification. She nodded several times and said, "I guess I better find you that information."

Drew told her the approximate time and type of car, and then added, "What my young friend here said about national security is quite true. However, that information is for your ears only. A word of it to anybody, either here or at home, and you could be in big trouble.

We've already had to lock up one person as a material witness for opening his big mouth."

The young woman nodded dumbly and handed over the rental contract she had just found. Jim quickly wrote down the credit card number, thanked her, and followed Holly outside.

As they were bringing Holly's car around, she said, "You two guys are something. You about had that girl wetting herself. 'Material witness'…give me a break."

Jim smiled and joked, "Before I met you and toned down, I would have just threatened to blow her kneecaps off if she didn't hurry up."

Holly punched him in the stomach. "Aw, shut up."

Drew went off chuckling to his car and got in, as Jim opened the door for Holly, then got in the driver's side of her car.

Once they got back to Drew's new house, they went inside, greeted Jessica (who had nothing new to report), and then Jim called the St. Louis FBI office. "This is Jim Scott. Has Director Engle arrived yet?"

"No, sir."

"May I speak to the agent in charge, please?"

Everyone in the St. Louis FBI office had been alerted that the name Jim Scott was to open all doors—at once. In less than ten seconds, he was speaking to the Special Agent in charge of the St. Louis office.

"How can I be of assistance, Mr. Scott?"

"Jim's fine…and the help I need is two-fold. I have four credit card numbers belonging to *known* terrorists. I'd like you to run them down and find out how big a credit line they presently have. Then I'd like to borrow an agent—well, actually six. I have two rental cars that I'm going to put in place for some of my men, a street over from where they are. I'd damn sure like the cars to be there when they need them."

The Agent-in-Charge bristled slightly and asked, "You want me to have my men stake out empty cars of yours, just to make sure they aren't stolen?"

"Precisely. Two men per eight-hour shift, three shifts per day, until we get what we're here to get."

"Mr. Scott, are you speaking from a secure phone?"

Jim noticed that his invitation to use his first name had not been utilized as he answered, "Yes, and I'm in a bug-free environment."

"Is that nuclear bomb actually coming to St. Louis?"

"Not if we can help it. As we speak, we're all over the people waiting on it. We've got everything but their assholes bugged, know the name of the courier, and when he is due to hit town. We are even pretty sure that they plan to use the train from Alton to St. Louis in their plan. What I'm attempting to do now is garner further information, and make *damn sure* we have no surprises, like my men having to run rather than ride when the bomb gets here."

The Agent-in-Charge could hear the ice in Jim's tone of voice and remembered that the Director had told him personally that until this nuke was in their hands, he was to treat any request from Jim Scott as though it had come from God himself. So he said, "Sorry if I got a bit touchy. Where will the cars be?"

Jim told him and gave him the credit card numbers.

When he hung up, Holly said, "From listening to you and the way your voice changed, I gather he wasn't too pleased to have the FBI's finest guarding empty cars for the good guys."

Jim smiled. "Can't blame him. Come on, Jessie, Holly. Let's deliver these two cars for Billy and Hector."

The two women followed Jim over to the street that ran parallel to the stake-out house. There Jim had them park the cars and told Jessica to stay in one of them until the FBI team showed up, at which point she could walk back to Drew's house, some four blocks away. He jokingly told her the exercise would do her good. He also told her to put the keys to each car in the ashtrays.

Before Jim and Holly left, Jessica asked, "How will I know if the FBI guys are here?"

Jim smiled and said, "When two guys pull up in a car and park, go ask them if they are the FBI guys to watch the cars. When they say 'yes,' ask to see their identification. After they show it to you, tell them the cars are for Hector and Billy, and give them your best description of those two."

"And if they say 'no'?"

"Shoot 'em."

"No, really, Jim."

"Take your gun out and tell them that Jim Scott said if they aren't FBI, you were instructed to shoot them."

"Jim, will you stop it."

Jim chuckled and said, "Call me on my cell phone if they say 'no.' But do it after you get back in one of the cars and have your gun out and safety off."

Seeing the confused look on Jessica's face, Holly said, "This jerk that I'm married to is *trying* to be funny. If two guys pull up in a car and just sit there, they'll be FBI, and they *will* show you their identification when you ask."

18.

On the way back to Drew's new house, Holly said, "That wasn't very nice. She doesn't know you well enough to know when you're pulling her leg. After that big lecture you gave her about doing exactly as told in the field, you could've gotten two FBI Agents killed."

Jim noticed the grin on Holly's face. "Nag, nag, nag…that's all I get."

That netted him a punch on the arm as they pulled in the drive. Once inside, Jim asked, "What does a person have to do to get a drink around here?"

"Walk himself into the kitchen and pour what he wants…or send his female slave to get it for him," joked Drew.

"Slave, hell," replied Jim, as he headed for the kitchen. "Either of you want anything, you better speak up while I'm in the mood."

Holly sighed. "Make mine water on the rocks, you know, baby and all."

Drew saw his daughter looking his way as she spoke and grinned. "Beer's fine, Jim. Thanks. Should I call Billy and Hector and let them know wheels are now available for them?"

"Yeah. Tell them directly behind them, in front of the back neighbor's house. The one with the two dogs."

Drew made the call, then asked, "Jessica with the cars until the FBI shows up?"

"Yeah," answered Jim, as he brought the drinks in.

Holly asked, "Dad, what about food? Jim and I haven't eaten since breakfast."

"I've got enough to feed an army in the kitchen. Why don't you start something, honey? For all four of us…Jess should be along before you finish."

•

In the Holmes' home, Billy and Hector were discussing how to go about placing the homing devices on the new terrorist cars, when Gary said, "I could do it when I walk the dogs."

Betty rolled her eyes, but Hector asked, "How?"

Gary avoided looking at Betty. "Just let loose of one of their leashes when we near the cars and, as I bend down to grab it or something, I can put them on—if you'll show me how to do it."

Billy and Hector looked at each other. Billy shrugged his shoulders and Hector said, "Well, they are pretty easy to attach. They're magnetic. All you have to do is reach up under the rear fender and stick it on. We can show you how in the garage on your car."

Betty just shook her head as the three men headed for the garage. Soon, Gary and the dogs were on their nightly walk. He walked down to the corner, where a tall, well-built, very attractive brunette met him walking down the connecting street. He smiled and greeted her pleasantly. She did the same, bent down, and petted both dogs, then was soon on her way. He noticed that the view from the rear was nearly as nice as it had been from the front.

Then he followed her across the intersection and made a left-hand turn to head back up the slight hill. When he reached the terrorist house, he stumbled and "accidentally" turned loose one of the dogs. It scooted down between the cars there. In a matter of fifteen seconds, the bugs were placed and Gary had both dogs back in tow as he continued up the street.

His great "performance" was missed by the terrorists, as none happened to look out their front window at that precise time. Across the street, however, Betty, Billy, and Hector watched, and all silently approved of his work.

After he completed the walk and returned home, Betty waited until the dogs' leashes were off before she said, "Nice job, you old fool."

Then she walked up to him and gave him an exhilarating kiss. Gary smiled and thought it was the best kiss he'd received in at least five years.

•

Holly had just finished figuring out what she was going to make when Jessica arrived. Jim asked, "Everything go okay?"

"Fine. I asked the guy and gal who showed up if they were FBI and they said, 'yes.' Then I told them Jim Scott said I got to shoot them if they didn't show me their identification. They showed it, but didn't smile a lot at my 'passed on' funny. Told them they were looking for a short, stocky Mexican and a tall, thin Indian."

"Sounds about right," replied a smiling Jim, before he asked, "How was the walk?"

"Good. Met some nice old guy walking two dogs. He was coming down the street from the direction of where Billy and Hector are."

"Probably Gary Holmes, Billy and Hector's landlord and assistant sleuth," Jim said.

Just as Jessica was about to ask for a clarification of that comment, the phone rang and Drew answered. "Just a second, Director."

Drew handed the phone to Jim. "Jim here."

"Hi, Jim. John Engle. I just arrived at our St. Louis office and understand you've been busy."

"Hi, John. Haven't done much. However, I *am* interested in the results on those four credit card searches."

"Have it right here for you. All four have between six hundred and twelve hundred available at this time."

"Do you have a computer wizard there who could manage to block those accounts for about forty-eight hours?"

"If we do it, we'd need a court order."

"If I come downtown, can I borrow one of your computers?"

"Sure, if you don't tell me what you want it for," John answered with a chuckle.

"I'll be there in about twenty minutes. Please have it set up for me to enter your parking garage without hassle."

"Will do—and I'll have someone down there to escort you up, so the weapon you're carrying doesn't cause any problems."

"How do you know I'm carrying a weapon?"

"See you in twenty minutes."

Jim hung up. "We need another car. Holly, I'll drop you and Jessica at one of the cars we left for Hector and Billy. Use it to get another car. Then put the one you use back where you found it. Drew, let Billy and Hector know they're down to one car."

Without waiting for any replies, Jim left and, after dropping off Holly and Jessica, drove to the downtown St. Louis FBI office. When he arrived, he spent half an hour at one of their computers, and then said to the hovering John Engle, "That should take care of that. I want to squeeze these guys all I can. The more problems I make for them, the better chance we have of them making a mistake."

"I agree," replied John and, with a twinkle in his eye, added, "I have no idea what you just did. While you're here, is there anything we can do for you—except guard your empty cars, which my man here is not too pleased about?"

"No, not at this point. We're all waiting on the guy with the bomb to make an appearance. Until he does, we can only wait and listen."

"Okay. Good luck."

"Right. See you."

John had Jim escorted back to his car, then Jim returned to Bellefontaine Neighbors. When he arrived back at Drew's house, the women were back and another car sat in the driveway. Once inside, Jim asked, "Everything go okay?"

"Fine," answered Holly. "Now I think I'll go back into the kitchen and start the cooking job I *tried* to start hours ago."

Drew shook his head. "My daughter, the martyr."

Jim laughed. "Yeah, and sired by a wanna-be poet."

From the kitchen, Holly said, "Hey, buster, if that's supposed to be support for your wife, you missed the mark…by a damn-long way."

A grinning Jessica quietly went into the kitchen to lend a hand.

After they had eaten, Jim asked, "How're we fixed for beds, Drew?"

"One, and I'm sleeping in it. Jessica, you're welcome to join me. You other two can sleep on the floor. Extra bedding, I have."

Jessica smiled. "I'll try the floor, thanks."

"Suit yourself," replied Drew, as he got out two sheets and a blanket from his now well-supplied linen closet.

Just as Drew was ready to hand the bedding to Holly, the phone rang. It was Billy, who said, "The 'Illinois observers' are about to leave…four of them in one car."

Drew nodded, told Billy to hold on a second, and relayed the message to Jim.

Jim said, "I'll go. Holly, come on. No, hold it. Jessica, you come with me. Holly, you better stay here. I doubt that it'll come up, but if someone here has to go out alone for some reason, you're more experienced."

"Right," agreed Holly.

Then Jim said, "Drew, please bug their other cars when you get the chance, or have Billy and Hector do it."

Drew just nodded.

As Jessica followed Jim out the door, Drew told Billy that Jim and Jessica would follow the four terrorists and told him to put tracking devices on the remaining terrorist cars.

Hector laughed. "Already done…Gary did it for us."

Drew laughed before hanging up.

Holly then said, "Well, I guess we better try to get some sleep."

Just as Drew started to answer, the phone rang again. It was Billy. "Four more headed for the Alton train station, to check things out."

"I'll go," said Drew, before he paused and added, "Holly better go with me…some of these guys got a look at me."

"Good luck," replied Billy.

Holly groaned and asked, "Who needs sleep?"

Drew just smiled and swatted her on the behind as he headed out the door.

●

As Jim drove well back of the four terrorists, he explained to Jessica how to read the monitor connected to the homing device on the car they were following, glad the terrorists were using a car that already had a homing device on it—not knowing they all now had them. Once she got the hang of it, Jim said, "Jessie, we may well run into a killing situation. Do you think you're up to it?"

"Oh, sure. I'm an old pro now. Just hope I don't puke again."

Jim recognized the mild sarcasm and self-doubting humor, reached over, and patted her leg. "Killing isn't an easy thing, but, when necessary, it's either kill or be killed. I plan to confront these guys at some point, and my guess is they won't give in too easily. I would like to question them, but not at the risk of one of us dying."

●

As Jim was saying that, the terrorists readied themselves to dispatch another team…this one to check on the security at the St. Louis train station. Billy groaned and asked, "Well, Hec—you or me?"

"I don't care," answered Hector, as he pulled out a coin, flipped it, and said, "call it."

"Heads."

"See you later, Indian scout. Have a nice trip."

Billy just nodded, picked up a piece of paper, and wrote Hector's cell phone number on it. "I better give this to the FBIs and have them call you with their number, in case you run out of people to chase these guys."

Then he picked up one of the homing device monitors and headed for the back door. Before he left, Gary Holmes said, "If it's just a matter of following them to the train station to watch them watch security, I could do it for you."

"Naw," replied Hector. "Betty would be madder than hell with us if we got your butt blown off."

Betty, who was in the kitchen washing up from the dinner they had all finished before the terrorists started sending crews all over the area, said, "I sure would be…I think."

Billy laughed. "Thanks for the offer, Gary, but you forgot one thing. They know you and don't know me. They just might wonder what you're doing down at the train station."

"Oh, yeah. I hadn't thought of that."

Betty said, "That's why you're a CPA and these gentlemen, who are *much* better trained, are more suited for spy work."

Billy simply left by the back door, without saying anything else. Hector, who was in the living room with Gary, whispered, "Don't worry, Gary. We're married, too."

"I heard that," emanated from the kitchen.

Billy was soon over the back fence and then the front fence of the backyard neighbors. He was quite pleased that their dogs were not outside.

When he reached the street, he spotted the FBI car and walked over. The agent nearest him rolled down the window and Billy said, "Hi, I'm with Jim Scott's crew. We're starting to run short of people to follow these guys. I'm about to go after the third car to leave in the last fifteen minutes or so. This is the cell number of my sidekick, still in the stake-out house. Please give him a call with your cell number, so he can call you in case we need some help following."

The FBI agent took the piece of paper. "Be glad to help. Sure would beat sitting here watching empty cars."

"Know you've probably had better assignments, but we sure do appreciate being able to count on our cars being here, and in one piece. Our cell phones are secure. If yours isn't, please use good phone technique when you talk to him."

"Oh, you mean I shouldn't say, 'Hi, I'm an FBI agent sitting here a block away from your stake-out of terrorists'?"

"Sorry. See you later," Billy said, after chuckling at the obvious rebuke.

Billy was soon in his car and following the four terrorists, heading for the downtown St. Louis train station.

As soon as he left, the FBI agent called Hector's cell phone and said, "Hi, I just met your Indian friend. He said you could get me a hot woman tonight, and all I had to do was give you my cell phone number."

Hector thought, *"Sounds like Billy pissed this guy off,"* but said, "Sure. Give me the number and I'll see what I can do."

•

By this time, the first group of terrorists were on the bridge across the Mississippi River, heading to Illinois. They drove on to a pre-selected motel and went in to register. One of the previously good credit cards was submitted for payment and the motel clerk gave them the bad news that their card charge was rejected for lack of funds.

They had enough money to pay cash for two nights in the room and, after settling up with the clerk, went to their room, grumbling about the continuing money crisis.

Jim had stopped across the street from the motel and waited until he saw the men had taken their things inside before driving onto the motel grounds and parking in a spot about four units away from where he had seen the men go.

Jim then turned to Jessica and asked, "You ready for this?"

"I guess."

Jim smiled and got out of the car, then walked around until he found a linen storage area. With Jessica watching with a curious look on her face, Jim quickly picked the lock and took out a stack of towels. Those he handed to Jessica. "I want you to knock on their door and announce that you have additional towels for them. Put your gun—safety off, please—under the stack and hold it in your right hand—the towels on top of it."

"You think they'll fall for this?"

"If they don't, I'll shoot the damn lock off. But if they do, it may make it easier to get at least one of them alive for questioning."

"*May* make it easier?"

"Yes, *may*. If I shoot the lock and barge in, we are more likely to have the element of surprise on our side. However, if they go for the towel gambit, it may relax them just a bit."

"Okay, if you say so."

Jim gave Jessica a funny look and headed off toward the room occupied by the terrorists.

Jessica followed behind and said, "I said I would do whatever you told me to in the field. I didn't say I wouldn't ask questions—and I didn't say I had to agree with everything you said. Just that I'd follow orders, which I'm doing."

"Jessie, you're a bigger pain in the ass than Holly is."

"Is that a compliment?"

"No."

When they reached the door of the room they were seeking, Jim stood aside and indicated for Jessica to do her thing. She dutifully held her stack of towels on her right hand, which held her gun and knocked with her left hand. In a moment a voice from inside the room asked, "What is it? Who's there?"

Jessica held up the stack of towels so they could be seen in the peephole of the door and answered, "Extra towels. The manager said you might need them."

The man on the other side of the door started to open the door and another voice said, "No!"

He was too late to suspect a problem, as Jim shouldered into the room, pushing the man behind the door down with the force of his action. Jessica saw one of the men pulling a gun out, dropped the towels, and fired in one fluid motion. The almost-silent puff of the gun sent a bullet on its way. The man was moving slightly and the bullet missed Jessica's target of between his eyes, but shot out his left eye and a good portion of the brain behind the eye.

Jim spun around and fired at another man going for a gun, then swung to a third man, only to see him falling from a direct hit from Jessica's second shot. Quickly Jim swung back toward the man who had opened the door. He was going for his gun, also. Jim shouted, "Jessica, no!" and shot the man in the hand wielding the gun, then shot him in the stomach for good measure.

With little wasted motion, Jim gently moved Jessica aside and shut the door. Next he walked over to the wounded man and told Jessica to check the pulses of the other three.

He saw the man was bleeding profusely from the stomach wound and said, "Here's the deal. You can talk at once and I'll get you immediate help and save your life, or you can lay there and bleed to death and join your three friends in hell."

The man glared at him and said nothing.

Jim said, "Your choice," turned his back on the man, and walked away.

Jessica looked at Jim, looked at the dying man, and watched without saying anything as Jim calmly took a pillow case off one of the pillows and bent down and started going through the pockets of one of the dead men. He put the contents he found in the pillowcase, and then did the same thing with the other two dead men and put their pocket contents with the other things he had found— except for the keys to their rental car, which he tossed on one of the beds in the room.

Next he picked up all four guns, which had belonged to the terrorists, and dropped them into the pillowcase. He then looked at the dying man and asked, "You ready to talk yet?"

The man gurgled something, then slumped over. Jim went to him, felt for his pulse, said, "Shit," then went through his pockets, putting the contents in the pillowcase.

Jessica asked, "Now what?"

"Go out and see if we drew any attention to ourselves. If not, back their car in as close to the door as possible and open the trunk. Then come back in and let me know when the coast is clear, so I can start putting their bodies in their car."

As Jessica picked up the keys and left, Jim started going through their luggage. What he found didn't surprise him, but he wasn't pleased nonetheless. He found Geiger counters, very dark goggles, and thin, but obviously sufficient, anti-radiation pullover suits.

Jessica, meanwhile, saw no one about and did as instructed. When the car was re-parked, with the trunk near the door, she came in. "Car ready, coast clear."

Jim nodded, dragged the first body over near a dressing table with a large mirror, and hoisted the body part way up on the dressing table. He took the dead man's hands and put them against the mirror. Then he hoisted the body up and carried it out to the trunk of the car. He then looked around and said, "Stand near the trunk. If anybody shows up, shut it and warn me."

Jessica did as told while Jim went in for the second body and repeated the procedure he had used on the first body. After dropping that body in the trunk, he decided he didn't have room for another in the trunk, so he shut the trunk and opened one of the back doors on the car.

With Jessica watching, he followed the same procedure with the last two bodies as he had with the first, except he placed the last two in the rear of the car. Then he shut the car door and went back into the room. On the way, he gave Jessica a head tilt in the direction of the room and she followed him.

Jim then said, "Shut the door, but keep a look-out through the drapes while I make a call."

Jessica just nodded and did as told.

Jim then called the St. Louis FBI office and asked for John Engle. When the Director was on the line, Jim asked, "Do you have pen and paper handy?"

"Just a second. Okay."

Jim gave John the motel name, address, and the room number he was in. "Okay, here's the deal. Jessie and I followed four of the terrorists here. For deniability purposes, you don't want to know what happened, but when your guys get here, they will be gone. I was unable to get any information from them, but found some stuff you're not going to like any more than I do. Also, if you check the mirror over a dressing table, you'll find their fingerprints. With those and the gear you'll find here, you should be able to help build a case against the other terrorists at the house we're watching in Bellefontaine Neighbors."

"What exactly are we looking for there?"

"Geiger counters, black lens goggles, and radiation suits."

"Oh, Jesus."

"Exactly. These guys were referred to as the 'Illinois observers.' The obvious conclusion is that these guys were to check the results of the nuke going off somewhere near downtown St. Louis from a safe distance. Maybe the idea was to start here, then drive across the bridge and go toward the explosion site, until it got too hot."

"I take it what you aren't telling me is that their bodies are going to disappear."

"*If* there were any bodies, it would be a good idea if their friends have no idea what happened to them. Plus which, I don't think it would be a great idea to try to explain all this to the press just now."

"Agreed. And thanks for the deniability in the use of the word 'if'."

"You're welcome. See ya."

After Jim pushed the 'end' button on his cell phone, he said, "Okay, Jess. Get our car and follow me."

"Where are we going?"

"There's a place upriver a few miles, where cars have been dumped since there have been cars," Jim answered with a smile, "an infamous dumping ground for unwanted cars…nice of the terrorists to pick my old hometown for their crap. This way I know things about where to dump unwanted cars…and, in this case, the cargo in the unwanted car."

19.

While Jim and Jessica had been up to their terrorist-elimination process, Drew and Holly followed their four terrorists to the Alton train station. When they arrived, Drew parked down the street half a block, took out a small pair of binoculars, and looked at the four men as they left their car. He recognized one of the men and said, "Okay, honey. You'll have to take this one. One of those guys has seen me. I'll wait here. While you're up there, get the current train schedules…just in case there have been any changes since you and Jessica checked on them."

"Okay, dad. See you later," Holly replied, before she got out of the car and walked toward the train station.

Once Holly reached the station, she walked up to the information desk and asked for train schedules. After she got what she wanted, she looked over the schedules without really looking at them, as she was more interested in the reaction of the terrorists as they watched the tight security on those people boarding the train. She almost laughed at the looks of consternation on the faces of the terrorists, who could hardly believe their eyes at how much security had tightened since their last visit to the station— when there had been *no* security at all.

Holly casually left the station and returned to the car, where her father waited. When she got in, she said, "Well, dad, those guys aren't real happy campers. The extra security Jim asked John Engle to lay on has them more than a bit upset."

Drew smiled as he watched the terrorists leave the station and get in their car. As they did, Holly asked, "I've been up this way with Jim a couple of times when we've been in the area and that road back to north county would be a prime spot for an accident to happen."

"Yes, it would. However, I want these guys to report back about what they found. In addition, I have a feeling that the guys Jim and Jessica followed aren't coming back, or reporting in. The idea is to put pressure on them, not scare them off entirely."

"I see your point. We have to get the damn bomb, and if they get too freaked out, they may just tell the courier to abort."

"Right you are."

•

Billy experienced much the same thing as Holly had. He went into the downtown train station and got current schedules. He smiled with silent pleasure to see the looks on the faces of the terrorists there at the increased security. When he had seen enough, he returned to his car to wait for the terrorists to leave.

Drew and Holly arrived back at the house before Jim and Jessica, and decided to have a drink, water on the rocks for Holly, while they waited up for them. While they waited, Billy reported in what he had seen. A short time later, Jim and Jessica returned.

After Drew told Jim what Billy and Holly had seen at the two train stations, Jim reported on what had transpired in the motel, and what he had found after the four terrorists had been killed.

When everyone had finished discussing the night's activities, Holly said, "Well, as I said two days ago, I'm for bed."

After everyone had washed up, taking turns in the two bathrooms, Drew went to bed, Holly tossed a cushion from the couch on the floor, stripped to her bra and panties, and said, "I'm for sleep."

Jim helped her spread the sheets and blanket, stripped off his clothes, down to his underpants, and laid down next to Holly, under the top sheet and blanket. Jessica stood there for a minute, then went into the bedroom with the bed.

She took off her clothing down to her bra and panties. "Move over. And if you do anything you shouldn't, I'm telling Tom."

Drew grunted, moved over to the other side of the bed, and slapped Jessica on her behind when she got in. "Good night."

Jessica said, "Good night," and lay there wondering how it would be with Drew.

Drew had a similar thought, but felt he *knew* it would be good. He also thought he'd be sorry in the morning, so he tried to go to sleep.

With Jessica gone, Holly suddenly had thoughts other than sleep. She soon had Jim thinking along the same lines.

In the morning, Jim was first up, and put on coffee before heading into one of the bathrooms. His moving around woke Holly, who had to go through her father's bedroom to get to the other bath. She chuckled when she saw her father and Jessica snuggled up together.

Holly's shower woke both Jessica and Drew, who, on realizing their close proximity to each other, both eased back from the embrace. Drew smiled and said, "You're damn cuddly for such a skinny young broad."

Jessica blushed. "I slept well, that much I know."

After all were dressed and breakfast completed, Jim said, "Now we wait."

•

During the night in Columbia, Boris had asked Roland to take the main portion of the night watch, so the others could sleep. Roland understood the need for his new friends to be well rested, and stayed up listening to nothing but the sounds of sex from across the street, followed by light snoring from one of the two remaining occupants of that house.

Billy and Hector asked Gary to do the same thing as Roland had done, and he also understood and let the two men get a good night's sleep. He heard more grousing about the money problem facing the terrorists—even more conversation about tightened train station security—and then a good deal of snoring.

•

While Jim and the other Janitors had been sleeping well, Sa'd Kahdi had been less fortunate. At midnight he had been awakened from a sound sleep and escorted to the parts shipping center, where his 'coffin' (as he called it), awaited. There he found a small stool in the large box. He tried it out and the unhinged cover was put on, to make sure there was adequate room for him, the stool, and both pieces of his luggage. When the cover was removed, his female companion asked, "Are you going to be comfortable enough?"

"Not very comfortable, but I will manage."

As he sat on the stool, she knelt down in front of him, reached out to undo his belt and said, "One parting gesture of my esteem for you before we have to put the cover back on and I must leave."

After she had finished, he pulled his pants back up and said, "Goodbye," before the cover was put on and nailed shut.

There were several very small air holes, enough so that he could breathe, but not enough or large enough to be noticed. There he sat for nearly five hours before he heard sounds and then felt movement, as he was loaded on the truck inside the box.

His trip to Detroit was one of the worst experiences of his life, and he felt almost re-born after the box was again moved—this time, off the truck—and it was finally opened. The man who opened it said, "Come quickly. We have to get you to your car before anyone notices."

Kahdi could hardly stand, but grabbed his two pieces of luggage and hurried along after the man. Outside the building, the man handed him the keys to a car. "This one."

Kahdi nodded and opened the door to the blue sedan. After putting his luggage in the rear seat, he got in and drove off, heading for Chicago and the address there where he was to leave the car. He had gotten little sleep during the drive to Detroit and was quite weary as he drove. Twice he stopped for coffee, to remain alert enough to complete the drive.

When he got to Chicago, his ordeal was to worsen. After parking the car where he had been told to leave it, he spent nearly twenty minutes getting a cab. Then, when he got to the car rental agency and filled out the paperwork, he handed over his credit card.

He waited impatiently until the clerk came back and said, "I'm sorry, sir, but your credit card was refused. The notation read 'no funds' available."

Kahdi was stunned, but quickly recovered and said, "I can pay cash."

"I'm sorry, sir," replied the clerk, "but we don't accept cash. Only credit cards. Do you perhaps have another card?"

"No," answered Kahdi, "will you please call me a taxi?"

When the taxi arrived, Kahdi gave the driver the address of where he had left the car and thought, *"My friends might not be pleased that I'm going to take their car the rest of the way, but this seems to be the easiest way to handle things."*

When they reached the address, the car was gone. Kahdi was upset at that fact, but not totally surprised. As the cab driver looked at him, he wondered what to do next. Being sore and tired from the trip, he decided to go to a cheap hotel; at least there they would accept cash.

He asked the driver if he knew of such a place and the driver assured him he did. After he had checked into the hotel and reached his room, Kahdi pondered his next move. First, he decided he must call Al-Sharif and let him know of his troubles. Maybe he would have a suggestion;

Kahdi just hoped the young fool wouldn't tell him to hurry up with the nuclear weapon.

He sat slumped in the hard-backed chair, which was the only piece of furniture in the room, except for the bed and a small nightstand, trying to summon the strength to make a call he really didn't want to make. Finally he dialed the number of Al-Sharif's Columbia house. The female answered and Kahdi asked, "May I speak to Ibrahim, please?"

"I'm sorry," she answered, "but he isn't available. May I ask who is calling?"

"I have a package for him. 'It' was to be delivered today. However, I've been delayed."

"Ibrahim is dead. I will be accepting 'it'."

Sa'd Kahdi was stunned. He asked, "Dead? How dead?"

"Automobile accident. The fool ran into a truck and was killed. What is your situation?"

"I have a shortage of funds. I have evidently overspent my credit card and am unable to rent a car with cash."

"How do you plan to travel?"

"I haven't determined that just yet."

"Where are you?"

"Chicago."

"Oh."

"Do you have any ideas?"

"We could come get you."

"That is a possibility; however, I'd like to think about it for a while. I'm very tired, so perhaps I'll just get a good night's sleep and call you back in the morning."

"Very well. I think we will go to our original meeting place. I'll give you my cell phone number and the number there. You can call us in the morning."

"Fine."

After she gave him the two numbers, she hung up and told her companion what the situation was. Even as she was doing that, Boris was on the phone to Jim. He quickly passed the information on, then asked, "Do you think it would be a good idea to put additional pressure on them by taking these two here out of the equation?"

"I think that would be a very good idea," Jim answered.

"As we speak, she is calling St. Louis to let them know what is happening. Um, I think it likely that they will resist being taken."

"So do I. Do something with the bodies. I doubt they have any information that will be of use, so give them every opportunity to resist."

"I understand," replied Boris, knowing full well that Jim wanted both of the terrorists across the street dead and disposed of.

After hanging up, Boris said, "Sergey, Tom, come on. We're going across the street to ask those two a few questions. Then we'll turn them over to the FBI."

Roland watched as the three men quickly headed for the garage. From what he had heard Boris say on his part of the conversation, he had the feeling that nobody was going to be turned over to the FBI. He was sure Boris had said that only for his benefit. He had been around these men long enough to know what would probably happen across the street and—as much as he knew everything in his life had trained him to abhor violence—down deep he knew he would like to be part of the coming operation, and wished them well.

In the garage, Boris pushed the button to open the garage door and said, "I'll drive."

When all three men were in the car, he added, "Jim feels—and I agree—that these two have little additional information to offer us. Their disappearance will put more pressure on al-Qaida's operation. My comments inside about turning them over to the FBI were just for Roland's benefit."

Both Sergey and Tom knew full well what Boris was saying, and neither bothered replying to those comments.

Boris backed out of the driveway, rapidly drove the few feet to the terrorists' driveway, and pulled to a stop at their garage door. As he got out, he said, "Sergey, you go through the back door."

Sergey said nothing, but hurried around the building as Boris walked up to the front door, shot out the door lock and the deadbolt with two almost-silent shots, and pushed the door open. The terrorists were stunned at first and reacted much too slowly. They both went for their guns, even as both Tom and Boris fired. Boris shot the female just above her upper lip, turned, and shot the man in the right eye, as he was falling back from Tom's shot, which had hit him in the throat.

Sergey came in from the back, where he had given the back door much the same treatment as Boris had the front door. Seeing both terrorists down, he knelt to feel for a pulse of the man as Boris did the same to the woman. Both were dead. Meanwhile, Tom had shut the front door and was looking out the window to see if any activity was going on outside.

Knowing Roland would be listening across the street, Boris said, "Not too smart of them to go for their guns. Sergey, you look for anything of value upstairs. Tom and I'll check things out down here. Then we'll dispose of the bodies. We don't want their friends in St. Louis knowing what happened to them. Oh...as we search, let's collect all the bugs Drew and I left. There is one in every room and on each phone."

Across the street, Roland thought, "*Good old Boris...trying to protect my sensibilities.*"

Without further conversation, all three men put on surgical-type gloves that they carried for just such situations and started searching the premises for any information that might be useful. When they were convinced they had looked everywhere they could, they spread out what they had found on the dining room table.

After looking it over carefully, Boris said, "About what one would expect. Not much. But at least we have some names and phone numbers. Bring it with us. Did we get all the bugs?"

Tom answered, "I couldn't find the one in the kitchen."

"On the back of the refrigerator," Boris said.

While Tom went to get it, Boris and Sergey carried the two bodies into the garage and put them in the trunk of the terrorists' car. When that was done, they gathered up all the items they wanted from their search and Boris asked, "Tom, you've driven around quite a bit…do you know a good spot to dump their car?"

"Not really."

"Okay, let's drive back over to Roland's and ask him. Sergey, you drive their car."

When they got back across the street, Roland was standing in the open doorway. He said, "I take it they didn't want to talk. And I bet you want to know a good place to dump their car and bodies."

Boris smiled. "That would be helpful."

Roland smiled back. "Since my car is 'hot,' I'll drive yours and one of you can follow me. I know just the place. You can drive it right into the river."

"Tom," Boris said, "you take care of that while I give Jim a call and report our success."

20.

Jim took the call from Boris, and after hearing about the successful operation and writing down the pertinent information, said, "Good job, Boris. You may as well head for St. Louis. There are two motels near us…you better check into one of them. Drew has limited sleeping facilities in this new house of his. Get a separate room for Tom. Jessica slept with Drew last night and is anxious to compare notes."

That comment netted Jim a hard poke by Holly and an obscene utterance from Jessica.

Boris, however, found it quite funny and he chuckled before Jim gave him directions to the two motels, which were less than a mile from Drew's house.

When Tom and Roland returned, Boris said, "Let's pack up our gear and head for St. Louis. Roland, you can leave whenever you want. Give the house keys to your real estate lady and Drew will give her a call about selling the house when he gets a chance. I want to give you a phone number to call, in case you run into any problems about your car, but I better call and warn him."

That said, Boris called the number he had for Ted Kuntz. When Ted answered on the first ring, Boris smiled and thought, *"All the world round, those below the very top always had to answer their own phone."* Then he said, "Hello, Ted. This is Boris."

"Hi, Boris. What can I do for you?"

"We had to use a car belonging to a nice chap by the name of Roland Wheeler for a little thing we did here in Columbia. In a day or two—maybe three—he'll be driving it from here to Kansas. Just in case he should get pulled over, I want to give him this number so you can keep him out of harm's way."

"What kind of 'little thing' did you use the car for?"

"We caused an accident…fatal."

"Oh."

"Don't say 'oh' that way. It was quite necessary and the deceased was a terrorist with a capital 'T.' Roland just loaned us his car…he wasn't anywhere around. I doubt there will be any problem because the police don't have a good description of the car—but just to be safe, I don't want any problems for him. This gentleman has been of great assistance to us here in Columbia."

"Sure, give him the number."

"Thanks, Ted," Boris said before pushing the "end" button on his cell phone, writing Ted's number down, and saying to Roland, "this number is to be used for the purpose of getting you out of trouble about your car only. Please burn it when you reach Kansas safely."

"I heard your conversation, but do you mind if I ask who Ted is and where he is?"

"He's an assistant to an advisor to the President. The number is to his office in the White House."

"Holy shit!"

●

After the call from Columbia about the delay, the terrorists across the street from Billy and Hector discussed the matter. Mohamed said, "Further delay, but we could still be on schedule for tomorrow night. I'm more concerned about the train situation. Increased security, I can understand, but from what our people found out at both train stations, it will be very difficult to board the train. Maybe there's another way."

One of his subordinates said, "We know the route the train takes, and since it moves slowly when it starts out, perhaps we could find a way to attach 'it' to the moving train."

"That's an idea. Tonight, take a man or two with you and try to find the best place to accomplish such a feat."

"What about our 'Illinois observers'…should they be told of the new delay?"

"No reason. They aren't expecting anything before tomorrow night."

Across the street, Hector let out a sigh of relief on hearing that. "For a minute there, I was afraid Jim's fun and games last night were going to cause a problem."

Billy nodded. "We sure don't need them to get so panicked that they change their plans and just decide to blow up Chicago or something."

•

In Chicago, that very thought had gone through Sa'd Kahdi's mind as he lay in bed the previous night. However, he had come up with what he felt was a much better idea, and one that would allow the mission to be carried out as planned. After counting his money, he found that he still had nearly three thousand American dollars. With that much, he could *buy* a car—perhaps not a grand one, but one that would make it to St. Louis.

That decision reached, Kahdi packed up his things, left the hotel, and summoned a cab. He asked the taxi driver to take him to the bus station. There he placed his two pieces of luggage in a keyed locker and wondered at the panic he would cause if everyone in the bus station knew there was a nuclear device in the locker. He could just imagine people running for the exits. Not for the first time, Kahdi felt a surge of power run through his body at what he had been entrusted with.

Next he bought a local paper, bought a map of Chicago, another of Illinois, found a small diner to eat at, and settled in to fill his empty stomach. While he ate, he looked through the "classified" section and found several used car dealers. After consulting his map, he determined that none was near enough to walk to, so when his meal was complete, he found another taxi and gave directions to one of the used car lots.

There he found one car that had a price tag of
eight hundred dollars and looked it over. When the lot
owner approached, Kahdi said, "This car hardly seems
worth the price you ask. I'll give you four hundred for it."

The dealer responded as though he had been shot
through the heart and replied, "This fine car deserves more
respect than that."

Kahdi looked in at the odometer and said, "It has
two hundred and seventy-five thousand miles on it. I'll
give you five hundred and not a penny more."

The dealer thought for a second—and, since he
had paid only fifty dollars for it from a dealer who had
taken it in for trade—decided that four hundred and fifty
dollars profit on a 1992 Chevrolet Cavalier station wagon
with two hundred and seventy-five thousand miles was
quite a nice profit.

After paying for the car, Kahdi asked, "How long
do I have to get license plates for it?"

"Thirty days. I'll put a temporary number in the
rear window."

"Thank you."

Kahdi got in and started the car, which seemed to
run well, and drove off the lot, back toward the bus station.
There he found a place to park and went into the station to
retrieve his luggage. He put his key into the lock, but it
wouldn't turn. Instantly sweat started to form at his
armpits and he was almost ill. After breathing rapidly for a
few moments, he took a deep breath and pulled the key out.
He looked carefully at it and soon realized he had tried the
wrong locker.

After placing the key in the correct locker, it
turned and Kahdi took out his luggage with an almost
audible sigh of relief. As he walked from the station, he
was almost faint, but got to his new car and put the two
pieces of luggage in the rear.

After consulting his map, he set off on his trip to
St. Louis, planning to stop in Springfield, Illinois for lunch

and to call the woman with news that he was well on his way.

•

In Columbia, meanwhile, Boris, Sergey, and Tom had loaded up all their equipment. While they had been doing that, Roland had called a moving company and had arranged for them to come out. He had decided there was no reason to delay his return to Kansas, since there was no longer a reason for him to be in Columbia.

When the others got ready to go, they all shook hands with Roland and again thanked him for all his help. After they left, he waited for the moving van, told them what to take, and asked them to lock up when they left. Then he too left.

His trip was a short one. Just as he was turning onto the two-lane highway, where his car had been used to cause the accident that ended the life of Ibrahim Al-Sharif, he was pulled over by a Missouri State Trooper.

It was the same trooper who had delivered the news across the street from Roland's old home that Al-Sharif was dead. He had never been made aware that Al-Sharif was a terrorist, but had received the general description of the car responsible. On seeing a car that matched that description pulling out onto the highway from the same street he had used in going to and then from the house of the deceased, he stopped Roland on a hunch.

The Trooper walked up to the driver's side window, which Roland lowered, and asked, "Sir, may I see your license, please?"

With a sense of dread, Roland handed it over and asked, "What did I do?"

"A car similar to yours was involved in a fatal accident not far from here two days ago. Do you happen to know anything about that?"

Roland considered lying and trying to bluff, but decided he wasn't a good enough actor, so he said, "I have a number I would like you to call about this."

Now feeling that his hunch might pay dividends, the trooper cautiously asked, "What do you mean?"

"May I reach into my coat pocket and take out my cell phone?"

The Trooper nodded and answered, "Very slowly."

Roland did as told and handed the phone to the trooper, along with the piece of paper Boris had given him and he had put in the same pocket with the phone. As he did, he said, "If you'll call that number, I'm sure we can settle this matter at once."

Not sure just what was afoot, but curious, the trooper opened up the cell phone and called the number. Good fortune was suddenly smiling on Roland as Ted Kuntz answered on the first ring and said, "Kuntz."

The trooper said, "Hello, this is Missouri State Trooper Elston speaking. I've pulled over a fellow by the name of Roland Wheeler concerning a fatal accident we had here two days ago and he asked me to call this number. May I ask who you are?"

"Ted Kuntz."

"*What* are you Mister Kuntz?"

"An assistant to General Bradley, who is the Military/Intelligence Advisor to the President."

"The President of the United States?"

"Yes."

"How do I know you're telling me the truth?"

Ted put his hand to his forehead, ran it down his face, sighed, and answered, "Let me give you the number to the White House exchange. Call it and ask for me."

After Ted gave the number to the trooper, who wrote it down carefully, the trooper ended the call and placed another call to the main White House switchboard and asked for Ted Kuntz. The operator asked who he was and what he wanted. The trooper told her who he was and that he had called another number and spoken to Ted Kuntz and to verify he was actually whom he said he was, he had been told to call this number.

The operator, satisfied with what she heard, connected Trooper Elston to Ted's line. Ted answered on the first ring and asked if the trooper was satisfied.

Trooper Elston replied, "I'm not sure. This could be some sort of a game."

Ted sighed, looked over to General Bradley's desk, saw he wasn't on the phone, and said, "Just a minute."

Quickly Ted explained the situation to the general, who then walked over and took the phone from Ted and said, "This is General Bradley. This *is* the White House. And we really don't have time for foolishness. What can we do for you?"

"Well, I don't know who you are either. This could still be a game."

"Hold on, please."

General Bradley put the call on hold and said, "Ted, give me the full details on this."

Ted told the general everything he had been told by Boris. When he finished, the general said, "Damn." Then he called the President's direct line.

When the President answered, the general said, "Sir, we have a small problem."

"What is it?"

The General told the President the entire story, including the fact that he had a Missouri State Trooper on the line who wasn't sure he was really talking to the While House. When he finished, the President sighed. "As much as the Janitors have done for this country, the least we can do is help out someone who has assisted them. Put the trooper on the line."

The general said, "Yes, sir," then put the President on hold. He then got Trooper Elston back and said, "I'm going to transfer you to someone whose voice I hope you recognize."

After the long time he had been on hold, Trooper Elston was getting rather impatient, but said nothing.

When General Bradley buzzed his line, the President said, "Hello, Trooper Elston. This is the President. May I be of assistance?"

Trooper Elston definitely recognized the President's voice and said, "Hello, sir. It's an honor to talk to you. I must admit that I feel a little silly at this point."

"Not at all, officer. You're just doing your job to the best of your ability. Keep up the good work. I understand this concerns Roland Wheeler. I would appreciate it if you would let Mr. Wheeler go on his way unimpeded. He has been of great service to our country in the fight against terrorism."

Trooper Elston swallowed and replied, "Yes, sir. Nice talking to you, sir."

"The pleasure was all mine. Good day."

Trooper Elston pushed the "end" button on the phone, handed it, the slip of paper with the phone number, and Roland's driver's license back to him. "Do you know who I just talked to?"

"From what I heard from your end of the conversation, I'd guess someone pretty high in the administration."

"Yeah, high—the *President* himself. The damn *President!* I can hardly even believe it."

Roland could hardly believe it either. He never guessed when Boris gave him that phone number that the *President* himself would get on the line to get him, Roland Wheeler, out of a jam. However, he made every effort not to show his own amazement when he replied, "I'm flattered the President took the time to talk to you about me."

"Well, *Mr.* Wheeler, I'd say you should be. And I'm honored to know someone who has actually been in the fight against terrorism. Please be on your way, with my thanks. May God look over you."

Roland muttered his thanks and drove off, filled with emotion and pride.

●

While Roland had been getting into and out of his situation, Sa'd Kahdi was nearing Normal, Illinois. He decided to stop there rather than go on to Springfield, since the events of the last thirty-six hours had taken their toll on him. He pulled into a truck stop and filled his car with gasoline. The car had been acting funny as he drove it, so he used a premium grade, hoping that would improve the car's performance for the remainder of the trip. While there, he decided to eat. When he finished, he got back in his car and dialed the female terrorist's number. There was no answer. While he couldn't understand why they weren't anxious enough to hear from him to keep their phone turned on, he tried the Bellefontaine Neighbors number.

There his call was answered on the first ring. "I have reached a point nearly halfway to you. I have 'it' with me. I was unable to reach those west of you, so thought it prudent to call you."

"They are on their way here. They may be in an area where there is no cell for their phone. When do you think you will arrive?"

"Yet tonight, if necessary. If not, I'd like to go on for a while longer, then find a place to spend the night. I'm quite tired."

"That will be fine. Please call us in the morning."

"I will do so."

On hearing that conversation, Billy immediately called Jim and reported what he had heard. Jim said, "Well, the plot thickens. I'd guess he's in the middle of Illinois somewhere. We know he was in Chicago and is driving. If he can read a map, he'll be taking 55 south, so from what he said, I'd imagine he's still somewhere north of Springfield. It sure would be nice to know what kind of car he's in…we could meet him part way."

"Yeah," replied Billy, "that *would* be nice. However, since we don't, we can't very well stake out the highway looking for southbound Arabs doing God knows what speed."

Jim chuckled. "Guess not. We'll just wait for better information."

Jim no sooner ended that conversation than Boris called and said, "We're here and checked in. Tell us how to find you."

Jim did and told him to be sure to bring the electronic equipment he had with him.

When Boris, Tom, and Sergey arrived, the latter was introduced to Holly and Jessica. Then Jessica gave Tom a ravishing kiss and asked, "Jim, may I steal my husband for a while?"

"No, not just yet. We need to have a little meeting first."

Jessica pouted as Jim continued, "First off, Boris set up our monitoring equipment so we can listen in on the lads across the street from Billy and Hector. They're only two blocks away, so we'll be able to hear everything they do. You'll have to calibrate in on their phone bugs, but that shouldn't be too much of a problem.

"Next, we know that the terrorists are sending out a team tonight to find a place to put the bomb on the train from Alton to St. Louis. It would be real prudent to know where they plan to do that little trick. So, I'm thinking, we'll follow along. I'll take Boris and Holly with me for that operation.

"Then we come to the matter of the nuke itself. I have a set of blueprints on the design of this type of weapon. I gave a copy to Hector and Billy. They've had some time to go over the data and I'm going to get one of them over here so we can do some brainstorming on how to handle the thing if we lay our hands on it."

"*When* we lay our hands on it," corrected Drew with a smile.

"I stand corrected," joked Jim, before he added, "Tom, take your wife back to the motel before she climbs your frame right here in front of God and everybody. Don't be gone too long."

Jessica grinned. "How long is *too* long?"

Jim ignored her (but smiled) and called Billy. When Billy answered his cell phone, Jim said, "I need you or Hector over here to talk about disarming the nuke *when* we get it. Maybe one of you could get in the back of Gary's car while it's in his garage and he could cover you up with a blanket and you could come over...or something of the sort."

Boris cleared his throat and said, "Sorry to interrupt, but that may not be necessary."

To Billy, Jim said, "Hold on."

Then he asked, "What do you mean, Boris?"

"Just shoot the damn thing. We, the Soviet Union, were fixated on electromagnetic impulse and those things have old vacuum tubes. So a well placed shot or two will render them useless."

Jim nodded and asked, "Billy, did you hear that?"

"Yes, and I'm damn glad to hear it. Hector and I have had a devil of a time trying to figure out a way around their safeguards once the things are armed. We think we came up with a way, but it might take more time than we'd have. Now that Boris has given us the key, it's easy. Break one of those tubes and the whole thing would shut down."

"Good, that's solved then," Jim said. "Just stay where you are."

"You mean we aren't needed?"

"No."

"Pity, it's Hector's turn. I was gonna make him climb in the back of Gary's car."

21.

Sa'd Kahdi was nearing Springfield when his car started making sounds he didn't like. What Kahdi, the used car dealer, and the new car dealership all failed to know was that the previous owner of the car had bought it new, and from the time he drove it home and put an oil additive in his oil, the car had always been run on the oil additive. And, like the German vehicles captured during the World War II, the first oil change without the additive proved near-fatal to engines pushed past their prime, but still functioning due to the use of the formula that additive was based on.

Kahdi saw a truck stop with a nearby motel, pulled into the motel parking lot, and went inside to register for the night. He was then torn between whether to put the bomb and his other piece of luggage in the room or leave them in the car until he went to the truck stop to see about having his car looked at. In the end, he remembered the sick feeling when the bus terminal key wouldn't work when he put it in the wrong lock, so he left the bags in his car when he went in search of a mechanic.

After a lengthy wait, the car was finally looked at. Kahdi stayed in the area of his car, to keep a close eye on it and to make sure nothing happened to the bomb. After a seemingly endless wait, the mechanic walked over to Kahdi and said, "You have one sick car, mister."

"How sick? Will I be able to make it to my sister's house in St. Louis?"

"With a lot of prayer."

"Is there nothing you can do?"

"Short of a new engine, the only thing I can recommend is an oil additive. But no way will I guarantee that you'll make St. Louis, or even the other side of Springfield."

"Try it, please."

•

As the additive was being poured into Kahdi's car, his friends in Bellefontaine Neighbors were starting to be concerned that their two co-conspirators from Columbia had not yet arrived. Mohamed said, "Even allowing for bad traffic and stops for food, they should have been here two or three hours ago."

Another member of the terrorist cell said, "Maybe they got a late start."

"No, she said they were about to leave when I talked to her."

"Well, what could have happened to them?"

"I can't believe they had an accident. On top of Al-Sharif's accident, that would be too much bad luck."

"Could they have been arrested?"

"How? For what reason?"

"I don't know. Maybe speeding, and whoever was driving didn't have a proper license."

"They all had proper licenses, just as we do. That is why we all have been here so long, to take care of little things like that."

After discussing the matter for several minutes more, Mohamed said, "I suppose we'll just have to wait to hear from them. If they don't arrive, we'll just go ahead with the plan as if they were here. But it makes me nervous just the same. Too many things are starting to go wrong with this operation, small things *and* large things, like our money disappearing."

"Should we call someone for advice?"

"No, we will just do our job and hope nothing else goes wrong. I've been thinking about the problem with increased security at the train stations. I'd like you to find a large magnet we can attach to 'it.' If all else fails, we can just drop 'it' from a bridge and hope it sticks to the train."

"Where do I look for magnets?"

"Do what Americans do. Look in the *Yellow Pages* under 'magnets'."

•

Listening in at Drew's new house, Boris said, "If they drop it far enough, they may break one of the tubes."

Jim replied, "Let's hope they don't ever get that close to success. That does give me an idea, though. I better call John Engle and tell him to have an agent at the train station tomorrow night, so if we call they can stop the train from ever leaving the station."

After Jim made that call and John Engle agreed it was a good idea, Jim said, "I for one could use something to eat."

Holly smiled and asked, "Should I count on Tom and Jessica being here for supper?"

Jim grinned and answered, "Yes. They've had plenty of time to catch up. I'll call them."

After Jim called Tom and Jessica and 'invited' them to eat, he said, "Guess I better help the old war horse in the kitchen, or my name's 'mud'."

From the kitchen Holly offered, "Hey, 'mud'…your new name's 'celibate'."

Jim had taken two steps toward the kitchen when his cell phone rang. "Jim."

General Bradley replied, "Hi, Jim. Bradley here. The boss asked me to call you to see if anything was cooking on the nuke front."

"We're pretty sure the guy carrying it is somewhere in Illinois. Probably around Springfield. Their plan, as of now, is for him to arrive sometime tomorrow. *Our* plan is to follow the guys who go to greet him and take it away from them."

"Any way to make a try for him on the way from Springfield? Maybe set up roadblocks somewhere along the line?"

"I doubt it. Damn guy sees a roadblock, he might just decide to arm it and set it off right there. Wouldn't cause near as much damage as if they set it off here, but the people at the roadblock sure wouldn't like it very much. Plus which, it sure wouldn't do the public's nervous system much good to have a nuke going off anywhere in the country, no matter what the damage."

"You're right there. Just, please, don't let the damn thing go off anywhere."

"Try not to. Boris did give us one little piece of information that should help us. He says about all we have to do—even if it *is* armed—is to shoot it. If you look at the specs for these things, you'll note that they use vacuum tubes. Boris says if one of those tubes is shattered, the whole thing just shuts down. Billy and Hector said they could disarm it even after being armed, but that it would take some time because the thing has a very good anti-tampering system."

"Yeah, that's what our experts came up with also. Guess the ball's in your court…don't drop it."

"Yes, sir."

Finished with his conversation with the general, Jim said, "The President—or at least General Bradley—is getting itchy. Can't blame them. We mess this up and there will be hell to pay."

"Then let's not mess it up," intoned Boris, before adding, "I thought you were going to assist in preparing our meal, which I'm very ready to eat."

Drew said, "Hey, Russian, you could help, too."

Jim joked, "Never mind, I'll help. I'm not too fond of red cabbage soup."

After they finished eating, and just as Billy and Hector started eating at the Holmes' home, everyone in both houses froze, as a screaming terrorist ran to Mohamed and said, "I found this in the basement!"

Mohamed looked at it and instantly realized what he was looking at. "We are being listened to! This is what the Americans call a 'bug.' Quickly, let's search this house for more. Be very careful what you say from this instant forward."

Billy said, "Shit," looked at Betty, and added, "excuse me."

Betty smiled and said, "You took the words right out of my mouth."

At the other stake-out house, Drew said, "This could complicate things a mite."

Then everyone at both houses quieted down as they listened to the search. It wasn't too long before another of the terrorists ran in from one of the bedrooms. "I found this one in my bedroom."

Mohamed said, "Check the phones."

Within three minutes all five phone bugs had been found, as well as another from a different bedroom. Mohamed thought for a few seconds, and then asked for the cell phone of one of the men least likely to need one.

He smashed it open and found nothing suspicious. "At least the cell phones are secure."

Drew looked at Jim, remembered that Jim told him he had only bugged three cell phones and said, "God, you're lucky."

Jim asked, "Me, lucky? How about you and your house hunting? Right across the street in Columbia, and two blocks away here, all within an hour of looking. You're the luckiest man alive."

"No, the luckiest man alive is the guy who goes into the kitchen to eat his breakfast and his son's picture is on the cereal box, his girlfriend's picture is the centerfold in his girlie magazine, and his wife's picture is on the milk carton."

Holly said, "Hey!"

Jessica smiled, looked at a laughing Tom, and said, "If you want more of what you got this afternoon, you better stop laughing…soon."

Boris, having spent much time in America, understood the "milk carton" portion of the joke, but

Sergey didn't. Nonetheless, both men smiled and looked at each other as they thought back to the times they had ribbed each other in similar fashion to the back-and-forth between Drew and Jim.

Then they all listened as the terrorists found the living room bug. Soon thereafter the bugs from the other bedroom and the bathrooms were all found. The search then concentrated on the dining room and kitchen. After locating the dining room bug, Mohamed said, "Now only the kitchen is left."

That one, Jim had taken the time to quickly get to his knees, reach around behind the electric stove, and place it below the oven in a small opening that had a metal lip protruding out less than an inch.

While the search had been going on, friendly wagers were made in Drew's house as to which bug would be the last to be found. Jim thought the one in the dining room, nicely placed on an inside lip of a built-in china cabinet, would be the last. Tom, Boris, and Sergey all bet on the living room, after having been told by Jim that it was inside the sofa, where he had cut a small hole in the bottom dust guard.

Since Holly and Jessica had been clearing away the remains of the just-eaten meal, they opted for the kitchen. Drew had chosen one of the bathrooms. Now, as they all laughed at the sounds of kitchen appliances being moved with a great deal of groaning, Jessica and Holly were having fun with the men on the team.

At long last, Mohamed said, "They may not have put one here. However, we will watch carefully what we say just in case we have missed any. Now the question becomes, who did this?"

One of the other terrorists said, "That is a good question. I wonder, though, if we should worry about the police or FBI coming after us now that they know we have found their listening devices."

Mohamed realized the man was correct and quickly wrote on a piece of paper, "Leave at once. Check to be sure you aren't followed. I will call you on your cell phone if I feel it safe for you to come back." Then he showed it to four of the terrorists, who quickly got their jackets and went out the door.

When Billy saw them, he said, "Hec, four of them are leaving. No time to call Jim. You go."

Hector didn't even reply as he picked up one of the homing device monitors, hurried to the back door, ran across the backyard, over the fence, over the backyard neighbor's front fence, and to one of the waiting cars. He hadn't taken time to worry about dogs, and the neighbor's dogs (who happened to be outside) stood dumbfounded until Hector was a few feet from the second piece of fence. Their barking caused the four terrorists to look around. However, from where they were, they were unable to see Hector as he cleared the fence.

The two FBI agents across the street watched as Hector got in his car and waited for the blip (signaling the terrorists' car) to start moving.

Back in the Holmes' home, Billy called Jim and reported what had happened. Jim told him to stay on the line and immediately said to Drew, "Four of them just left their house. Take Holly and get ready to follow any more that leave."

Even before Drew and Holly were out the door, Billy said, "Four more."

Jim said, "Right. Drew, go."

Even as they started their car, Jim said, "Tom, you and Boris take the next batch."

Both men nodded and Boris picked up one of the monitors. They only had to wait about a minute before Billy told Jim four more were leaving. Jim tilted his head toward the door and said, "Go."

After they left, Billy and Jim listened intently as Mohamed said, "The rest of us will stay here. Have your weapons ready, in case we get an unwanted visit."

Billy and Jim couldn't hear that well because the only bug left was in the kitchen and the remaining terrorists were in the living room of the house. However, they were able to hear enough to know that it appeared the others wouldn't be leaving.

Jim, still on the phone with Billy, said, "Okay, Billy, let's just monitor things the best we can. I'll talk to you later. If any more start to leave, get back to me."

"Roger."

In the terrorist house, Mohamed said, in Arabic, "From now on, we use our language…enough practicing English. Now we must try to figure out who did this. If it was the FBI, they may not arrest us now that we know. They might want to follow us to meet Kahdi."

Another of the terrorists said, "I don't see how it could have been the FBI. How could they have done it? We have had someone here at all times."

"That's a good point. We must have a spy amongst us."

"But who?"

"I don't know, and I don't know how to find out. I do have another thought, however. I should call the Illinois observers and warn them."

That said, Mohamed tried the cell phone of the lead man of the team sent to monitor the nuclear blast. He naturally got no answer. Then he tried each of the other three cell phones and got the same result. After a few moments of thought, he rooted through the pile of papers on the living room coffee table and found the number of the motel they were to have checked into. He called that number and an FBI agent John Engle had decided to station at the motel answered it.

Mohamed asked if he could be connected to the room of the man who headed the team. When told that man wasn't registered there and never had been, he next asked for each of the other men in turn. He was told that none of those men had ever registered either.

Mohamed thanked the agent for his time and hung up. Then he said, "We may have just found out who planted the listening devices. Our Illinois observers never checked into the motel."

Another of the terrorists said, "Maybe they were arrested."

"I don't think so. They would have called the attorney we are supposed to use in that case, and he would have called us."

"What if the FBI didn't allow them to call an attorney?"

"This is America…you know their rules. Anyone arrested is allowed to call their attorney. If we assume that one or all of those men were responsible for the listening devices, we still don't know why, and we don't know who was listening to us."

"What do we do?"

"We carry on with the operation until stopped. I think we will forego looking for other places to get 'it' on the train as planned and go to option two."

"Option two! We don't have the timing down well enough for that. What about option three?'"

"Our timing on option two is close enough. Option three is out. We saw the increased security. I'm sure it is even more so now, if the FBI has been listening to us."

"We could check it out."

"Maybe tomorrow."

While Billy and Jim were picking up only part of what was being said, they both clearly heard the words 'option two.' Since both were fluent in Arabic, the change in language mattered little to them. In fact, it helped them because the heavily accented English was at times harder to understand than clearly spoken Arabic.

Jim, however, realized that the continued use of Arabic could pose a problem for Tom and Jessica, the only two members of the Janitors who weren't fluent in the language. That fact faced, he made a mental note to keep those two out of any situations that would require them to listen into conversations of the terrorists.

His immediate concern was "option two," especially since "option three" seemed to have been discounted. He called Billy and said, "I assume you picked up that 'option two' reference. Since we have no idea what that may be, I think we better plan on staying on all of these guys like glue. Maybe when he talks to this Kahdi fella, we can get a better idea."

"Yeah, we could be in the soup if he just tells the guy to drive the bomb downtown and set it off. We don't know if the courier is a suicide guy or not."

"I doubt that he is—or that may have been the plan from the beginning. Though putting it on a train is a nice touch, suicide or not. Give our public another form of transportation to worry about."

"Jim, if I was the bad guys and was going to do this, I'd just check into a downtown hotel, go to my room, arm the thing, and split."

"You're right, Billy. But there must be a reason for why they were going to do it on the train. With bin Laden, one never knows what he may be thinking. We do know, however, that he likes symbolic gestures. For now let's think about this and get back to our listening."

"Roger."

As an afterthought, Jim called John Engle, and when he had him on the line, said, "John, I've got a hunch. The Arch. How is security down there?"

"It's been quietly increased since the attack on us. Do you think that's the target?"

"No, not really. Just an itchy feeling. How about some added security there, but not obvious, like at the train stations. A few of your guys in plain clothes, maybe dressed as tourists."

"Okay, Jim, but I better start calling in more help from other offices. I'm starting to run short of people at this office."

"You better hurry. I think tomorrow is going to be the day the damn thing gets here. Maybe you could borrow some DEA guys and maybe some Marshals."

"I'll see what I can do."

•

Meanwhile the three cars full of terrorists drove around the north St. Louis County area aimlessly. The five Janitors in three cars followed at a very safe distance. From time to time they would call each other or Jim with situation reports.

After more than two hours of this, Hector called Jim and said, "Amigo, these guys are just driving around to stay away from their house. I bet they are just trying to avoid arrest by the FBI if they go back. What do you think about reducing the odds, if we get the chance?"

"No, not just now, Hec. We still haven't figured out why they had so damn many people involved in the operation if it was just a simple matter of someone getting the bomb on the train and having it go off somewhere along the line. Half a dozen guys, maybe. The four guys to watch the blast from a safe distance, sure. However, counting the three in Columbia, the courier, and the twenty in the house here, we have a grand total of twenty-four. For craps' sake, if this was our job, any one of us could do it with no help. Why the army?"

"Well, why not make the army smaller?"

"It's a thought, but not now. I still want to figure out what all these guys are for."

"Okay, amigo. I'll keep driving around in circles."

"I doubt if it'll be for much longer. Their head guy will decide that if an arrest was coming, it would have already come. He's already tripped onto the idea that we plan on following him to the bomb."

"Diversion?"

"Come again?"

"Could all the extra guys be for some sort of diversion?"

"Maybe. Let's think about it."

22.

Abdullah Mohamed was doing some thinking of his own. He realized his part of the plan would have to be put on hold until the nuclear device was safely on its way to the general area of the target. However, even as he had that thought, he tried to remember if there had ever been any discussion of his portion of the plan in the house, which had been so thoroughly bugged.

After careful consideration, he was sure that there had been no incriminating conversation in that regard. He had—including his own—five teams of four men each. One team was to observe the nuclear blast, the other four were to set off non-nuclear explosive devices, which had been pre-situated at the various places of detonation. The idea had been that, with the emergency response teams of the St. Louis area concentrating on the nuclear blast area, his other teams would have an easier time with their respective duties and cause more terror with their detonations *after* the nuclear device went off.

Ibrahim Al-Sharif was to head the team responsible for the nuclear device. With Al-Sharif dead, and his two Columbia companions missing, Mohamed had to face a serious decision. Should he—who was obviously now responsible for the entire operation—send out the four conventional explosive teams (one short a man since he would have to be with the nuclear team) to do their job as planned? Or should he send them out first, causing confusion and forcing the authorities to run around in many areas, thereby possibly overlooking the more serious threat?

He had come to know the St. Louis area rather well, as he spent many days driving around from one potential blast sight to the next and then back again. He had selected the four sites with care, always with an eye toward his al-Qaida training to look for sites that would cause the most psychological damage and/or the maximum financial strain on the area.

With the Gateway Arch and downtown area the target of the nuclear device, Mohamed and his assistants had selected the Boeing Aircraft plant in St. Louis as their prime target. However, they found the security there too difficult to breach. They also considered landmarks such as the St. Louis Zoo, but in the end decided on the financial impact of destroying four of the main bridges leading to St. Louis or St. Louis County.

Over a period of months, they had secreted explosives on all four bridges. All that was left to do was to affix detonators, arm them with timers, and leave. Since they had planned to leave the St. Louis area using those four bridges as they dispersed into the countryside to wait their next assignment, Mohamed in the end decided that the nuclear operation would be done first, as originally planned. That way he could also have all his men in the area when they would place the nuclear weapon on the freight train, which was 'option two.'

While Mohamed had been thinking, the other three terrorists still with him had been instructed to carefully re-check one of the bathrooms, to make absolutely sure there were no more listening devices in it, or the bedroom it was attached to.

His decision made, he asked one of his men, "Are you *sure* that there is nothing in either that bathroom or bedroom?"

"I would stake my life on it."

"You may very well be doing just that."

With no response expected or forthcoming, Mohamed went into the bathroom, shut the door, turned on the water in the bathtub, and placed a call to Sa'd Kahdi. When he had him on the line, Mohamed said, "We have had some serious problems here. Not the least of which is the failure of the two from Columbia to arrive. Tomorrow, when you get to the train station in Alton where you were to be met, *don't go in.* Instead call me, and I will tell you what to do. That call should come to me about eight at night. If you arrive early, find something to do to occupy your time…something that doesn't cause suspicion. I would like you to be south and east of the station when you call."

Kahdi asked, "Are we not going to use the train as planned?"

"No. Security there has been increased from nothing to something a good deal more than nothing. I will not go into it during this call, but there are other concerns as well."

"I also have a problem. The car I bought to travel in has been acting quite poorly. I worry that it may not make the remainder of the trip. I, like you, don't want to go into detail, but if the car quits, I wonder what you might think of coming for me. Would that be possible?"

"It would be possible, but certainly not desirable. Especially with the problems we are having here."

"Very well, I will call you tomorrow night at eight. If I call earlier, it is because I have had further car problems."

•

While Mohamed had been thinking, Jim had a conversation that started when he said, "Sergey, when I spoke to your President, a thought occurred to me. How would you like to go home after this is over and set up a sister operation to ours?"

"Be the Russian Janitor?"

"Yes. I'd fund it, and I'm sure there are other ex-KGB types who you trust to help you. As things work now, when information needs to go to Russia from us, or other agencies, the proper channels must be observed. Sometimes that can prove to be bothersome. If you and I had a direct, secure link, we could funnel information directly to our Presidents, without all the hassle."

"Would our respective Presidents approve such an idea?"

"Both have already agreed in principle to the idea."

"What about Boris?"

"I think he's quite happy here. Just something to think about. Play around with it in your mind."

"I will. I can tell you right now that I like the idea in general, and I do miss Russia. I was about sick to death in Iraq, but one has to live and the pay was *very* good."

Just as Jim started to reply, Mohamed made his call to Kahdi and Jim listened in intently to the conversation and smiled broadly when it was concluded. Jessica, who hadn't understood one word of it, asked, "Why the smile that looks like you just ate the canary, Mr. Cat?"

"Our friendly neighborhood terrorists are having all kinds of problems. On top of the disappearance of six more of their people, the bugs they found at their house, security at that tiny train station in Alton, now the guy bringing the nuke to town is having car problems and isn't sure if he can even make it."

Jessica smiled. "I didn't understand what they said, but I sure could hear the water running in the background. Was that to keep us from hearing what he said?"

"Yeah, since he thinks his cell phones are safe, he wanted to make sure we weren't listening some other way. That was the bathtub water running that you heard. Them finding the bugs may turn out to be a blessing. The guy'll figure his cell is safe and may say something he shouldn't. In fact, he did say more than he should have. I now know that the bomb will be here at eight tomorrow night, and I've got a pretty good hunch our boy will meet and then lead Kahdi to wherever they plan on using the bomb. If this guy was more experienced in the spy business, he would have gone over all his cars with a fine-tooth comb and wouldn't have assumed all his cell phones were okay, just because he broke one open and found nothing. Now, all we have to do is follow him around until he meets Kahdi...and following him will be easy, with his car bugged."

In a more serious vein, Jessica said, "Jim, I've been meaning to ask you something. You took me to Illinois with you, when you could have taken Holly or someone else. How come?"

Jim joked, "You're a fox and I like your company."

"Yes, she is," put in Sergey.

"Yeah, sure. You're married to the best-looking woman I've ever seen. Most of the women on the planet would kill for her body...and I've seen the way you look at her, rightfully so. Hell, Tom looks at her the same way. Not that I've ever noticed, of course."

"Okay, Jessie. I took you to Illinois as sort of a test."

"You already knew I could kill...you saw that at the Joint."

"That was spontaneous. You just reacted to what you were presented with. This time I gave you warning of what was to come. You had time to think about it. I wanted to see how you'd react under that kind of a situation...just fine, I might add."

"Yeah, 'old killer Jess,' that's me. If my parents could only see me now—their gun totin' little darlin'."

Jim just smiled and said nothing. Shortly thereafter, Mohamed was on his cell phone again, this time calling in one of his teams. Soon he called the other two and told them to come in as well. By the time he finished the last call, Boris called and said, "Hi, Jim. Looks like they're headed home."

"I know. The boss man summoned all three teams back to their cubbyhole. Come on back."

Next, Hector called and said, "Hi, amigo. They're homeward bound."

"I know. Stop by here on your way back to Billy."

"Will do."

Drew didn't bother calling, he just returned to his house, arriving before the other three. Tom and Boris arrived next, followed through the door in a matter of seconds by Hector. After Hector had been introduced to Sergey, Jim said, "Hec, when you go back, tell those FBI guys…"

"Guy and *gal*."

"…to be ready tomorrow night for a little action. Let them know that if you give them the high sign, they should follow you in a loose tail. We might wind up needing them. I'd also like you or Billy to show Gary how to use a Walther…do you have a spare with you?"

"Naw."

Jim opened up one of the cases he had brought along and took out one of the extra silenced Walthers. As he handed it to Hector, he said, "Anyhow, show him how to use it and tell him that if anyone from across the street comes calling, he should open the door and plug the guy. Tell him 'no joke'… just shoot the bastard. Our head terrorist has let it slide for now, but at some point he is going to think about just where the signals from those bugs were going. I'm hoping if he does, you and Billy will still be there if he comes calling. But, if for some reason you're not, I don't want Betty and Gary getting into the soup."

"Me either…that lady can *cook.*"

Holly joked, "The way to a Mexican's heart is through his stomach."

"Nah, that's gringos. The way with a Mexican is through his…you know."

Jim shook his head in feigned disgust. "Get out of here."

•

In Springfield, Sa'd Kahdi was snuggled in bed, but he couldn't go to sleep…and not just because it was so early. His mind was filled with thoughts of what tomorrow would bring. He was far from a religious man and had no desire to die, tomorrow or anytime soon. When he joined al-Qaida he knew that death was a possibility, but suicide was not his idea of a way to accomplish this…or any other…mission. However, his mission must be completed; there was no other option.

Kahdi was very concerned about the "problems" they were having in St. Louis. Beyond the disappearance of the Columbia team, what other problems could they be having? He mulled over the possibility of just driving his car—assuming it would make it—to as near the Arch as possible, arming the bomb, and then leaving the area by any means available.

The obvious problem with that was his shortage of funds, and no one to contact besides Mohamed. In the end, he decided to trust Mohamed to help him accomplish what he set out to do, and he drifted off to sleep. Some while later, however, he woke in a cold sweat at a dream that had been all too real. In it he had felt a searing pain, then had been floating in the sky, surrounded by female forms. In disgust he said aloud, "Probably virgins," before he had a chilling thought, "*I wonder if this is my last night in a bed*?"

●

While Kahdi went to bed, Mohamed had things on his mind he wished to communicate with his men. After they all returned to the house, he asked, "Was anyone followed?"

After being assured that they had not been, he gathered up writing paper and a pen and told his men to follow him to the dining room. When all were gathered around the dining room table, he began to draw, using the legal-sized lined pad he had brought with him.

The map he drew was to a place north of Bellefontaine Neighbors, on Highway 367, which lead to Alton. About two thirds of the way to Alton, there was a rock quarry with train tracks running alongside. The map led to the quarry, which could be reached from the southbound lanes of the highway. Someone traveling north had to go up to an access road between the north and southbound lanes, then turn left, and left again at the southbound lanes.

When he finished the map, he wrote, "This is the best site for option two. I have decided that everyone—except one man I will take with me to drive—will be at this place. I will want everyone to conceal themselves the best they can. The cars should be parked out of sight from the highway. I will lead Kahdi and his bomb to the spot marked with the 'X.' I do not want any conversation about this at any time in this house. We can't be sure we have found all of the American 'bugs.' If anyone has any questions, write them down."

One of the other terrorists wrote lower on the page, "What about our other missions, to blow up the bridges?"

Mohamed flipped over a page and wrote, "When Kahdi's bomb is taken care of, we will carry out the remainder of the mission. Each bridge will be detonated by the team already assigned to it."

Another of the terrorists took the pad and wrote, "What about money? None of us has enough to reach our escape destinations."

Mohamed thought for a few moments, then wrote, "I have an emergency number to call if needed. I will give it to each of you." He then flipped over another page, wrote down the phone number several times, and tore off the number for everyone there.

Next he said, "If there are no more questions, I think it wise that we all try to get as much sleep as possible."

When no one reached for the pad, they all headed to their respective sleeping spots.

•

The Janitors had been listening in when Mohamed asked if any of his men had been followed. Then, after a long silence, they managed to pick up a few words, including 'sleep,' and assumed the terrorists were heading to bed.

At that point Jim said, "If they're needing sleep, it's probably a good idea for us, too. Boris, you and Sergey may as well head back to your motel. If anything comes up, I'll call you. Tom can take one of our cars. Tom, before you and Jessie leave, I want to go over the use of night vision goggles with Jessie."

As he said that, he got up, went to one of the equipment bags, and took out a pair of the goggles. He also picked up a case with a sniper rifle equipped with a night vision sight. While he did that, Boris and Sergey wished everyone a good night and took their leave.

Jim then led Jessica out the back door and told her to put the goggles on. He then explained as much as he could about them. Next he opened the gun case and showed her how to assemble the gun. When that was done, Jim said, "When you get ready to shoot, raise up the goggle protrusion to get it out of the way and use the gun sight in its place. This is the same gun Ted told me he used in your rifle training. The scope automatically adjusts to the surrounding light emissions. The darker it is outside, the more illumination it will give you. Try it out."

Jessica did as told and said, "Should be just like shooting during the day. It almost seems too easy. Is there something I'm missing?"

"No. I did, however, forget to tell you something about the goggles. Don't—repeat, *do not*—look directly at any light source with them on. If you do, you'll be temporarily blinded. Since the guy with the bomb is coming in by car, at night, take care not to look at his headlights…or any other headlights, street lights…even the moon."

"Gotcha."

They then went back inside and Drew said, "I sure hope none of my new neighbors saw you two out there. I'd hate to get a reputation."

"Dad," said Holly, "you already *have* a reputation."

After a few chuckles, Holly added, "Now, I'm for bed….or should I say floor? Good night, Tom. Good night, Jessica."

They both took the less-than-subtle hint, offered parting comments, and left.

A short time later, Jim and Holly were snuggled up together on the floor, when Drew's voice came from his bedroom, "If you two plan on any extracurricular activities, keep it down."

•

On the drive to the motel, Tom said, "Honey, we've never really had a chance to talk much about your involvement with the Janitors."

"That's because every time we're alone, we don't have much time—and what time we do have is better spent doing what we should be doing—namely, making love. I really like doing it with you."

Tom smiled and replied, "Me too. What I wanted to ask, though, was how you're doing with being a Janitor?"

"Just fine. I like everyone, and think I can hold up my end. Though, I must admit, I never dreamed I could kill someone. These guys being involved with the attack on us makes it easier, but still somewhat unsettling."

"Just wanted to make sure you're doing okay with it."

Jessica reached over, rubbed Tom's arm, and said, "Sure nice to have my man worry about me. I'm just fine. I'll sure have something to tell our grandkids. I can see me now, all hunched over with gray hair, saying, 'Granny used to run around killing people in the good old days.' Really, Tom, I'm okay. Just wish I knew more. Wish I had trained with you guys. I'd sure hate to mess up and get someone hurt because I didn't do the right thing at the right time. Especially since we're going to be responsible for getting that nuclear weapon back."

"You can't worry about things like that, honey. Just do the best you can. You'll do fine. I've got a world of confidence in you."

"Thanks. At least I married smart."

23.

The next morning, Sa'd Kahdi was the first person involved to climb out of bed. He was still shaken from his dream, but put it behind him as he dressed and loaded his car. He drove out of the motel parking lot in search of a place to eat, where he could watch his car while leaving the bomb in it.

As he drove, he noticed that the car didn't seem to be running much better, but at least it *was* running. Finally he spotted a café that had a parking lot in front of it. He went inside and got a seat at a front window. Kahdi played with, rather than ate, his breakfast. As he did, he wondered if this was the last time he would eat breakfast. He tried to shake off the feeling, as he realized that was the second time in a matter of hours he had suffered a fateful premonition.

Unable to even look at his food any longer, he paid the waitress and left the café. Once back in his car, he headed toward St. Louis. From looking at his map, he knew to drive to Interstate 270, and then go west to Illinois Route 3, where he would turn north toward Alton.

●

As a despondent Sa'd Kahdi drove south, the Janitors were finishing breakfast…Billy and Hector at the Holmes' home, and the remainder at Drew's house. There, Jim said, "Okay, here's the drill. Since we have no idea what 'option two' is, I want us to at least know the surrounding area. I know it well, Drew to a lesser degree, and Holly's vaguely familiar. Therefore, Drew, Sergey, and Jessica ride in one car; Holly, Tom, and Boris in another. Just drive around until you know every street in a five-mile radius, both sides of the river…actually rivers. The Mississippi is a mile east of us, and curls around about six miles north of us. The Missouri flows into it, about three or four miles north of where we are. While you're out, be sure to check out Alton carefully."

Drew asked, "What about Billy and Hector?"

"I'll call them in a while. Have them go out one at a time and do the same thing. We don't know where these guys will try to strike, but I bet they at least try to make contact with the bomb guy somewhere in the area. When they do, I want to be there and take the damn thing away from them. I'm also going to try to figure out something with John Engle. I want enough of his forces handy to shut down highways and roads, in case it becomes necessary."

Without much further conversation, Holly kissed Jim and left with Sergey and Boris. The other three soon left as well. Jim then called Billy and Hector and told them what he wanted them to do. Next he called John Engle and said, "John, from the way their lead guy talked when he spoke to the courier on the phone, I'm pretty sure they will meet him somewhere in Alton or North St. Louis County. The meeting is set for eight tonight, so I'd like you to have as many men and cars in this area as possible at that time. My thinking is for you to close highways and streets behind them. Hopefully I'll know at some point what car we are looking for and, if we miss him, you can cut him off."

"Okay, Jim. I have about forty men, and about twenty cars lined up: DEA, ATF, and the Marshal's office are all going to help out. You know the area…is that going to be enough? Or should I get more?"

Jim did some fast calculations in his head and answered, "That should be enough. I think you should have one team in Alton, to close the bridge from there into North County, and another team at the I-270 bridge, called the Chain of Rocks Bridge. Near it is an exit to Granite City, Illinois. At that exit there are places for your team to hold up without attracting attention. There is a casino boat in Alton near that bridge. Your guys there could just plop down in the parking lot. There is one a distance from the casino that uses a shuttle system, so two people sitting in a car could just be waiting for the shuttle."

Jim chuckled. "Of course about the third time around, the shuttle driver will wonder if the guys are just trying to build up their nerve to go gamble, so it might be a good idea if they just drove around until I gave you the high sign that the courier is getting close to the area."

John smiled to himself. "I better find a team that doesn't like to gamble. It wouldn't be a very good idea to have them inside on a roll when they're needed."

Jim let that pass without comment. "Your other teams will have to be spread out around the area, basically out of sight. You'll have some planning to do there. Maybe get a blown-up map of the area and sort of pre-plan who will be in charge of blocking what road. With any luck, they will use the bridge from Alton and we can cut them off somewhere on Highway 367, heading south. Hopefully, one or more of your guys will live up north here and can help out with planning. While I think of it, I'll need one of your cars with a radio in it so I can stay in constant contact with you. Also, be damn sure all of the other agency cars are on the same frequency."

"All ready thought of and organized. As to one of our cars, we'll bring it to you when you ask. I could ride with you, if you'd like."

"Might not be a good idea, John. I play by a little different set of rules than you do and I wouldn't want to be restrained by concern for following proper procedure."

John wasn't happy at that, but said, "I take it you aren't planning on any arrests."

"One shot fired in anger by these guys and you can bet on it. And you can damn well count on that shot being fired. These are terrorists and they aren't going to give up if we say, 'Please lay down your guns so we can arrest you.' I'd like to give the President the option of this never being made public…the fact that a nuke was intended for use in America and made it all the way here before we stopped it."

"As you can guess, I'm not real happy about that, but reluctantly agree. I don't want a wild shootout that could endanger the public, however."

"John, you know we'll try at all costs to avoid that. Running gun battles in automobiles is not my idea of fun. We do have, however, sixteen terrorists in a house two blocks from me, and another on the way, and I have no idea what their plans are. It is possible that one or two of them will go out to meet this Kahdi guy. If that happens, you can have the guys in the house if you want. Though, it might be more efficient if we took them out."

"More deadly, you mean."

"That too. But what I meant was, my people know this neighborhood now and are trained to deal with these guys. Some of your people are also, but *all* of mine are."

"All right, we'll do it your way. You call the shots…just don't leave me too big a mess to clean up."

"Try not to. One other thing—well, two actually. We should have a Geiger counter and a radiation-proof suit. One to fit Boris, since he's the one who knows this particular bomb the best. In case you've forgotten, he's about six two, two hundred thirty pounds."

"No problem with getting both those items for you. Anything else?"

"No, that should do it."

"When do you want me to bring your car and the radiation equipment up?"

"About seven should be okay."

"I'll see you then, unless I have any questions or ideas. If so, I'll give you a call."

"Right. Talk to you later."

•

While that conversation had been taking place, Mohamed had seen to the feeding of his men and then indicated to them to follow him back into the dining room. Once they were all there, he wrote on his pad, "I want everyone to carefully check his weapon. Then during the day, besides eating, I want everyone to get as much rest as possible. After we send the bomb on its way, and blow up the bridges, we have long drives in front of us. The money we have will be divided up evenly among those in each car. I will take Kahdi in my car. The three good credit cards we have left will go one to a car, except mine. If Kahdi has any money left, I will use it instead of a credit card. If not, I may have to use the emergency number I gave all of you."

After everyone had read the message, Mohamed carefully took all the pages that had been written on and tore them into small pieces. Those he took to the bathroom and flushed down the toilet. Next he turned on the bathtub water again and called Kahdi. When Kahdi answered, Mohamed said, "A slight change in plans. Do not call until nine tonight."

"As you say."

"How is your car running?"

"It is still making awful noises, but is also still running."

"I have a question to ask you that I really should not ask, but since it is crucial to our timing…how long will it take to arm 'it'?"

"Less than a minute."

"Thank you. We will speak tonight. Nine o'clock sharp, please."

Mohamed had changed the time for Kahdi to call because he wanted to reduce the time the bomb would be in the area by as much as safely possible. "Option two" was a simple shift in trains. The passenger train leaving Alton for St. Louis used tracks on the Illinois side of the river before crossing a bridge near St. Louis. There was a freight train that used different tracks, ones that came through North St. Louis County running parallel to Highway 367, before bending around and heading downtown through, among other places, Bellefontaine Neighbors. On this night, that train was due to pass the quarry at Highway 367 at approximately 9:15 p.m.

Mohamed's plan called for him to speak to Kahdi on the phone at nine o'clock, with both men being in Alton. He would direct Kahdi to cross the bridge at the same time as he did, then lead him to the quarry. Even if they were followed, with his men pre-positioned, they would be able to hold off any authorities until Kahdi could arm the bomb and toss it on the slow-moving train. Then they would mount an all-out attack on anyone who had followed them. With luck, the train would go on toward its destination and explode somewhere near downtown St. Louis.

•

Jim, sitting alone in Drew's house, heard the conversation between Mohamed and Kahdi, smiled at the running water in the bathroom, and pondered the change in time and wondered if it had any particular significance. He had an itchy feeling on the back of his neck that he was missing something. Something besides the lack of information he had. From long years in the military and later dealing in espionage, he had learned that trying to force a thought forward was futile, so he concentrated on planning the best he could to cover all eventualities.

In the middle of that thought process, he stopped and called John Engle to let him know of the change of time for the meeting between the terrorists. Then he went back to his planning and kept at it until the others came in for lunch.

•

Long before lunch was being served at Drew's house, Sa'd Kahdi reached Alton. He drove past the small train station and could easily see from the road that a station thought to have no security now had two uniformed officers in clear view, and an unmarked FBI car that looked very much like just what it was.

Kahdi's heart sank still further, in spite of having been told what the situation was. Somehow, he knew their plot had been uncovered. To what extent he had no way of knowing, and worried that he was heading right into a trap…that he would never be able to complete his mission and that he was doomed to die before the day, or night, was out.

Not really paying any attention to where he was, he drove aimlessly around Alton until the first pangs of hunger, heightened by tension, began to be noticeable. Then he paid more attention to where he was. As he passed the bridge leading to Highway 367, he noticed a sign advertising a casino. From his earlier trips to America, he knew that casinos routinely had quite good food at reasonable prices.

Soon, therefore, he was driving to the casino parking lot. It turned out to be one of the floating casinos in Illinois that had originally plied the Mississippi River before the state allowed them to be permanently docked. Kahdi pulled up to the valet parking area, received his ticket from the parking attendant, and went into the casino. As he walked away from his car and bomb, he almost secretly hoped that one or both would be gone when he returned. What he would be able to do with the remainder of his life if that happened, he had no idea. *"But,"* he thought, *"at least I will still have a life."*

Once inside, he went to the dining room and had a nice lunch. After paying for that, he stopped at a slot machine on his way out and put in five dollars. In a matter of minutes, he had won over five hundred dollars. Not knowing too much about casinos, he was still able to figure out how to get his money.

After filling his coin buckets up, he went and cashed in his winnings. His mood suddenly much better, he walked around the casino until he found the gaming tables. With hours still to wait until time to complete his mission, he sat down at a blackjack table. He decided to risk only one hundred dollars of his winnings and asked how to play the game. The dealer was very patient in explaining the game, and other players offered to help when he asked for their help.

When he had won three straight hands, one of the players whose help had been sought suggested he might want to raise his five-dollar bets to ten dollars. He seemingly was unable to lose. After winning three more hands, he again doubled his bets. Within twenty minutes, he was playing each hand for one hundred dollars and had already won over five hundred.

While he occasionally lost a hand, at the end of an hour he was over two thousand dollars ahead and had inched his betting up to three hundred dollars a hand. His winning kept on and, by the time he had raised his bet to the maximum bet of five hundred dollars a hand, he was nearly five thousand ahead.

He was over ten thousand dollars ahead before he started losing. One of the other players suggested to him that his run of luck was ending and it was probably a wise idea to quit while he was still far ahead. This drew a dirty look from the pit boss, but Kahdi thanked the man and picked up his chips and left the table.

He cashed in over seven thousand dollars worth of chips and looked at his watch. He still had hours to wait and decided that the casino was as good a place to wait as anywhere. Since it wasn't time to eat again, he decided to risk only five hundred of his new-found supply of money. He found another table game, called three-card poker, and sat down. Again the dealer and other players were helpful in explaining the game. Here, however, his luck wasn't near what it had been, but he was able to avoid losing much of his allotted five hundred dollars, and played on in bliss for hours, totally removed from the task that still awaited him that night.

•

While Kahdi gambled, others were busy making plans for his arrival in Missouri. In the FBI office in downtown St. Louis, John Engle had assembled his task force. Including himself—but not including his people who would be watching Hector and Billy's cars—he had forty-four agents and deputy marshals from four different agencies: the FBI, DEA, U.S. Marshal's office, and ATF. Of those forty-four people, only one lived in North St. Louis County. He was an ATF agent nicknamed "Tank," due to his muscular build. Tank had lived in Bellefontaine Neighbors before moving a few miles further north and had spent his entire life in the area.

With a large blown-up map of the area spread on a conference table, Tank was in the process of explaining how to best isolate the area just south of the bridge across the Mississippi from Alton into North St. Louis County. He said, "As soon as Scott says he knows the car is on or over the bridge, the team there shuts down the southbound lanes of the bridge. At the same time, we shut down Highway 367, both northbound and southbound, then Highway 67 (which is called Lindbergh by most in the area because it *is* Lindbergh before it becomes 67). Now we would have him trapped on 367.

"Since there are turn-arounds in three places on 367, those would have to be systematically closed off as well. The timing of that could prove to be a problem, because the first one shut down should be the one nearest the bridge. There are filling stations at the first two heading south, so we could have a team at each. When the word came that the bad guys were past each of those exits, our teams could jump out and close them off. But they couldn't use lights or anything like that because the terrorists would probably notice."

"Question," said John, before asking, "I can see the fella driving the car with the bomb catching wind of us and turning on one of these turn-around strips and just falling in with the traffic northbound that was already on the road before we closed it off. How do we stop that?"

"We don't," answered Tank. "We just make damn sure he doesn't catch wind of us. When you see Scott, you can tell him to let us know when we can close them off. If the guy *does* turn around, someone is going to have a quick decision to make on what to do. At least by that time, we'll know what kind of car we're looking for."

"About what I was thinking," replied a less-than-happy John. "Please continue."

"All right, the next exit he could use to turn around is also easily closed when word is given. There are a few businesses down there for our team to hide out at. One thing you all should know…these north and southbound lanes are *well* divided in this area between the two rivers—something like twenty or thirty feet—and it isn't flat ground. The northbound lanes are about twenty feet higher than the southbound ones. With the rain we had last week, there is no way to turn around anywhere except at the proper places.

"Okay, that takes care of the possible left-hand turns. Now, on to the two possible right-hand turns. The first one is easily blocked and our guys can just pull off to the side of the road, out of sight, and wait for word to pull up and close it. The other one leads to the West Alton area and it's easily cut off, also. We should have a team on the other side of the railroad tracks that go over the exit road. It's only one lane under the tracks, so real easy to shut down. The problem here, however, is that there is no good place for our people there to hang around without drawing notice. They could, I guess, stay around one of the gas stations on the other side of both north and southbound lanes with the team that will close that exit, then just drive straight across, after Scott gives the word that he has the car spotted. That should just about cover that area. Any questions?"

John asked, "What if there is heavy traffic and the car with the bomb in it just keeps on going?"

"There shouldn't be heavy traffic that time of night. If he plans to go on—as I'm sure he probably will—it'll be up to Scott to stop him somehow. If it was me, I'd just force the bastard off the road and take my chances. As much as I hate to say it, if that bomb goes off, it would cause a good deal less damage there than anywhere else in the area."

John nodded. "I agree, but the people who live there might not like the idea—and I can sure predict the President wouldn't care for it. The idea is to keep that bomb from ever being used. If you just force him off the road, he might just decide to cut his losses and detonate it. Of course, we don't know how long it takes to arm it."

Tank was an experienced ATF arson investigator and he replied, "I wouldn't think it would take very long at all. However, from what you told us about Scott, I doubt that he'd give the guy very long to try. We sure don't want the damn thing getting past 67. If we have the thing corraled on that stretch of road, best to take our chances on taking it out right there."

John smiled and said, "I'll pass your suggestion on to Jim. Knowing him, I'd say he'll probably agree. He's from St. Louis and probably knows the area pretty well, and won't want the thing to get into more-populated areas."

24.

John Engle and his people weren't the only ones going over their plans. Abdullah Mohamed wasn't having a conversation with his fellow terrorists, but he was in deep thought. He knew he was cutting it close to attempt a rendezvous with Kahdi only fifteen minutes before the train was due to pass the quarry…maybe too close. He decided to give himself more time by calling Kahdi at 8:45 rather than waiting for the 9:00 o'clock call.

In the study of the trains, they had found out that the freight train was much more punctual than the passenger train. The ten times they had checked on the freight train, it had never varied more than two minutes from the norm of 9:15. By calling Kahdi at 8:45, there would be more than ample time, no matter where he might be. Chances were that he would have to instruct Kahdi to circle around so they could time his arrival at the bridge at about 9:05, leaving only ten minutes to hold off any possible attack on them by the American authorities.

That part of the plan now firmly set in his mind, Mohamed turned to the timing of placing his men around the quarry. If they left the house at 8:30, the no more than ten-minute drive would give him time to instruct his men as to where he wanted them and still be able to reach the bridge in plenty of time.

Then he re-thought the entire thing through again and decided to leave the house at 8:15, again to allow for slightly more time, without risking overexposure. He finally decided that further thought would only cause doubt and worry—and, like his men, he needed all the rest he could get.

•

As Mohamed lay down on his bed, Jim said, "Okay, gang, when you go back out for more driving around, let's change the teams. Holly, you'll go with your dad and Boris this time. You other three go in the other car. I'd like everyone back here by three, and we'll all try to get some rest. Let's eat about 6:30. I'm thinking soup will serve. I'll put a pot of something on while you guys are out driving and just let it simmer until we eat."

"For God's sake, not potato soup," joked Boris.

"Nor cabbage," chimed in Sergey.

Drew started to say something, but Jim cut him off and said, "I was thinking along the lines of either chicken or bean. Take your pick. Show of hands for chicken."

Five hands went up and Jim said, "Chicken it is."

Drew said, "There's two chickens in the freezer."

"Good," said Tom. "It'd sure be stupid for someone to cut one as we're trying to sneak up on the bad guys, and bean soup gives me gas."

"Sure does," joked Jessica.

•

While the Janitors joked, John Engle was going over the plans for his group again. Finally sure that everything had been covered, he went over the call signs each unit would use one last time. He also made sure how each section of roadway would be cut off—and that each had been assigned numbers.

Jim's car was assigned the call sign "Control," John's "Abel," and John's teams in the immediate area with specific assignments "Abel" plus their respective number, starting with "Abel 1."

He looked around at his team and sighed. "One last thing. No red lights, unless you're told it's okay—and maintain radio silence. Hold it. One *more* last thing. If locals show up at any of our roadblocks, tell them we're holding an unannounced anti-terrorist drill and part of it is to see how long it took them to get word of roads being shut off and what kind of cooperation we get. Ask them to help with the roadblocking. Any questions?"

Since they had been over the plan a dozen times or more, there were none. After looking around the group with him and seeing no inclination to ask anything, John said, "Fine, let's all get as much rest as we can. We'll head north about six-thirty."

•

As the day wore on, Kahdi was gambling away, neither winning nor losing much. However, with each passing hour, his tension level increased, even though time seemed to be standing still. No matter how much water he drank, his mouth seemed to be filled with cotton. He wanted to eat, but knew it was too early. Finally, unable to sit any longer, Kahdi got up, cashed in his remaining chips, left the casino, and went for a walk. He went up a block, looked in storefront windows, circled around, and went down to the river, which he followed back to the casino and went in to eat. It was six o'clock.

•

In the Holmes' home, Betty was serving supper for herself and the three men with her as Kahdi walked through the front doors of the casino. She and Gary had been kept abreast of things and knew that the night to follow was going to be the climax to this frightening but— she had to admit to herself—thrilling adventure.

With that thought in mind, she said, "Before you two go off tonight to perform your deed, I want you to know how proud Gary and I are to have been of assistance, however small. I also want you to know that I'm sure you'll do just fine. I'd really appreciate it if neither of you got yourselves shot."

As Betty took a breath before going on, Billy joked, "That's not the way we do things. We shoot the other guys."

Betty frowned and replied, "I hope you're right. Having spent this time with you while you've been here— getting to know about your wives and, in Hector's case, children—I'd just be sick if anything happened to either of you."

Gary reached over and patted Betty's hand. "I feel the same way, fellas, so be damn sure to duck if the other guys shoot at you."

"Thanks, we will," Hector said.

"And," Gary added with a smile, "thanks for letting me play spy."

•

Across the street, the terrorists were also eating. Mohamed was starting to tense up as the time of action neared. He had become quite testy, severely admonishing two of his men for seemingly trivial matters.

He tried to relax, but the more he tried, the tighter he got. Any efforts at thinking through his plan again proved futile. He tried to run through his mind what could go wrong, and what to do if it did. Nothing, simply nothing, would come in the way of constructive thoughts. Finally, in desperation, he went back into his room and laid back down, since he was nearing the point of being ill from worry and tension.

•

Quite a different scene was taking place at Drew's house. All seven people there were eating Jim's chicken soup, with the comments ranging from "not bad" to "where's the beef?"

As they ate, Jim said, "When we go out tonight, Sergey will be with me, we'll follow the first car. Tom, you go with Boris. You two will follow the second of their cars to leave. Jessica, you'll be with Billy. I'll call him and tell him to take the third terrorist car to pull out. With the homing devices, he'll have time to pick you up. Holly, you'll go with Hector and follow the fourth car, same deal.

"Drew, when the last one leaves, you go over to that house and see what you can unearth. I doubt that they are stupid enough to leave anything of use behind, but one never knows."

Drew nodded and replied, "With these guys, I wouldn't be totally surprised to find something. Hell, he still thinks his cell phone is okay and hasn't even bothered to check his cars for bugs. With an idiot like bin Laden for a teacher, no wonder."

"Damn," said Holly, "I just found a piece of bone in my soup. Shame on you, husband, trying to kill your loving wife."

"You're too mean to die, daughter," Drew intoned with a smirk.

•

Downtown, in the FBI office, John and his people had eaten and were going over the highlights of the plan one last time. Finally, with nothing left to say on that subject, John said, "I guess we may as well get this show on the road. Tank, I'll drive the car for Jim. You drive my car. I'll follow."

"Uh," a smiling Tank said, "I don't have the address where he's at."

John chuckled and replied, "Neither do I. We've been planning this all day and can't even start the operation without calling Jim for help. I'd bet a dollar to a donut that I never hear the end of this."

After John called Jim for the address of Drew's new house, listened to witticisms from Jim, and gave the address to Tank, they left. While John had made the call to Jim, his other teams filed out of the office for their date with destiny.

Tank knew just about exactly where the house was located and drove there in just under twenty minutes.

As he followed along, John thought of all the good people he was bringing into this situation and hoped all would survive the night. An atomic blast would be an awful way to lose the best and brightest law enforcement people offered to him. He hadn't bothered to tell Jim that he carefully picked the best of over ninety law enforcement officers. John had gone over the file of each of those ninety plus with a fine-tooth comb. He was looking for those who would follow orders to the letter, but still have the initiative to act on their own, if it came to that.

Beyond the obvious, he had stressed to all those selected that the bomb *would* be stopped, somehow. That if the courier managed to get through the initial net, he was to be apprehended with the use of any force necessary, that his death would not be questioned.

John had also informed everyone on the team what Jim had passed along that the easiest way to disarm the bomb was to shoot it, explaining about the vacuum tubes.

When Tank stopped in front of the house, John pulled in behind him, got out, signaled Tank to follow, and walked to the door.

Once they were inside, John and Tank were introduced. Then John said, "Something smells good in here."

Holly made a face and said, "Jim's idea of chicken soup. Help yourself, but watch out for bones."

John replied, "No thanks, we ate. However, chicken soup sounds better than what we had. I hope not to eat another hamburger and fries for at least a month. That and eggs is all I've had since I've been here."

"Keep that up," joked Jim "and you won't live through your term as Director."

"I know. So does my wife. She always asks me what I ate when I'm away from Washington. I lie, but she gets it out of me eventually. On to business. Jim, I've got a map I'd like to spread out and go over with you."

Jim nodded and replied, "Okay, gang. Let's clear off the kitchen table."

The kitchen was a mess, but room was made on the table, while Holly and Jessica started washing the dishes. When the map was spread out, Jim said, "Girls, can the water noise and get over here. This concerns all of us."

Not needing to be told twice to stop washing dishes, they complied with smiles.

When everyone was gathered around the table, Tank explained their plan in detail, with call signs and location identification numbers.

After Tank completed what he had to say, Jim said, "Great. Good job. This bastard slips by us once we get him on 367, and we all ought to be shot."

"Or blown up," said Sergey with a grim face.

"Yes," replied Jim, "there is that to consider."

While the others looked over the map and asked a few questions, Jim called Billy and gave him as much detail as possible over the phone. He also told him the plan for following the terrorists as they left their house.

When he finished the call, Jim asked, "Anybody have any questions about tonight?"

Jessica got a puzzled look on her face and said, "Well, not exactly, but I do have a question. I thought you said that train from Alton used tracks in Illinois until it got near downtown. If so, what are all these tracks I've been seeing all day as we drove around trying to learn the area?"

Jim looked like he had been shot and said, "Son-of-a-bitch! Of course! The damn freight train!"

Those in the room with Jim exchanged glances before Tank said, "There is a freight train that comes through this area three or four times a week, southbound and the same northbound. It seems to me that they switch it off as to the days and nights it goes each direction."

Jim said, "I'd bet there is a real good chance we'll find out that thing is coming through tonight about nine, headed south. John, how about trying to find out for us."

John wasn't familiar enough with the area, but could tell by the words and body language of both Jim and Tank that they might be onto something, so without reply, he quickly took out his cell phone and called the FBI office, telling them the information he needed.

Within half an hour, he received a return call. When he hung up, John said, "Good guess, fellas—a *southbound* freight train is due to be on the tracks running next to Highway 367 at roughly nine tonight. Should I have it stopped, Jim?"

Jim thought for a few moments before he answered, "I don't think so. We've been putting all types of pressure on these guys for days now. One more thing might spook them. Our guy across the street from Billy and Hector is cutting this pretty close, telling the bomb-toter to call him at nine. He may be planning on actually *seeing* the train before he makes contact. I wonder what kind of speed that thing is doing when it gets to our target area?"

"Don't know," answered John. "My man at headquarters didn't say. Should I give him a call back?"

Tank said, "Don't bother. It doesn't roll through there at a very high speed. I'd say no more than twenty or thirty miles an hour. Too much residential property down the line a short distance."

Jim nodded and said, "Okay, here's the deal. We'll just play it the way we planned. If…*when*…I spot the guy with the bomb and know what his car looks like, we'll just seal the bastard off on that section of 367 and take our chances. If we keep him from getting as far as 67, he'll have a hell of a time trying to get that bomb on the train, no matter how slowly it's moving.

"Remember, at some point he will have to stop and arm the thing. Even if that only takes a minute or so, if he's alone in his car, he still probably has to stop the car to do his thing."

"Jim, a question, please. Do we know for certain that the courier will be coming across that bridge?"

"No, Tank, we don't. However, everything we've heard indicates that to be the most likely scenario. At one point the head guy told the courier to be south and east of the train station when he called. Depending on how far south and east he goes, he could be right at the bridge. Remember that the courier has no more to go on than we do, so when he finds out what to do, we should find out at the same time."

"Makes sense," agreed Tank, as John (standing nearby) simply nodded.

Jim then said, "If you guys have nothing else, pardon us while we check gear."

John nodded and handed Jim a bag Tank had brought into the house when they arrived. It had the radiation gear for Boris. Jim opened the bag, pulled out the suit, and handed it to Boris, who quickly tried it on.

He looked like a being from Mars and received a good deal of ribbing from his cohorts. He grunted. "You're just jealous."

"Yeah, we are…sure, Boris," joked Drew.

As Jim started opening one of the equipment bags he had brought from Washington, Holly said, "I don't know if you've noticed, darling, but it's starting to rain."

She had been standing near one of the windows at the front of the house and was shutting the drapes when she noticed the rain. Jim walked over, pulled back one of the drapes slightly, looked out. "Sure glad I brought plenty of camouflage ponchos along."

Then he dialed Billy and asked, "Do you guys happen to have rain gear?"

"No."

"We'll put a set in both cars for you. What about rifles?"

"Yeah, we're covered there."

Jim told Billy he would talk to him later, turned back to his bags, and said, "Tom, grab a hat and poncho for yourself and two of each for Billy and Hector, then run them over to their cars, please."

"Will do," replied Tom, as he walked over to the bag Jim had opened up.

Jim then asked, "John, have you got rain gear with you?"

"No. Didn't even think about the weather. Tank, how about you?"

"I thought about it, but didn't bring anything either."

Jim nodded and tossed both men a poncho and hat. He also passed out emergency first-aid kits that could be worn around the waist. Knowing that both Billy and Hector had night vision goggles, Jim started handing out goggles to everyone in the room. When he got to John and Tank, he gave an inquiring look and John said, "Don't know how to use the things."

Tank said, "Nor do I. Do you think we'll need them?"

"Probably not," answered Jim as he started passing out small headsets with mini-microphones attached.

Next, Jim said, "Okay, Billy, Hector and Jessica will take rifles in addition to their Walthers. The rest of us will just use our Walthers. Everyone check weapons and make sure you have plenty of ammo. I hope we don't get in some big damn shoot out, but one never knows."

When silenced guns suddenly appeared, John excused himself and went to the bathroom. Tank stood and watched quietly as the Janitors checked their very illegal guns. When Jessica started going over her sniper rifle, which was also silenced, he shook his head and wondered at the influence these people had—to be openly displaying an illegal arsenal in front of not only an ATF agent, but also the *Director* of the *FBI*! He had to admit to himself that John had warned him to be prepared to turn his head the other way when around these people. Now he knew why.

Jim noticed the look on Tank's face and smiled. "If we don't get this guy, you can arrest all of us for our weapons."

Tank grinned. "If you don't get him, we'll probably be dead."

At that point, John returned, happy to see guns all put away. "Tank, I think it's about time for us to leave."

Holly came over and kissed John on the cheek. "You should have had some of Jim's great chicken soup."

As he walked through the door, John said, "Yeah, the soup with the bones in it. Good luck, people. Nail the bastard."

In the car heading north toward Alton, John said, "Tank, as Director of the FBI, I should be upset about some of the things Jim and his crew do…and the weapons they use. However, we wouldn't even know about this bomb if they hadn't already been to Iraq since the attack on us and raided a sizable al-Qaida facility there, killing seventy or so terrorists in the process. Then a couple of Iraqi generals make a try for Jim—or I should say, 'tries'—and Jim goes back to Iraq, kills one of the generals in Saddam's Palace, and gets back in time for this operation."

Tank swallowed and said, "Jeez, I had no idea we, the U.S., was even thinking about Iraq at this point."

"Oh, yes. But keep that to yourself. Oh, I forgot two more interesting things that have happened with the Janitors in the last ten days or so. Jessica, that good-looking tall drink of water you met, single-handedly wiped out an eight-man hit team that came for Jim's scalp when he wasn't in."

"You're kidding!"

"No, I'm not. Blew six of them to pieces with claymore mines and shot two right between the eyes. That, by the way, you also get to keep to yourself. I'm not really supposed to know about it, especially since the bodies all disappeared. Jim, and others, want to keep the bad guys guessing as to how many men they're losing and how. The others in question live and/or work in a big White House in Washington. Oh, yes, before I forget…that fella

Sergey tried to kill Jim less than a week ago. Now he's working for the man he came to kill."

"Crying out loud…is this guy real?"

"I don't know. I doubt it. Anyhow, the reason I'm telling you all of this—which I obviously shouldn't be—is because I don't want you preoccupied with thinking about all those illegal weapons and my seeming numbness to them. Now you know why."

"Thanks, Director. You didn't have to explain to me, but I'm glad you did. I really appreciate it."

John patted Tank on the shoulder and replied, "You've been at this crime-busting business a lot longer than I have, and with your record, I felt you deserved to be told."

25.

Sa'd Kahdi again played with rather than ate his food. His palms were sweaty and beads of perspiration welled on his head. Finally, at a little after seven, he paid for the mostly uneaten food and went back to the slot machines. He idly pumped quarter token after quarter token into the machine, without much to show for it. By eight-thirty, he had lost over fifty dollars and found he didn't care in the least.

He stood up and walked on less-than-steady legs out of the casino and gave the valet attendant the numbered stub for his car. As he waited, nerves overcame him and he vomited the little bit of food he had eaten. When his car was brought around, he paid for the service, got in, and drove off.

As he did, the attendant said to a co-worker standing nearby, "Cheap bastard...tipped nothing and puked all over our sidewalk."

Kahdi was, of course, oblivious to such niceties, and drove around the curling road to the exit of the casino grounds. As he drove by the car designated "Abel one," with a Deputy U.S. Marshal and an FBI agent in it, they both noticed the Mideastern looking driver, but said nothing to each other. Kahdi didn't notice the occupied car. Once on the street, he just drove two miles heading east, then turned around and headed west.

Then he turned and headed east again.

•

Meanwhile, across the street from the Holmes' home, Abdullah Mohamed was pacing the floor as Kahdi gambled. At eight-twenty, he said, "Everyone check your weapons one last time, then let's go."

•

Mohamed had spoken near enough the kitchen to be clearly heard by the Janitors, and Jim said, "Looks like they're leaving together, so let's get ready to roll. Don't use the headsets until they're in their cars. Then he quickly called Billy and imparted the same message. While talking to Billy, the latter said, "They're outside...no sign of scanners. They're getting into their cars now. Hec and I are off."

Jim said, "Go with the headsets."

Then to Sergey, he said, "Let's go."

As the terrorists piled into their four cars, Billy and Hector were out the back door, over the side fence, over both of the fences belonging to the neighbors next door to the backyard neighbors (to avoid the dogs), and running for their cars.

When the terrorists drove toward Highway 367, Sergey followed the blips on the monitor held by Jim. By the time the terrorists reached the highway, Sergey and Jim were only two blocks away and the other Janitor cars had fallen in behind them.

Jim said, "Okay, gang. Sergey and I'll drop in behind them, slowly falling back to about half a mile in the rear. The rest of you stay back, about a quarter of a mile behind us."

Then he keyed the radio in the car and said, "John, they're on the move, heading north on 367. We're in pursuit."

John radioed back, "Message received. Good luck."

Mohamed was in the lead car of the four terrorist vehicles. They drove straight to the first of the turn-arounds past the quarry and used it.

As the blips slowed, used the turn-around, and headed south, Jim said, "They're heading back south. Slow your speed until we figure what they're up to."

Less than a half-minute later, the terrorists took the small road heading down to the quarry. Sergey and Jim were approaching from the opposite direction and could clearly see them leave the highway. Jim quickly said,

"Team, turn left at 67 and go up to Jamestown Road—the first road west of 367. They're going down into a quarry. About half a mile up Jamestown, there is a gate with parking area. Blow the gate—quietly, please—and go overland by foot to get behind them. Sergey, we'll go on down to the third turn-around and use it, but pull off the road between it and the second one."

Tom, driving with Boris next to him, was already past the Highway 67 exit and drove on past it. The other two cars were able to make the turn and did as told. Tom relayed his problem and Jim said, "Just go to that first turn-around and head on back."

•

Back in Bellefontaine Neighbors, Drew was already in the terrorist house and searching for anything of use he could find. It took only about two minutes to spot the pad Mohamed had used for all his written messages. He turned on the dining room lights, held the pad sideways, saw indentations on it, and took out a mechanical pencil from his pocket. He ejected a half-inch piece of lead and carefully rubbed the lead across the paper. After blowing off the excess lead, he was able to read what was there, enough to pick out the word "bridges" and enough other words to realize what he had found.

Sure that Jim by now would be out of range of the headset, he called his cell phone number. When Jim answered, he said, "Jim, Drew here. They're going after bridges when they finish with the nuke. Suggest you alert Engle."

"Roger," replied Jim, before pushing the "end" button on the phone and keying the radio.

Into it, he said, "John, Drew is at their house and has found information that they have bridges in mind for possible destruction. We now know what all the extra guys were for. My guess is that by bollixing up their plans as we have, the head guy wants everyone involved to make sure they take care of the nuke first. I'd bet that they have to set detonators to blow the bridges, so no real emergency on them…unless some of the guys slip through our fingers."

"You're probably right. But as soon as this is over, I'll have teams check out all the bridges in the area."

As they spoke, Tom and Boris had turned around and were heading for the spot where Jim wanted them.

In the quarry, amid much grumbling about the rain, Mohamed quickly explained to his men where he wanted them, then got back in his car and drove out of the quarry toward Highway 67, where he turned around and headed north again.

Jim saw the single blip on the move again and told Sergey to start moving.

Meanwhile, Billy and the others had arrived at the back gate to the quarry and Hector had shot off the lock with his silenced Walther. It was a walk of only about two hundred feet to the upper rim of the quarry from the opposite side from the terrorists. With their night vision goggles, they were easily able to see their foes.

Billy surveyed the situation as he watched the terrorists climb the far side of the quarry and settle into various positions in the foliage atop it. As Tom and Boris walked up, Billy said, "Jim, we're on the far side of the quarry from them. I see what they have in mind. When the bomb guy gets here, he can drive up an access road all the way to the top without too much trouble. From there it'll be an easy toss down to a passing train. I'm going to leave Jessica here to concentrate on him when he arrives. The rest of us are going to work our way around. Sound good to you, Hector?"

"I agree fully, amigo."

"Then do it," said Jim, just as Mohamed reached Highway 67, made a left, and then another left back onto Highway 367, heading back toward Alton.

Jim saw Mohamed's move as Sergey passed the last of the turn-arounds. He told his companion to step on it too and follow the same route. Next, he called John on the radio and said, "Close off 367 northbound and 67."

John replied, "Right," then added, "Abel 3. Close Point 3, now. Abel 2, wait one minute and close Point 2."

The "Abel 3" team was parked at an abandoned filling station, not a hundred feet from the traffic sign at Highway 367 and Jamestown Road, where it intersected with the highway before crossing it and then swinging around to cross Highway 67 up to and past the point where Billy and the others had parked their cars before going through the back gate to the quarry. Within seconds, they pulled their car into the middle of the intersection and started signaling the traffic that they would have to turn around.

A minute later, "Abel 2" shut down Highway 67 at Highway 367 in the same manner.

By the time Sergey had made the two left-hand turns to get back northbound on Highway 367, Mohamed and his driver were halfway to the bridge. Without being told, Sergey floored the car and rapidly closed on the car they were following. When Jim felt they had closed enough ground, he held up his hand to signal Sergey to slow down. Sergey had anticipated the move and already had his foot easing off the accelerator.

•

Back at the quarry, Jessica had been instructed to stay right where she was, at the far edge of the gaping hole in the ground, and listen in until Jim gave a description of the bomb-carrying car. Then, her "one job" was the driver of that car, and/or the bomb. The others had started to circle around the top ridge of the quarry. About halfway around it, Hector had been dropped off to take up a sniper position. Billy led the remainder of the team further around the rim, until he felt they were close enough until further word from Jim. It was eight forty-seven.

At that precise moment, Mohamed called Kahdi, who nearly jumped out of his skin when the phone rang. He answered, "Yes?"

"Where are you?"

"In Alton."

"Where in Alton? How close to the bridge?"

"Less than a minute away?"

"Fine. Turn onto the bridge and tell me when you have done so. Keep your phone on."

"Yes."

Mohamed then told his driver to turn left off the bridge and go down to the light and make a U-turn.

Jim, who had pre-placed the listening device that allowed him to hear Mohamed's cell phone, got an evil smile on his face. He and Sergey heard both the conversation with Kahdi and Mohamed's instructions to his driver. Jim made a fast decision. "Sergey, turn right on the far side of the bridge. Fifty feet up is a light with left-turn lane. Get in it. When it's time to make the turn, we'll make up our mind if we should do that or make a U-turn."

They were just arriving at the bridge and Sergey nodded as he drove up onto it. By the time they reached the far end of it, Kahdi said, "I am now turning onto the bridge."

"Fine," replied Mohamed, then to his driver he added, "Get to the bridge and turn onto it."

Back to Kahdi he said, "Drive in the right-hand lane, below the speed limit. Let all traffic pass you. We will be behind you shortly."

"I will do so."

Hearing this, Jim said, "Sergey, make a U-turn at the light."

As he drove off the end of the bridge and made a right-hand turn, Sergey nodded and did as told. By the time he made the U-turn, Mohamed was already on the bridge and closing rapidly on Kahdi's blue station wagon.

Sure which car it was, Mohamed's driver slowed as he approached from the rear.

When they were less than three car lengths behind, Mohamed said, "Please turn your lights off, then quickly turn them back on."

Kahdi did as told, and Mohamed said, "We are right behind you. We will pass and pull in front of you. When we do, I will say 'now' and you can look at us to see what type of car we have."

When Kahdi had flicked his lights off and then back on, he had been at the far end of the bridge. Sergey and Jim had been just at the crest of the bridge, saw the light show after hearing the instructions, and therefore also knew what car was carrying the bomb. Jim quickly said, "We have a dark blue station wagon" into his head set, then got on the radio and said, "John, we believe the bomb is in a dark blue station wagon, just now leaving the bridge, heading south. Please close off the bridge."

John acknowledged by saying, "Abel 1, close the bridge."

Even as John spoke, "Abel 1" was pulling out of the casino parking lot. They ignored the stop light in front of them and pulled out onto the street, with another car dangerously close behind them. In less than a minute they had the bridge closed. Only four cars had gotten onto it after Sergey and Jim.

Soon, Jim said on the radio, "John, close Point 4."

•

At the quarry, the rest of the Janitors heard Jim's last statement and knew the bomb was on its way. At that point, Billy decided to move his group in closer. They were fanned out at least fifteen feet apart as they inched forward. At a place with no cover, Billy rushed across the gap in foliage, just as a terrorist who had been relieving himself behind a tree looked up. Stunned, the terrorist raised his gun and fired wildly. His shot at Billy didn't come close, and his miss was the last thing he would ever do.

Hector was looking in that general direction when the man started to fire. He quickly raised his sniper rifle and shot him. The bullet entered through one ear and out the other as the man fell dead. Unlike the shot from Hector's rifle, the terrorist's shots had alerted all his cohorts and soon a gun battle raged in earnest.

Billy spoke into his headset mike. "Jim, they're onto us. We're in a battle."

Jim didn't reply, as he was talking on the radio, "John, close Point 5."

While the terrorists had trouble seeing what they were shooting at, they were at least able to aim in the direction of muzzle flashes. One of the terrorists' more or less wild shots found home, in Hector's leg. He swore, dropped his gun, and pulled his pants down. He took out his emergency kit, bound the leg, and gave himself a shot of morphine before pulling his pants back up.

In short order, six of the terrorists were hit, and most had given away their places of concealment. Meanwhile, Billy and his group had circled further around and were now very close to a large group of the terrorists. With Hector back shooting, other terrorists sighted in on his position and fired away. That gave Billy's group ample targets and, within a minute, four more terrorists were down.

At that point, Mohamed drove down the exit road, with Kahdi close behind. With the rain still pelting down, it was hard to see just where he was going and it became harder still when the headlight on the right side of his car was shattered with an errant shot by one of his down-but-not-out men.

Quickly seizing on the situation, Mohamed jumped out of his car and ran back to Kahdi's vehicle. He opened the door and said, "Arm the bomb for thirty-seven minutes, then drive up that road straight ahead. When you get to the top, wait for a freight train that will be along in minutes. You must get the bomb on that train."

Jessica had been looking for the blue station wagon. When it stopped, she swung her gun around, saw Mohamed, and ended his term as the head of the terrorist cell. The bullet exploded in his head and he slid from the car. Kahdi reached behind him for the bomb, pulled it into the front seat, and opened it. He set the timer for thirty-seven minutes, then floored his car's accelerator.

Since Kahdi had been leaning down in his seat as he armed the bomb, Jessica didn't see him until he sat up and started up the incline to the top ridge of the quarry. From her angle, she didn't have a good shot, until the car reached the top edge of the quarry. Then she sighted in and squeezed off a shot. The shot would have surely killed Kahdi if his car hadn't hit a rut at that precise moment. The resulting bounce of the car caused the bullet to hit the steering wheel and deflect downward, into Kahdi's lower abdomen. In spite of the searing pain, Kahdi swung the car around at the end of the road and pulled to a stop at the far edge of the ridge.

As he opened his door and slid out of the car with the bomb in tow, he was hidden from Jessica. He could also hear the train coming.

Back at the base of the quarry, Jim followed the two cars in and radioed John with instructions to close everything down and move in. He got out of the car in time to see Sergey shoot the driver of Mohamed's car. Just as he was looking around for something to shoot at, he was hit in the shoulder. The force of the bullet spun him around and he fell.

Holly saw that, yelled "Jim," stood up, and almost immediately realized her mistake. Two of the wounded terrorists and the unharmed one all fired in her direction. All had saved their best shots for the last thing they would ever do. One hit Holly in the lower abdomen; one hit her in the upper portion of her left breast; and the last one hit in the head. She went down without even knowing she had been hit. Hector saw all three gun flashes, shot the one remaining healthy terrorist, then finished off another before Boris (who had slowly circled in behind the enemy line) sighted in on the other and finished him off.

Billy saw Holly go down and rushed to her. When he got to her, he immediately saw that she was seriously wounded. As he pulled out his emergency kit, he said, "Jim, Holly's hit…and hit hard."

Jim said, "Shit," pulled himself together, and climbed back into the car. He grabbed the radio and said, "John, we need an ambulance. Now. Holly's hit."

While John made the call for the ambulance, Billy worked on Holly the best he could. He quickly bandaged her head wound, then used a compress on her chest wound. Next, he did the same for the stomach wound.

26.

Jessica heard the word that Holly had been shot, but tried to concentrate on finding Kahdi. As the train engine went past him, Kahdi stood up to throw the bomb. Jessica saw him and shot. The shot traveled through his back and out his chest, but even as he was dying, he summoned a final surge of energy and heaved the bomb.

Both Jessica and Hector saw the bomb in mid-air and fired at it. It seemed to flutter downwards, soon out of sight. Boris also saw it, but didn't have a shot. Before he lost sight of it, he saw it land on top of a boxcar. He said, "The bomb is on a boxcar."

Jessica was the first to react. She turned and ran as fast as she could to one of the cars they had left some two hundred feet behind her. When she reached it, she tore open the door and jumped in. She started the car and drove off—the car door slammed shut from the force of her acceleration.

Once underway, she said, "I'm going to try to get to that overpass I noticed in Bellefontaine Neighbors that is just off Bellefontaine Road. The one with the light, just past the filling station."

"Go, Jess," said Jim before he walked back to John's car, which was just pulling to a stop behind his. To John, Jim said, "Jessie is going after the train. The damn bomb is on there somehow. Call ahead and have your guys let her through."

John immediately got on the radio and said, "All personnel. One of the Janitors is going to be heading south on 367 from 67—you'll know her because she'll be driving like a mad woman. Give her free access!"

Even as he spoke, Jessica flew around the corner at Jamestown Road and narrowly missed a car just turned around by the road-block. She swung around that impediment, up the ramp, and onto Highway 367 southbound.   At the first of four stoplights, where the northbound lanes of Highway 367 were shut down, she again nearly hit a turning car.

Traveling at speeds she didn't even want to think about, the next light on 367 taxed her driving skills to the maximum, as the light was green the other direction and cars from both directions were crossing the intersection. First, to avoid the stopped traffic, she swung into the empty left-hand turn lane, then swerved between the two moving cars, and somehow came out the other side unscathed.

Racing on down 367, she used similar tactics at the next light, which was also red. This time there was no oncoming traffic, so she just barreled through the light and approached the last of the lights on that section of road. Luckily, this one was green, so her derring-do consisted of simply driving on the shoulder, around the traffic, and on down to Highway 270, where she took the ramp and headed east on that highway.

Again she had to travel the shoulder of the road to get around traffic. This time she was spotted driving like a crazy woman by a Bellefontaine Neighbors police officer, who gave chase.

●

Tom, meanwhile, had heard Jessica and heard what Jim said to John. He told Jim he was going after Jessica and Jim simply said to John, "Another of my loonies is rushing off in the same direction."

John nodded and warned his forces.

●

When Jessica reached Bellefontaine Road, she took the ramp, passed another car by driving on the shoulder, and raced south, totally ignoring the policeman behind her. The road in front of her was empty and she raced the half-mile to the road she sought. It was called Shepley, and went over the train tracks about a hundred feet from Bellefontaine Road. When Jessica turned left onto it, the policeman was right behind her…so close that he almost ran into the rear of her car when she slammed on the brakes at the overpass and jumped out of her car, carrying the sniper rifle.

At the sight of the gun, he sat in his car, stunned for a moment, then hurried out of his car to approach Jessica from behind with his gun drawn. He said, "Drop your weapon."

Jessica all but ignored him as the engine of the train passed under the road. Without even looking back, she said, "I'm FBI and there's a nuclear bomb on this train. Shut up and stay back."

The officer stopped in his tracks. FBI? Nuclear bomb? He wasn't sure what to do, so he did nothing.

Jessica raced up onto the overpass and desperately looked for the bomb. It was riding on the twelfth car behind the engine. When that car passed under Jessica, she saw the bomb and quickly sighted in on it and squeezed off a shot. The bullet tore into the satchel bomb and blew it off the train.

When she shot, the policeman realized that her gun was silenced and thought, *"Shit, FBI or not—that gun is illegal,"* and started walking toward her, with his gun again up.

Jessica rushed to the far side of the overpass, saw the bomb lying alongside the tracks, sighted in, and squeezed off another shot. The long-since-destroyed bomb seemed to jump up and then landed back down on the edge of the track bed.

Now right behind Jessica, the policeman said, "Hands up, lady. I don't care who you are, that gun is illegal."

At that point, Tom, who had arrived as Jessica took the second shot, came up behind them both, and over the noise of the train said, "Officer, if you so much as twitch, I'll blow your ass off. Put that gun away. Now!"

Deciding that discretion was certainly the better part of valor, the policemen slowly re-holstered his gun and turned around to see still another silenced gun, this one pointed at him.

Tom looked at Jessica. "Did you get it?"

"Yes."

"Good. Call Jim and let him know. Better have him send Boris and his spacesuit around, too."

Then he got an evil look on his face and said to the policemen, "That woman—who, I'm happy to say is my wife—just averted a disaster. The thing she just shot was a handheld nuclear device, put on that train by a terrorist trying to blow up a portion of downtown St. Louis. You are going to forget you ever heard this. You are also going to forget you ever saw us. Not your wife—if you have one—nor your chief of police, nor anyone else will ever hear of this unless the President of the United States personally calls you and tells you otherwise. You got it?"

The policeman looked into the steely eyes boring in on him, swallowed, and nodded his head. His mouth was suddenly too dry to talk.

Jessica was spellbound. She had started to dial Jim's cell phone number and had stopped at the seeming transformation of her husband right in front of her eyes. She shivered slightly at the murderous look on Tom's face, felt a slight amount of fear, but also realized she was quite proud of her man.

After all those emotions washed over her, she quickly finished dialing, and when she had Jim, she said, "Got it. Shot it all to hell. Send Boris, please."

Jim replied, "Good work. Boris is on his way."

Just then another police car pulled up to the area, with lights flashing. He'd been summoned by the first officer while the chase after Jessica had been going on. Tom looked at the first officer. "Have that guy block off this road up there a bit. You do the same at the light."

The officer hurried off to do as told.

•

After ending the phone conversation with Jessica, Jim said into his headset mike, "Boris, Jessie got it. Shot it. Do you know where to go?"

"Yes," answered Boris, "I heard her when she left and I know the spot. Quick thinking by that young lady."

"I'll say," agreed Jim.

•

Between the time Jessica left and when she called Jim to report a successful mission, the ambulance had arrived and left with Holly. It had been directed in the back way that was used by the Janitors and drove toward her at the direction of Billy, until the ground got too soft. Then Holly had been carried to it.

Sergey had taken out his emergency kit and patched up Jim to the best of his ability, then set off with Billy to make sure all the terrorists were accounted for. He worked the lower areas, while Billy did the same above. Along the way, he had helped two on their way to the end of their lives. Billy did the same to three who were also not quite dead. In the end, they had a body count of the seventeen they were expected to account for.

Hector had left in the ambulance with Holly, as much to be with her as to have his own wound attended to. Since they were all on the upper rim of the quarry and Jim was far below, he had made the request that someone go with her. Billy had nominated Hector because of his wound, since Billy had the feeling that cleanup work would have to be performed.

He was right. After the call from Jessica, Jim said, "John, I think these bodies should disappear. I'll have Billy and Sergey take care of that matter, if you'd be kind enough to drive me to the hospital."

John thought about arguing, but decided Jim was right. "Sure."

Jim said into his mike, "I know you heard that, Billy, so I'll leave it to you and Sergey. When the bodies are gone, ferry their cars to some nearby parking lot and leave them there. The rental companies will eventually find them, if they don't get stolen."

Sergey was standing next to Jim when he said this and nodded. Billy said, "Will do."

On the trip to the hospital with John and Tank, Jim called Drew and said, "Drew, Holly was wounded, quite badly from all indications. She's at the hospital near you. I'm on my way there now."

Drew swallowed. "See you there."

After Jim left, Sergey said into his headset mike, "Billy, we need to get all these bodies in one place. I think down here would be best. It's a lot easier to bring them down than to take them up, though I only have two down here."

Billy asked, "Do you have any suggestions as to how we get rid of them?"

"I see some heavy equipment, and I know this type of equipment. Strip them, dig a large hole away from where the quarry people are working, and cover them up would seem like a good plan."

"Okay, sounds good. The guy who brought the bomb drove his station wagon up here. If it's still running, I'll load up as many bodies as possible and bring them down, then go back for a second load."

"You could just toss them down."

"Aw, hell, I thought of that. But if they get hung up on something on the way down, we could be here all night trying to dislodge them."

"Good point."

•

Back in Bellefontaine Neighbors, John and Tank arrived about the same time as Boris did. Boris was somewhat grumpy as he put on the radiation gear, but less so when he neared the thoroughly destroyed nuclear device, as the Geiger counter showed a positive reading of some magnitude. As he walked back toward the others, he pulled off the hood to the radiation suit and hollered up, "It's hot, but not extremely so. The disposal team should have no trouble."

John nodded and said, "I've already called them and they're on the way. I had them in the area. They should be here in a few minutes."

Then he turned and walked over to the policeman who had followed Jessica, introduced himself, and said, "What you have seen here tonight will have to remain with you. A team of specialists who report directly to the President have eliminated a large group of al-Qaida terrorists tonight. Our plan is to give the President the option of keeping this quiet. At some point, I'm sure he will inform the public of what transpired here, but for now will probably wish to keep the lid on it, to confuse the al-Qaida leaders. Much better for them to wonder what happened to their team—have to worry about loyalty and so forth—than to know they simply failed in their mission."

The policeman nodded and, as he glanced at Tom, said, "That point was made to me rather forcefully a while ago by one of your men."

John then looked at Tom and Jessica. "I'm sure you two want to be at the hospital with Holly, so why don't you go ahead. We'll stay here until that thing is taken away."

At that point Boris, who had climbed the embankment from the train tracks, arrived and said, "Nice shooting, Jessie. You hit the thing four times. Any one of the four was sufficient to render it useless."

Jessica got a puzzled look on her face. "But I only shot at it three times."

Boris shrugged. "Well, someone else must have taken a shot at it back at that quarry because it has four holes in it."

A sheepish look appeared on Jessica as she said, "I only shot at it twice here, so I must have hit the first time, along with someone else, so all my crazy driving wasn't necessary."

John interjected, "That may be, but we would have been going nuts with worry if it wasn't laying down there in pieces. I'd have been trying to stop the train and all sorts of problems could have reared their ugly heads."

Boris nodded agreement, finished taking off the radiation gear, and said, "Come on, Tom, Jessie. Let's go to the hospital."

•

When those three arrived at the hospital, they did not find a happy group of Janitors. Jim's shoulder had been repaired and—much to the dismay of the doctors and nurses at the hospital—he was walking around with his arm in a sling. Hector had been tended to as well and was in a wheelchair, being pushed around by Drew.

Holly was still in surgery and the prognosis on her wasn't good. All Jim had been told was that her prospects of recovery were slim.

After Boris brought him up to date, Jim sighed and called the White House. When he had General Bradley on the line, he said, "The bomb is destroyed, and all the terrorists are dead. Their bodies are being disposed of, so the President can play it however he wants. With considerable help from John Engle, we have pretty well kept the lid on things. Besides his team, only a small number of local police are aware of anything of note happening. A few came to John's roadblocks and one followed Jessica as she made a mad dash in one of our cars to catch up with the bomb, which had been tossed on a freight train. All of them have been told to keep quiet."

"You don't sound too good, Jim. Anything wrong?"

"Yes, sir. Holly's in bad shape. She took three hits and may not make it. Hector and I got scratches, but nothing serious."

"Oh, Jim. I'm so sorry to hear about Holly. Please keep us informed. If there is anything we can do to help, you know it's yours for the asking."

"Thank you, sir."

Shortly after that call was completed, Billy and Sergey arrived, their clean-up duties complete. Then the Janitors—and a later-arriving John Engle—sat around the hospital, waiting on word of Holly.

When that word came, it wasn't good. One of the doctors who had operated on Holly took Jim off to the side and said, "Your wife is in critical condition. She is in intensive care and may not make it until morning. Shortly, you can be with her. Amongst other things, she lost her baby. And if she does live, will not be able to get pregnant again. Her reproductive organs are destroyed. Her chest wound is the least serious of the three, but still quite serious. The head wound is the main concern at this point. The bullet that hit her there didn't enter the brain, but caused a good deal of damage nonetheless. We'll have to wait until the anesthesia wears off to determine more. I fear she will be in a coma when it does wear off."

Jim nodded numbly and muttered, "Thanks."

•

By early the next morning, Holly still had not regained consciousness and the doctors were growing more concerned as time passed. Jim had been by her side since being allowed in. The doctors had requested that no more than two of the others be in the room with him at the same time. That request had been totally ignored by the Janitors. Drew had been there almost constantly, and the others had come and gone with regularity, but for the most part at least three or four were in the room at most times.

Finally, by noon three days later, Jim, who had been talking to Holly on and off most of the time, decided it was time to try something outlandish. He called the White House and asked for Ted Kuntz, then said, "Ted, I need a favor."

"Sure, Jim, anything."

"This may seem off the wall, but would you go out to the Joint and get Bowser and bring him here?"

"Jim, if you think it might help, I'd bring the President if you asked. He's driving the general crazy with requests for updates on Holly's condition."

"I know. Bless his heart. He's called me a few times himself."

•

Less than three hours later, Ted arrived with Bowser in tow. The hospital staff wasn't too thrilled at a dog being led through their facility, but Ted's White House credentials eased his passage to the intensive care unit. When he entered, he shook hands with Jim and said, "Here's your pup. He was a good boy on the flight, but took a dump on the tarmac."

"That's Holly's dog," a smiling Jim replied, as he picked up the little dog and put him on Holly's bed.

Bowser snuggled down next to Holly's side as Jim said, "Honey, your mutt is here to see you, and expects some loving."

Holly's eyes flickered, and a tear rolled down the side of her head. She looked at Jim and whispered, "Hi."

As Jim bent over and gently kissed Holly, Jessica squeezed Tom, Boris rubbed Drew's back, Hector glanced at Billy who returned the glance—both men wearing huge smiles with tears rolling down their cheeks, and Jim said, "Nice to have you back with us, lover."

At that point a nurse rushed in, followed shortly by a doctor. Everyone else was shooed out of the room, including Bowser.

Later, Jim was allowed back in and Holly said, "Guess I got hurt pretty bad. Did we get the bomb?"

"Yes, honey. All the bad guys, too."

"How bad am I? What about the baby?"

"Are you ready for this?"

"I lost the baby, didn't I?"

"Yes."

"Oh, Jim, I'm so sorry. I did a dumb thing when I saw you get shot… How are you?"

"Fine, the bullet did little damage."

"Everyone else?"

"Hector took one in the leg. He's already hobbling around on a cane. Said he called Rosa and she's madder than hell at him for not ducking…doesn't want him to come home and expect to be waited on hand and foot."

•

Holly fully recovered from her wounds and in time recovered from the mental anguish of having lost her child and being told that she never again would be pregnant. An unannounced and quiet visit by the First Lady was of great comfort to Holly, a kindness she'd never forget.

•

The Janitors continued to help in the war against terrorism, with Sergey setting up a sister operation in Moscow.

•

Some months after the destruction of the bomb and al-Qaida network in St. Louis, there was a private ceremony in the White House. It was attended by all the Janitors, and honored Betty and Gary Holmes and Roland Wheeler for their help in the fight against terrorism.

the end